# Pennington's Heir

## K. M. PEYTON

*Illustration
by the Author*

A Magnet Book

*Other books in the Pennington trilogy:*

PENNINGTON'S SEVENTEENTH SUMMER

THE BEETHOVEN MEDAL

First published in Great Britain 1973
by Oxford University Press
Magnet paperback edition first published 1982
by Methuen Children's Books Ltd
11 New Fetter Lane, London EC4P 4EE
First issued in New Oxford Library 1980
© K. M. Peyton 1973
Cover artwork © 1982 Methuen Children's Books Ltd
Printed in Great Britain by
Cox & Wyman Ltd, Reading

ISBN 0 416 24700 8

# Chapter 1

Ruth didn't know what was going to happen when Pat came out of prison. To her, that is. Pat's future was arranged. He was going to live with the Professor. But the Professor didn't approve of Ruth. She distracted Pat from his work and to the Professor Pat's work was all that mattered.

She wanted to discuss it with him during one of her monthly half-hour visits, when they confronted each other through a sheet of glass like zoo animals and stared hopelessly at each other under a warder's bored supervision, but Pat seemed disinclined to talk about the future. Or the present, come to that.

'Are you all right?'

'Yes, of course.'

'Are they nice to you?'

'If they feel like it.'

He had got nine months for knocking out a policeman and didn't look as if he would think twice about doing the same thing again if he got half a chance, sitting there scowling and restless. She hadn't expected to find Pat resigned and philosophic and smiling; she had expected his characteristic attitude of contained, aggressive energy to be exacerbated by the frustrations and humiliations of his new way of life, and she wasn't wrong. It didn't seem tactful to mention her own worries about the future. She didn't even know if she was really engaged to him at all, from the oblique way he had put it before the trial, but she was only too well aware that she loved him desperately whatever his humour. She just stared and stared at him and the half-hour was gone. But when she got up to go, he leaned forward and said urgently, 'You will come next time? Promise?'

'Of course. I'll always come.'

But next time they said she couldn't see him. No reason. She went to Chelsea and called on the Professor, who opened the door to her, forbidding as usual, impeccably correct. He frowned when he saw her.

'Please,' Ruth said.

'Come in.' He was resigned. 'What's wrong?'

She only ever saw him when anything was wrong. He taught Pat. Pat was his star pupil, the only one of his pupils, as he had told Ruth at their first meeting, to whom nine months sewing mail-bags could be considered a complete disaster. But in fact he had arranged with the authorities for Pat to go on studying in prison, and he visited him once a week to give him a lesson.

'Have you seen Pat this week?' Ruth asked. 'They said I couldn't. Why?'

'Poor child, come and sit down, and I will tell you why.'

He led the way into his marvellous music-room with its two pianos and book-lined walls and gave her the elegant armchair before the fire-place. Although he didn't approve of her, because she distracted Pat from his single-minded devotion to his job, he was kinder to her since their joint troubles. Their concern for Pat was a mutual bond.

'He has been in trouble, I'm afraid. He has lost his remission. Did they tell you that?'

'No!'

'He has also lost his "privileges" for two weeks, which include apparently your visit, my lessons and his practising. I saw him for five minutes and he said they were locked up all over the week-end and he got fed up and there was an argument . . . He doesn't remember much about it now. A perfectly logical sequence of events knowing Pat, but—' The Professor clutched at his intellectual forehead in a rare state of emotion. 'For heaven's sake, with so much to lose, you would have thought . . .' He shrugged, calming himself with an effort. Ruth could see the anger in his eyes. 'Well, that's why he's in there, I suppose, for his lack of self-control. What a waste of time and talent! I can never understand what moves that boy, that he is capable of such remarkable control and application where his playing is concerned, and yet his behaviour—we've covered all this ground before, haven't we?'

'Yes.' They had indeed. Ruth had covered it many times with her parents too. 'He's had to fight to get where he has with his music,' she said. 'Nothing's ever been easy for him.'

'He's never had to fight *physically*! Good God, it's criminal for him to use his hands to such an end, apart from the ethics of the thing! He couldn't play for the next two weeks, the state he's in, even if they were to allow him. He's got a splendid black eye as well—what does he gain by it? You tell me!'

A release of a kind, Ruth supposed. Not the one he wanted, though.

'The sooner we get him back here into a civilized atmosphere, with a routine of hard work, the better for all concerned. He's costing the country heaven knows how much a week in that damned place, and it's of absolutely no use to anyone at all. Least of all to him. Fantastic material going to waste here, all for want of a little restraint, a quite normal modicum of commonsense.'

Ruth noted that the Professor considered Pat as 'fantastic material'. He wasn't a person; he wasn't Patrick Pennington, twenty years old, six-foot two and fourteen stone, mixed-up, aggressive, gentle, thoughtful, violent, extraordinarily sensitive in some ways and thick as a mule in others. The product of a useless pair of parents and a devoted music-master at an otherwise lousy school, he was to Ruth the light of her world—to the Professor an incipient concert-pianist of such remarkable promise that

3

anything which deflected his mind from his work was to be deprecated with vehemence. And although the stumbling-block at the moment was Pat's incarceration for nine months in Pentonville, Ruth knew that when that was over, the stumbling-block, in the Professor's eyes, would be herself. He had told her so quite bluntly, at their very first meeting. Pat was not to waste his time on girls. Pentonville had been unavoidably prescribed by the law, but girls were another matter. After Pentonville, the Professor would be the law. The Professor had great influence over Pat. Ruth foresaw an almost impossible situation for herself.

'The best thing you could do is forget him and get on with your studies,' her mother told her sharply. 'If he chooses to spend more time in prison just because he can't keep his temper, what sort of a husband is he going to make?'

Nobody transgressed society's rules in Ruth's family, which lived calmly and without ambition in a small Essex village. It occurred to Ruth that if her mother was in prison, no harm would be done; she had no soul to struggle with; she would not go berserk being shut in a little room all through an April week-end with the blackbirds trilling on the roof of Pentonville itself. Pat was *human*, that was his trouble.

'And if he marries you, what are you going to live on?'

'He plays in concerts and gets paid for it,' Ruth said.

'Not as soon as he comes out, surely?'

'No, but as soon as he gets going again. Everyone's got to start, haven't they? You know he can, you saw him with your own eyes. It's not just my imagination, you know. I don't make it all up. When he comes out he's got an audition with Backhaus to play a Beethoven concerto.'

'Hmm.' Her mother pursed her lips.

It did seem a far cry from his present situation, she had to admit when she saw him again. It was hard to remember him in white tie and tails on the concert platform, this morose figure with the awful haircut and the fading remains of a black eye darkening his face, hunched into the drab prison clothes.

'Don't say anything about it,' he warned her. 'I can't change anything. It happened. I got a lecture from the Prof but why does he think I can change? I can't change myself.' For Pat, this was bordering on the philosophical.

'What did you do?'

'Oh, there's no point—you wouldn't understand. I told you right from the start I'd lose my remission, so you can't say you're surprised.'

'No. Only disappointed.'

'Yes. Well, I'm good at disappointing people. Ask the Professor.'

'He can't wait to have you under his thumb!'

'No.'

'I wish you weren't going there afterwards. He disapproves of me so.'

'Well, that's his bad luck. Clarissa's mother offered me a room. Would you prefer that?'

Ruth was stung. 'No! She hasn't—she hasn't been to see you?'

'No. She wrote.'

'You wouldn't—'

'God, no!'

Pat's scorn was a comfort. Clarissa had been at College with him. Although she was an *ex*-girl-friend, Ruth was deeply suspicious of Clarissa, who was both talented and gorgeous. She also, for good measure, had musical parents who could be extremely useful to Pat in his career, her mother being a self-confessed Lady Bountiful to struggling talent and her father a concert impresario. Pat couldn't stand them.

'Oh, Pat—'

It always came round to this, for Ruth: an agony of what her mother called her adolescent passion, just looking at him. She knew that in bed tonight she would just cry and cry, remembering him, but now, while she was with him for these incredibly mean thirty minutes, there was no way of expressing anything at all, not even his hand to touch. They were neither of them talkers, and the confrontation, controlled and supervised, stifled their natural reticence into a hopeless failure at communication. She always went away feeling far worse than at any other time during the intervening months.

When, eventually, the day of his release came, she went to meet him outside the prison. She was trembling like a leaf. The Professor's car was parked by the gate.

'It's lucky I'm thick,' she thought, acknowledging him. Otherwise the frost in his eyes would have withered her.

'Wait in my car,' he said. 'The wind is cold.' He had perfect manners. But she knew better than to believe that he was pleased to see her. When Pat came, she was too shattered to say anything. He smiled at her, then past her at the Professor, very equal. He looked shattered too.

'I thought it would never come,' he said. 'I can't believe it.'

The Lotus was a two-seater, so Ruth got in the back, which was almost non-existent, and Pat got in the front, next to the Professor.

'I thought we'd go straight back and talk things over. Clemmie's making a special lunch to celebrate, and I've nothing on until this evening.' The Professor spoke to Pat, and Ruth wondered for a moment if he would dare to exclude her from the gathering. No, she was being too sensitive. Her heart was thumping like a steam-hammer, her cheeks burning. But Pat was pale and cool, his eyes watching the walls outside, past the Professor's head. He half-turned in the seat and looked back at her, not smiling. He shifted his elbow over the back of the seat and his hand came down and rested on her knee. She put her own hand over his and their fingers caressed. She could feel his bones. After all the time apart it was almost too much to take in, that in the space of a minute—after all the agony of the nine months—he had come out of the gate and got into the car and was there in the flesh, holding her; the very expression that she had sought so desperately to recall during the intervals of not seeing him through the long shady months of the sentence was there before her eyes to drink in: the delinquent scowl and the restless eyes, the untrusting, untranquil, nervous energy in the quite normal features that had the power to transfix her. She was like a camel come to an oasis. And, drinking him in, she knew she was as dotty as a camel too, dotty enough to burst, and she was shivering with the excitement of it, holding his hand while he talked to the Professor, and his hand stroked her knee, and her other hand came up quite without her willing it and touched his wrist and felt the pulse beating through his artery, soft underneath and on the other side bony and hairy. She could hardly stop the idiotic happiness bursting out, especially after her doubt, and the Professor right there talking about some old concert he wanted Pat to go to at the week-end—God, what a vulture the man was! Driving and pecking. No wonder Pat blew up at intervals.

'Funny to see it from the outside,' Pat said.

The sun was shining and the road smelt of tar, blown newspaper, and a whiff of chips frying. The Pentonville walls were ugly to the point of obscenity. Ruth, always early for visits, had tramped all round them on several occasions, and was familiar now with the decaying streets, the boarded windows, the thud of demolition machinery. And the walls, and walls within walls, so high and blind as to suggest some secret religion, some monastic order, even the plane-trees lopped and tonsured to conform . . she never wanted to come here again. The car slid away down the Caledonian Road.

'Never again,' said the Professor, feeling the same. The Royal Borough of Kensington was his province. Pat grinned.

'No. It's like being *born*, getting out of there.'

Ruth felt born too. Everything was sharper, more positive; there was a purpose again. She did not know where they were going, but life had flowered suddenly like a cherry-tree in April.

'My God, but you've got some work ahead of you,' the Professor said to Pat. Ruth's cherry-blossom felt the frost, contracting. But Pat nodded affably, as if the prospect quite pleased him.

The car nosed through the traffic, deft with its expensive acceleration, jousting and thrusting. Ruth, anticipating the formal lunch with the Professor, had a twist of longing to be making for her home-ground with Pat, out on the marshes along the sea-wall with the tide flopping against the stones, the track dried into its clay cracks and warm underfoot. But for Pat, with his most civilized of professions to pursue, it had to be the city and all its contacts. But better Kensington than Pentonville. The Professor's house, for the time being Pat's home, was a stucco Regency villa in a quiet road. He had recently moved, and Ruth could see the attraction: the village atmosphere, the pink roses over the porch, the shade of pollarded lime-trees, yet all within a stone's throw of Knightsbridge. She thought, 'It stinks of money.' She saw Pat's expression and knew that he was not keen on this patronage. He looked uneasy, taking it in. The Professor parked the Lotus neatly in its allotted resident's bay.

'You've gone up in the world,' Pat said to him.

'You like it? It's fantastically handy.'

'A bit of a change for me. I—' He shrugged, frowning. Ruth could sense the struggle already, the Professor's pressure taking hold. It had taken less than half an hour. The Professor led the way up the steps, groping for his key, and Pat followed. He put his hand on Ruth's shoulder, pulling her with him, a quick hug. Ruth felt rather than saw Hampton's expression, cool, quick. She could feel herself rejected, even while she was stepping over the doorstep. But stubbornness was one of her characteristics; she had been told so all her life by her mother. It would support her now.

The atmosphere was improved by Clemmie, the Professor's housekeeper, an elderly, motherly, entirely uncomplicated soul whose joy at seeing Pat again swamped the nuances among the three of them.

'My word, you look as if you could do with a bit of fresh air and a square meal—I'll bring some coffee, and then in an hour when you've had a bit of a chat, I'll serve the lunch.'

'I'll help you,' Ruth said. She was always more at home in kitchens. Clemmie, she sensed, was sympathetic. By lunchtime she knew she would have had her fill of being excluded from the Professor's conversation with Pat, which would be all about work. All he ever thought about. He was a maniac, Ruth thought. She remembered then what Maxwell had said about Pat's first sentence: 'Three months—the first holiday he's had in years.' It was a bit funny really, to think that Pat might be returning refreshed from his nine months in Pentonville, to resume his studies at full bore again. Only the Professor could provoke such an idea.

'Doesn't he ever think about anything else but music?'

In the small kitchen the coffee was already percolating with a comfortable, expensive aroma. Clemmie reached the cups down from their hooks.

'No, dear. Music and chess, that's all.'

Clemmie had a sort of brisk, nannyish demeanour that emanated good sense and comfort. It occurred to Ruth that she could, in fact, very likely have been Hampton's nanny when he was a little precocious Kensington boy. She would have liked to ask, but didn't dare. It fitted.

'He doesn't like me getting in the way.'

'No, dear. He's very single-minded. But he can't expect a boy like Pat not to have a bit of fun. It would be unnatural. Pat's not one of those droopy, dreamy sort like some we get, like dish-cloths wrung out. He will work ten times harder than any of them, and then be ready for the next thing. I suppose it's all this energy that gets him into trouble.'

'He doesn't think.'

'Reckless. He'll grow out of it . . . a boy of twenty. A steady girl like you, just what he wants.'

Ruth smiled. 'Will you tell Professor Hampton that?'

Clemmie smiled too. 'I'm not paid to give him advice. Only meals.' She was watching the milk, its surface just starting to crinkle. She warmed a jug with hot water, ready.

'Did Clarissa come here?'

Clemmie's smile faded. 'Yes, she did.' From her expression she might have added, 'The hussy!' Or was she imagining it? Ruth wondered. Clarissa was so fantastically attractive one could not easily get her out of mind. Why had Clarissa's mother invited Pat to make his home with them? Ruth had tried to bury this bit of knowledge like a dog with a bone, but—like the dog's bone—it kept reappearing, unearthed by the uncontrollable, jealous, despicable streak in her nature.

This uncontrollable bit of her now pressed Clemmie, pouring out the hot milk. 'Did Professor Hampton object to Clarissa in the same way that he objects to me?'

'Professor Hampton is a great friend of Clarissa's father. It was a bit different, you see. Clarissa came here to play duets with Pat, for lessons.'

But a lot more than lessons had passed between Pat and Clarissa. Pat had told her so.

'But she *distracted* him too!' Clarissa had been suitable, herself unsuitable. What a hurtful thing it was to discover! She was quite surprised at the feeling. She had gone too far and it served her right.

Clemmie said, 'Settling down would be good for Pat, in my opinion. A man will work all the better for a bit of home comfort.'

Ruth followed her out of the kitchen door into the garden, with this vision of carpet-slippers, sleeping cats and hearth-rugs all mixed up with her Clarissa complex. The garden was small but perfect, the high walls hung with roses, shaded by next door's acacias and cherries. The garden furniture was arranged on the stone terrace where Pat and the Professor sat talking.

Pat looked up and smiled at her, and Ruth's heart gave its great uncontrolled leap of adoration, seeing him face on, receiving his whole attention, like the sun bursting out of cloud. He didn't move or get up—gentlemanly manners being one of the attributes he conspicuously lacked, as Ruth's mother had pointed out often —but sprawled comfortably, his physical presence, even in repose, very positive, very active—('Or is it just me?' Ruth wondered uncertainly. 'Like a poor moth to a candle?').

There was a garden chair for her, she was relieved to see. Clemmie put the tray on the table.

'Would you like to pour it, dear? The Professor takes his black, no sugar.' She gave Ruth a sense of belonging, which was a relief.

'We've got the top bedroom ready for you, Pat, the one that gets the sun. It's only small, but there's a big cupboard for your things.'

'I haven't got any things,' Pat said. 'They're still at Mrs. Bates'. I'll have to go and collect them.' He was wearing his concert suit, the one he had appeared in court in, to look as respectable as possible. 'If I take Ruth home this afternoon, I could collect them then.'

'You're working this afternoon,' the Professor said.

Ruth saw Pat's face harden. He opened his mouth to say something, and shut it again.

'The water's hot if you want a bath,' Clemmie said. 'There'll be time before lunch, if you like.'

'Thanks, yes. I would like one. It would be marvellous. And the coffee—the smell—you can't imagine—'

Ruth thought she could imagine. Civilized living breathed here, from the very flagstones of the patio. To have come from breakfast in Pentonville to morning coffee here was as big a step as one could take in atmospheres. Ruth, aware that Pat set little store by his surroundings, could see that this time it was too much to take, and Clemmie's bath idea was far more practical than Hampton's programme.

Pat departed; Clemmie brought out a colander of peas for Ruth to shell; and the Professor put some Mozart on in the music-room, so that the sound wafted up out of the windows into the pale pink roses, a perfect affinity, an underlining of the exquisite surroundings to which the Professor had attuned himself. 'Life isn't like this,' Ruth thought. Life was the Caledonian road, or her mother vacuuming the carpet with the Jimmy Young show on the transistor and the milk boiling over. Beautiful music was apt to bring out a reaction in Ruth, so that sometimes it made her very sad and angry, thinking of starvation and Calcutta and South Africa, because the music was a perquisite of people who had the education, the leisure and the opportunity to listen to it and enjoy it. And yet a great deal of the greatest music had been born out of poverty and war and distress: her argument was full of holes. She was always getting moved and vehement about the injustices of life, and having great rows with her mother (her father didn't have rows, ever) but at the same time she was aware that she herself was completely powerless to change anything. She couldn't even win the arguments. Her mother's dogma enraged her, all the indisputable facts brought to bear like battle-ships on Ruth's poor little explosions against capitalism and Tories and inequality, the arguments levelled with all the same familiar tags . . . 'You'll find out when you're older that . . .' and 'Human nature being what it is, I'm afraid that . . .' Ruth got all tied up in her refutations, but amongst her frustrations her rage and her ideals burned all the harder. This was the effect her mother had on her. She wished she were calm and poised and terribly intelligent (like Clarissa). She had no confidence at all.

Clemmie duly served lunch, and afterwards the Professor, ever-anxious to remove Ruth, said, 'Perhaps you would like to go out for the afternoon while we work, and come back at tea-time?' How smoothly rude he was! Ruth said stubbornly, 'I would like to listen. I'll sit on the sofa. I won't say a word.' The sofa was under the front window, a carved chaise-longue heaped with cushions and looking most inviting after the lunch and the day's emotions.

The Professor said to Pat, 'Sit down and think about the C Major study. And I mean think.' He sounded cross, and was taking it out of Pat instead of her. 'I want total concentration, not automatic fingerwork.'

'Pig,' Ruth thought. 'Bullying pig.' But during the lesson they argued quite a lot. She had often wondered what Pat's lessons with the Professor were like; she now felt that the master-pupil relationship was fairly gruelling. It wasn't just a matter of playing pretty pieces through, punctuated by exclamations of encourage-ment and congratulation; it seemed to consist of agonized appraisals over a few bars, discussion and argument, and then great surging passages played with great power, broken off abruptly, restarted . . . Not at all restful, Ruth decided. All the same, she dozed off, and came to later, intuitively, to hear Pat playing in quite a different mood, something soft and lilting, very delicate, caressing. All her senses came awake at once, with a rush of joy and gratitude. The Professor had gone, and Pat was playing the Brahms waltz that he had once played especially for her. It was for her now, she knew. She got up and went over to him and put her arms round his neck, burying her face in his hair.

'Where's the Professor?'

'The phone rang. He's gone to answer it.'

She could see his hands moving over the keys like large spiders, very smooth and supple. They played the last notes and came up to take hers.

'What will the Prof say?' he whispered, smiling, moving his face against hers.

'He'll say I'm bad for you.'

'Good for me. I need you.'

'I love you.'

'Yes.'

They heard the ting of the receiver being put down. Ruth leapt back to the sofa and buried her face in the cushions. She heard the Professor come back into the room, and the voices talking again, and then Pat was playing what she thought of as 'properly', on and on; it was beautiful, all mixed up with the warmth of the sun on her back and the smell of the velvet cushions. She dozed again, and when she awoke, someone was offering her a cup of tea.

'I'm going to take you home,' Pat said. 'The rest of the day is our own.'

The Professor wasn't there. Pat put her cup of tea on a small table and sat on the sofa. He looked very tired.

'He says I can borrow the car. We'll go and look at the sea. I need it.'

Pat's home was near the sea, like hers. He had been born there. But he lived with a landlady called Mrs. Bates, the mother of an old schoolfriend, because he could not get on with his own parents. Mrs. Bates lived just across the road from his own home. 'We can call on Mrs. Bates and collect my things.'

'I've got your medal for you. Here.' She fished it out of her shirt collar, the little gold relief of Beethoven on a gold chain that he had given her before he went into prison. 'I never took it off.'

Pat smiled.

'You'll need it,' Ruth said. 'To play the right notes.' That was what he had said it was for, his luck.

'Cripes, I'll need it all right, if I've got to make my playing pay for my keep.' The smile faded. He had never been one for smiling much. Ruth hoped that things would change now. There was nothing to worry about any more.

'Come on,' he said. 'I can't wait.'

She drank half the tea, and they went out into the hall. The Professor came down the stairs.

'Here are the car keys. And a door-key. I don't have to tell you to drive as befits one so out of practice.'

'Thank you for having me. Thank you very much for the lunch.' Ruth felt very affable.

'A pleasure, my dear,' lied the Professor charmingly.

Pat and Ruth went outside, and got into the Lotus. 'At last,' Ruth thought. And yet there wasn't anything that needed saying; it was just to be free, at last, together. Pat didn't say anything either, only, 'It's so strange.' He drove very carefully down the road, watching everything. It was very hot, the shadows just beginning to draw out, the rush-hour traffic throbbing at the top of the road. It occurred to Ruth that it was very generous of the Professor to lend Pat his expensive car. Riding in it with Pat, just the two of them, was altogether more than she had allowed in her dreams—not that Pat had many moments through all the rigours of Hyde Park circus, Oxford Street, Holborn and the City in all their going-home chaos, to remove his concentration to her, but she was content. She felt like a girl in an advertisement.

'I've forgotten,' Pat was saying. 'I've forgotten everything.'

He was not carefree and laughing, as she had imagined it, even when they were out to the arterial with all the snarl-ups behind them and the Lotus zooming down the outside lane. The advertisement analogy faded from Ruth's mind. Pat's arm was not round her shoulders and her hair wasn't flying out in the wind. Pat was saying, 'It's as hard to come out of prison as it is to go in.'

'You can't mean that!'

'No . . . But you think when you get out all your troubles will be over, and then when it's happened, you see that they're only just starting.'

'Not *troubles*.'

'Difficulties.'

'You've got to adjust. You can't expect to take up exactly where you left off.'

'I didn't expect anything. What happened last summer—that concert and the notices—was too good to be true. Then the other happened to even things out. Now we're back to square one. Only worse off, because in spite of being able to work in the nick, it wasn't the same as being at college. I can't play as well as I should be playing. It's like climbing this ladder up the side of a skyscraper, and half-way up about six rungs break, and you drop back.'

'But you still have the Professor to help you, and a home—' She would have liked to add, 'and me,' but she was still very uncertain of how much she meant to him. There had been so little time before, and in prison he hadn't had anything much else to think about, but now—now she was back in competition with the piano and his ambition, and his musical friends and the Clarissas of the world.

'Yes, it's true, but to be dependent on Hampton is the worst thing of all. You must see that. It's being a prisoner in another way. Look at today.'

'Yes.'

'I don't want to live there. But he's not charging me anything. How can I afford not to? And I must have his lessons. He's not charging me for those either. But he virtually owns me in exchange.'

Ruth considered. 'You're looking at the worst side of it. You've got a home and food and lessons. Suppose you'd come out and there was no one who would help you? You might have had to give up altogether.'

'It might not have been a bad thing.'

'You wouldn't have said that before. Not after that concert. And that Backhaus man saying you were marvellous.'

'He didn't.'

'He wanted you to play with him again, didn't he?'

'He did. Two months from now. Beethoven's Third Piano Concerto. If he'd heard me this afternoon—cripes, he'd be a worried man! I can't see it happening.'

'Oh, Pat, stop it! How do you expect to feel, the first day out?

Only the Professor would have made you work, instead of letting you go out and wander around and look at the buses and the shops and go into a pub or a Wimpy bar or something. You couldn't possibly have felt like it.'

'No.' But she had merely gone round in a circle and caught up with the beginning of the argument, the Professor's possessive pressure.

'Don't,' she said. 'Don't think about it now.'

They turned off the arterial and headed for the lanes that went down to the marshes. Everyone else was roaring on for Northend. The sun was burnishing the fields, the flowering grass rippling in dusty pink waves, ready for hay, roses in the hedges. The elms cast long shadows across the road. Ruth thought of Pat locked away for all those months. And yet he had said he was glad he had done it and wouldn't have changed anything. How could he think that? The Professor had said he couldn't understand him, with so much to lose. 'You don't know how it feels,' Pat had said. 'There are some things you can't take.' She couldn't have taken what he had chosen. Would she ever understand how his mind worked?

They came to the village where he lived, and went straight through, past Mrs. Bates' and his parents' and the church, and down the dusty cart-track to the creek. This is where they had come before, and everything had been spoilt. 'It can't be like that this time,' Ruth thought. But she expected nothing. Pat was silent, looking across the fields. He parked the car by the boatshed and they got out and climbed up on to the sea-wall, scrambling up through the long grass. The sun was behind them and their shadows went right across the creek to the opposite side. The tide was almost gone, threads of gold water trickling out through channels in the mud. The yachts in the centre of the creek lay perfectly still; silence, save for a curlew. Pat stood looking, saying nothing. Then he turned and started to walk along the sea-wall, upstream, his hands in his pockets. Ruth followed. Three hours from the Royal Borough of Kensington and Oxford Street. Ten hours from Pentonville. The grass flowers powdered her thighs and the smell of seaweed and mud came like a draught.

Pat walked as far as the bend in the creek, and sat down, looking at the half-tide and the uncovered mud. He took off his jacket and sat chewing a blade of grass. Ruth sat down beside him.

Because of his mood, which she could not quite place, she felt that her own feelings were suspended, waiting for Pat. She was that much dependent on him.

But he turned and smiled, at last, and slipped down the bank so that he was lying facing her, his head propped on his hand. It seemed to Ruth that this was the very first time they had ever been alone, with nothing between them, the physical presence being enough to blot out all other thoughts. No problems, no past, no future. The feeling grew between them, surging so quickly, so passionately, so perfectly, that there was never any question of Ruth withdrawing, doubting. Afterwards, because she knew she always doubted, was always knotted by her suburban hang-ups, her groundings—grinding—of conventional morality, she could not understand her own release. It was something she had never known was in her, this power to unlock herself from every minute of the seventeen years of careful upbringing that had gone before. It would have terrified her, if she had been in the mood to think about it in everyday blood. But the evening was unique; it was not everyday. It would not happen again in just this same way, this coming together after all the time apart, this very first time. It could never be the same again. Ruth, aching, crying, 'undone'—and the word was in her own head, with its truly Victorian associations—and yet powerfully, fiercely happy, lay clutching Pat on the cold bank, not thinking of anything but her love for him, not—for once—thinking of what might happen, what might have happened. The sun had gone, and the familiar dank smell of the evening marshes, a lacing of hay with mud, and pollen with oyster-shells and crabs' remains and the stalks of tide-washed marsh-grass, came with the soft rising of the on-shore breeze. They lay feeling the dampness of the grass all round them, and their own warmth a cocoon, a private world. Pat was smiling. Ruth had never seen him, ever since she had known him, smile in quite the same way he was smiling now. She looked into his eyes, three inches away, with her own shadow in them, and at his eye-lashes and his eye-brows and the faint scar through his upper lip, and at his hair growing down in front of his ears and then shaved suddenly, the cheek pale in the dusk. Impossible. True. But not to analyse it: just to let it exist, to have him, to be perfectly happy. And she didn't think she had ever been happy before.

When it had got cold, and almost dark, they sat up, and Pat put his jacket on, and they walked back along the sea-wall to the car. It was too narrow to walk together, to hold hands. They walked separately. Back to normal, Ruth thought. Two people. Had it really made any difference? To her, the whole world was changed, but to Pat—she couldn't tell. That was what he was like. But at the steps he took her hand and put his arm round her, and when they got back into the car, he kissed her again, very gently.

Then he started the car. 'Mrs. Bates,' he said.

'Oh, God,' Ruth said. She didn't want to see anyone else. She looked in the car mirror and saw herself all white and dishevelled, grass in her hair. She combed it. It was too dark to do anything to her face. She had to go home, look her mother in the eye! Impossible. Inevitable.

'I wish I could come back with you.'

'Yes.'

'I wish—oh, Pat! I—'

He put his arm round her and she laid her face against his smooth concert suit. They drove into the village slowly, and he parked outside Mrs. Bates'. Ruth sat up. She didn't want to share the moment with anyone. But before they could get out of the car, there was a sharp tap on the window on Pat's side, and a face peered in. Ruth heard Pat's soft blasphemy, then the door was flung open.

'It is you then! God Almighty, let's have a look at you! Jim Purvis said it was you in a smart car and I said he was dreaming. And then I saw the car come back and I said to Bill, "There, I reckon it could be—the nine months is just about up." Well, now, what a surprise! Come out now and give your mum a kiss! Let's all have a cup of tea. Bring your girl-friend. Clarissa, is it? Do you remember me, dear? Come on, both of you.'

Ruth felt Pat's hand give her a quick, regretful squeeze, then he was climbing out, giving his mother a brief peck on the cheek, turning for Ruth.

'This is *Ruth*, Mother.' His voice was fierce. 'I just came to get my things from Mrs. Bates. I haven't much time. I've got to go back to London.'

'If you haven't time to come into your own home for five minutes to drink a cup of tea, after all we've had to put up with—' The voice had changed key, swerving into indignation. 'It's nearly eighteen months since I've seen you! D'you realize that? Come and say how-do-you-do to your father and have a drink in your own home. Then you can go off for another eighteen months. We don't ask much!'

'All right!'

Pat turned round for Ruth, scowling. She could see the apology in his expression, the mute gesture of despair. Ruth went with him, following his mother across the road and up the garden path of an unkempt council house. She had been warned about Pat's mother, but had never met her before, only the father.

'Come in then. Ruth, d'you say? Come in, Ruth. I'm pleased to see any lady-friend of Pat's, you know. Not that he brings his friends here very often. Not now. Ashamed of the place he is, now he's got so high in the world.'

'Pentonville,' Pat said.

'When did you come out then?'

'This morning.'

'This morning, eh? I thought you looked peaky. You did the full term then? No remission? You're just like your father. Can't keep out of trouble. What d'you think of him then, Ruth? Not much good to a girl if he's always getting put away. You'll have to see if you can keep him on the primrose path as they say. Here, I'll put the kettle on. You're looking very smart, Pat, I'll say that for you. Never a one for suits—mind up, let me get to the sink. At least you got a good haircut for once—never thought I'd ever have anything to thank one of Her Majesty's prisons for! What d'you think of him, Ruth? You missed him last year? You never brought her to see me before, Pat? Ashamed of us, I know. You don't have to tell me. We both know, your father and I—'

She went on and on, banging around the poky, dirty kitchen with a tin tea-pot and a bottle of milk. Ruth stood by the door, realizing gradually that, for all the questions put to her, she wasn't required to answer any of them. She remembered Maxwell's saying once, 'Have you met his parents? Try not to.' She could see that Mrs. Pennington was one of those fiftyish, embittered, hard-working, shrewish little women; she was lean and quick and bony, with frizzled brown-grey hair and sharp, evil eyes. She was horrible. Ruth, watching her, thought of the long afternoon in Kensington on the velvet sofa, listening to Pat playing the piano. The contrast was so sharp it was hard to believe. Pentonville to the sea-wall, the Professor's town house to this. No wonder Pat was mixed-up. It was all a part of him, what had made him. And she most of all, his own mother who had raised him, she was awful.

'We don't expect gratitude,' she said to Ruth. 'We don't ask much. We never said anything, not even when he moved his things across the road to the Bates'. But you can imagine it gave the village something to talk about—when a boy moves out like that—not *away*, mind you, but just across the road—'

'Pack it in, for heaven's sake,' Pat said. 'Let's just have the cup of tea.'

'And all those lessons we paid for, year after year. And him staying on at school when by rights he should've gone out to work—'

At this point the tirade was interrupted by the appearance of Mr. Pennington, a grizzled, burly man with Pat's scowl. Having sampled the mother, Ruth felt she now understood the family scowl. She thought that Pat might look like this when he was old if everything went wrong, but if everything went right he would be quite different, his truculence and his aggression smoothed, the charm that he now revealed on very rare occasions far more apparent, the smile more ready. Hard to imagine, glancing at him now. Back-to-the-wall, he looked like his police-record photograph.

'So it was you!' His father clapped him on the shoulder in welcome. 'The bad penny turned up again! How's things then? How long you been out?'

'Only today.'

'Cripes, today! How was it then? How is the old place these days? Better than in my day, I bet—they make it all easy now. I read all about it in the papers. Piece of cake today. Rest-home. I would've come to see you but I didn't seem to get round to it. I see you still got a lady-friend. How do you do, my dear. I think I saw you once before—in court, was it? I don't know, Pat, you always seem to have someone waiting for you! I don't know how you do it, always falling on your feet. That Professor bloke keeping you on, is he?'

'Yes.'

'You still at that College?'

'No. They stopped my grant. I've got to get a job.'

'Yeah, well, not before time. Playing in concerts and suchlike, you mean?'

'Oh, anything.' Pat wouldn't make the slightest effort to talk shop to his father. His mother poured out the tea and while Mr. Pennington questioned Pat about 'the old school' (Pentonville), Mrs. Pennington fastened herself on Ruth and asked her a lot of nosy questions about where she came from and how she met Pat and what she did and what she was going to do. And all the time Ruth was picturing Pat growing up with these two unsympathetic people in this untidy, depressing little house, meeting aggression with aggression, scolding with truculence, until the day he was inspired enough to move across the road to Mrs. Bates'. It explained a whole lot about him which she had only guessed at before. Mrs. Pennington embarrassed her acutely; she had no idea how to parry the prying, the self-pity, the veiled accusations. She was infinitely relieved when Pat, having finished his cup of tea, moved purposefully to the door.

'I've got to go back to London tonight, I can't stay. Come on, Ruth.'

'I was lucky to see you,' his mother said. 'Only because you didn't see me first—'

'Oh, stop beefing, Norah!' said Pennington senior. 'You don't expect him to care about an old bag like you when he's got a lady-friend with him. It's not his mother he want now, it's a—'

'For God's sake!' Pat shoved Ruth bodily out of the door. 'Why do you expect me to come back when you always carry on like a bloody tap dripping? It's always the same—'

Ruth scurried down the path, cold, harassed. She began to feel that the day had gone on for ever. Pat obviously felt the same, for he got into the car, slammed the door and drove off immediately.

'I thought we were going to Mrs. Bates'?'

'I can't stand any more people. Enough has happened today.'

'Yes.'

'I can't stand them.'

'No.'

'I didn't want—I'm sorry, sorry you got caught up.'

'It's not your fault, what they're like. I didn't mind meeting them.'

'I'll take you home and then I'll shove off back to London. I'll come down again at the week-end and we'll go to Mrs. Bates' then.'

The car sped down the dark lanes, rabbits' eyes gleaming, farm cats jumping into hedges. Pat did not speak again. Ruth sensed that he was very tired. She tried to feel just what the day had been like for him, after the nine months inside, but her brain could not stretch to it. It was impossible. Even in her mind it was a jumble now, only the time on the sea-wall sharp and warm and close, all the other things blurring together. Other places, other people. They didn't matter. She had no sense of guilt or shock or fear. She thought she ought to have, but she didn't. They drove through her home village and down the lane to her house. Pat turned into the drive and stopped the engine. 'You're sure you don't want to come in?' Her parents had promised that they would be pleased to see him, although she knew that it might cost them an effort.

'No.'

She was relieved, although she wanted the time with him to be stretched out.

'You'll come on Saturday?'

'Yes.'

He made no move to touch her, embrace her, but only said, 'I'm sorry about my parents.'

'It didn't matter.'

He shrugged, reaching for the ignition. It was very dark; she could not see his expression, but could feel the withdrawal. He had always been like this, retreating without warning into this slightly hostile silence. It always left her doubting, uncertain, although she was used to it. If he felt he wanted to withdraw in this way, he would not concede the smallest sign or gesture to alleviate the other person's uncertainty. Ruth put it down to his musical side, the side she could not approach, the part of him she had no hand in. It was part of what her mother called his bad manners. She thought of it more as artistic temperament. She didn't suppose he thought of it at all himself.

'Good-bye then.'

'Good-bye.'

'Saturday?'

'Yes. In the afternoon some time.'

'Be careful going back.' She thought he might fall asleep.

The car slipped out of the gate. Ruth watched the lights sweep round in a bright arc and head up the lane. What was he thinking? How could she tell?

She walked very slowly up the drive, not wanting to go in.

# Chapter 2

Pat, with three hours to go before his audition with Backhaus, had never faced any ordeal he felt less confident about, and—God only knew—he had played enough times now with plenty at stake: auditions and competitions and examinations and all the other heart-stopping, stomach-turning occasions that went to make up this masochistic profession. He was quite used to being sick before a concert, although everyone told him that he looked as if he had no nerves at all, but he wasn't familiar with not feeling pretty well on top of what he intended to do, which was how he felt now. The nine months had left their mark; he felt sapped of some vital ingredient in his previous make-up. Confidence, presumably. The prison life wasn't designed for improving one's self-confidence. Quite the opposite.

'Patrick!'

He opened the door cautiously. Clemmie's voice floated up the winding Georgian staircase:

'Telephone for you!'

Perhaps Herr Backhaus had been run over by a bus and wasn't coming? The audition was to be in the Professor's music-room, with the Professor playing the orchestra's part on the second piano. He went hopefully down the stairs.

'Hullo?'

'Pat, is that you?'

It was Ruth. Pat felt pleasantly ready to be distracted from his gloom and said, 'Yes, it's me. How's things?'

'Pat, I must see you! I'm in London. I've got to talk to you before I go home. It's terribly urgent.'

Pat had never heard Ruth speak in this vein before. She sounded upset, almost as if she was crying.

'Whatever's the matter?'

'I can't tell you on the phone. I must see you!'

'Cripes, but I'm playing for the Herr conductor tonight. Where are you?'

'Kensington tube-station.'

Pat glanced at his watch. Five past five. The Prof was due back from the College at half past six. Pat knew that it was more than his life was worth if he was discovered chatting up Ruth when his mind was supposed to be on higher things.

'How about the "Birdcage" then? If we both start walking now? Say, in ten minutes. I've got to be back here at a quarter past six, though. Will that be O.K.?'

'Yes. Ten minutes.' She rang off abruptly. Pat put the receiver down more thoughtfully. Peculiar. Not like Ruth at all. He felt slightly uneasy. Ruth never demanded things of him, least of all his time when he was bound up with work. She had a touching reverence for his work which sometimes annoyed him. He went out of the front door and down the steps, feeling in his jeans pocket for any hopeful signs of money. A fifty pence piece and a button. She'd be unlucky if she was hungry. But she didn't look hungry. She looked white and fragile, all eyes and hair. She was waiting for him outside the small café they sometimes used, not smiling at all. Usually, because they didn't manage to meet very often, she was laughing and eager and flatteringly pleased to see him. She didn't use the cool sophisticated ploy, which was a relief, and he didn't think she was putting anything on now. But cripes, whatever it was, he hoped it wouldn't take too long. Her timing was unfortunate.

'Oh, Pat!' It was close to a sob.

She came up to him and he put his arm round her, his heart sinking heavily.

'What's up? What's wrong?'

'I'm going to have a baby.'

Pat, having asked the question in the same way as one might comment on the weather, hadn't expected a straight answer, and certainly not the one he got. It was so completely unexpected that he could not take it in. He could not believe that he had heard her right. There was a long silence, and Pat realized that he was holding his breath, and let it out very carefully. He looked at Ruth closely. She was looking at him with an expression he could not make out, something beyond the obvious distress.

'Look,' he said. 'You *are* joking?'

'About a thing like this!' She blazed suddenly and pulled herself away. 'Some joke!'

'But we never—we *haven't*—'

'Only the once.'

'On the sea-wall?'

'Yes.'

'But you can't—not just the once—'

'I thought that too. Well, it's not true.' The tears came welling up and ran down her cheeks.

'Oh, Lord! Stop it!' They were standing in the middle of a swarming pavement, dusk just coming and the sharpness of autumn pinching, the buses flaring past in a haze of diesel fumes. He could not believe it. He felt furiously angry.

'Oh, come on,' he muttered. 'Not here, for God's sake.' He took her arm and steered her along the pavement, walking with the rush-hour mob. He felt so angry and confused. He could not say anything, because his brain wasn't coping. He wasn't sure if he believed it.

'How do you know?'

'Oh, don't say you don't know how it works! I came up today for a test, to find out. You read those advertisements and go to an address and they do a test and tell you if it's positive or negative. Well, it's positive. I knew anyway.'

Pat wanted to ask if it mightn't be somebody else's, but he daren't. If it was true, it was the biggest bloody disaster he could conceive of (and *there* was a good pun, he registered viciously)— worse than Pentonville.

'Cripes, but *once*!'

It was beginning to sink in. He was appalled. He couldn't find anything to say to improve the situation. He walked along staring at the pavement, and Ruth wept beside him.

'Does anybody know? Your parents?'

'Not yet.'

He pictured himself telling the Professor. It was impossible. He felt sick again—the prospect of playing Beethoven to Herr Backhaus was roses beside this. Cripes, Ruth must be *potty*—he glanced at her, and was smitten for the first time with a pang for her. She looked about ten, thin as a twig, crying in a silent, painless sort of way that made his heart lurch uncomfortably. He put his arm round her and gave her a squeeze. He couldn't think of anything to say at all.

There was a Wimpy bar, and he steered her in because people were staring. He ordered two coffees, and Ruth sat with her elbows on the table, her head in her hands, staring out of the window between the leaves of a large rubber plant. The tears were easing off; the expression remained difficult to define. Pat felt uneasy. The idea had sunk in; it only remained to discuss it. But he didn't know how to start. The waiter brought the coffees and wrote the price down on his little slip of paper. Pat glanced at his watch. It was twenty to six.

Ruth said, 'It's all right now I've told you. I've got to go home.'

'And tell your parents?'

She shrugged. 'If I *dare*—'

'And then?'

'Whatever you decide.'

'Me?' He heard the shock in his own voice. He hated being manoeuvred, and was angry, at a loss.

She said, 'It can't be decided in a hurry. Only one thing: I'm not going to get rid of it, whatever you decide. I only wanted you to *know*. I didn't know there was anything special on tonight. I'm sorry if I've put you off. I just couldn't go home without telling you.'

From anyone else one would have suspected sarcasm behind these sentiments, but not Ruth.

'No,' he said.

'What are you doing tonight?'

'Playing for Backhaus—Beethoven's Third. He's coming to dinner.'

'I'm sorry. It's important, isn't it? I didn't time it very well, coming today.'

'No. But your thing matters—God, it's more than—' It was *somebody*! His! Heavens, he was a daddy-oh! He pushed his coffee away, feeling sick. But it was the females who were supposed to feel sick. The jumping pre-concert feeling was knotting his stomach. But there was no running away from this one, just like a concert. They would soon all be gathering to pontificate: Ruth's parents, his parents, the Professor . . . the Professor! Even Clemmie, and Mrs. Bates, Clarissa. The prospect was dreadful. But, God—his mind lurched off again, it wasn't anything to ruddy well do with *any* of them!

'Look, whatever *they* say—' He spoke quickly, before he could change his mind. 'It doesn't matter. It's all right.'

'What do you mean?'

Pat could see the Professor's face, the charm wiped out, flint showing, the anger pinging like hailstones. It had happened before. He didn't have to let it matter again. Say it quickly, while the vision gave courage.

'We can get married. Get by—we don't need anybody to tell us what to do. Find a room somewhere.' Cripes, what was he saying?

'We needn't decide now,' Ruth said, but now her expression made sense. She was glowing; she could not hide it. She was like a thirsty white daisy given rain. He could not believe that she could want him so much. But his big foot was well in it now.

Ruth said, 'Listen, you don't have to say that!'

'No, but—'

'Honestly. You can't spoil your work. You must think about it properly.'

'It's no good the way it is now anyway, just being a parasite on the Prof.' This could be the shove he wanted. He'd just have to get by now on his own efforts. But the prospect was daunting. He leaned on the table, drawing a pattern in spilt sugar with his teaspoon. He felt strangely excited. To live with Ruth was a far nicer idea than living with the Professor. While he had been in prison he had thought about marrying her, but when he came out the idea hadn't seemed so bright; the flesh had been more than willing, but the resources non-existent. They still were. He looked at her, scowling thoughtfully. He didn't quite know what he felt about Ruth sometimes. He thought that he loved her as much as he was capable of loving anyone, but he did not rate himself highly at loving—properly loving, in the sense of caring for and looking after, not the sex thing which he had learnt with Clarissa and found very easy, much to his surprise, having worried about it considerably beforehand. (Clarissa had knocked the whole thing for six, but he did not ever think of Clarissa now.) He knew that he had worked so hard because work had mattered more than people. In fact, work had come as a sort of relief, in a funny way.

'You look terribly miserable,' Ruth said, all closed up again. Very earnestly she said, 'I couldn't bear for you to do anything you don't want to do, because you feel it's the right thing. It would be far worse than if you were just to say, "Oh, bad luck. Good-bye."'

'Did you think I would say that?'

'How can I tell?'

'No. I won't.' He didn't know what the hell he was going to do, though. Had he proposed marriage a few minutes ago? The desperate feeling came back. He tried not to let it show.

'We—look, we'll have to work it out.' It was ten past six! God in heaven, he'd have to gallop. 'The week-end—I'll see you. I'll come down. I'll meet you in Northend.'

'All right.'

'The station, about eleven?'

'Yes.' Ruth got up, following him. 'Will you—I mean, you'll have to, whatever you decide—come and see my parents?'

'Cripes, yes!' He heard the toughness in his voice—plain funk at the thought. The classic encounter. Not to think about it now! Think himself back into Beethoven where he belonged. But the evening was a dead duck already. He didn't want to say anything else, frightened to commit himself again. Having already done so, he was shattered by his impetuosity. He wasn't in a fit state to decide anything.

They went out of the café and Pat walked Ruth to the tube-station in silence. Ruth seemed composed, withdrawn. Pat was grateful for this restraint, having a strong suspicion that it was rare in such circumstances. For the first time, he felt her strength; he admired her. It steadied him. He had never been so thrown, he realized, not ever—even during his worst moments on the wrong side of the law. But at the tube-station when they got to the ticket barrier, she kissed him good-bye with a desperation that he could sense, although she didn't say a word. It was an electric current of emotion—compounded of God only knew what powerful, urgent ingredients . . . it left him mindless, drifting back to the Professor's in a state of numb shock, head down against the jostling pavement. Ruth's face, tightly not saying anything, yet with all those powerful feelings buttoned away behind the dark, silent eyes, would not go away from his vision. He had never felt so bewildered, so deeply involved.

It was a quarter to seven when he got back. The Professor was in the hall, cold and business-like.

'Where have you been?' Pat shook his head and went on up the stairs, quite incapable of speaking one word of sense. The Professor must have taken his trance as a sign of communication with Beethoven, for he merely stared after him curiously, and then went away into the music-room, and Pat was free to moan and groan about his bedroom, his mind freeing itself from Ruth's spell to concentrate with startling clarity and vision on his own plight. Away from Ruth, secure in his own pad, this was now taking on its true and awful proportions. He was being pulled into matrimony by the ears—a month away from the altar, and he had no money, no job, no home, not even a ruddy piano of his own . . . Was he dreaming? A *child*—!

He heard the doorbell ring. He changed quickly, and combed his hair and went downstairs. He had to go down. He didn't know what he was going to do. Not about Ruth, nor even with the Beethoven. He kept thinking that he must think of Beethoven, but all through dinner he could only think of Ruth's electric-current feelings and the seed inside her that had perversely chosen to grow into a human being, quite heedless of the train of chaos it thereby set in motion. Every time he looked at the Professor he knew that the Professor was thinking that his abstraction was due to his normal state of nervous tension before a performance. The Professor was benign, fatherly (*fatherly*, a very relevant word!). Pat could imagine him when he knew, the anger, the scorn, the white fury—he had experienced it all before. All his life he had had the knack of inspiring this emotion in his elders and betters: his parents, teachers, and various elements of the law. It was nothing new, nothing he did not know how to accept. But getting married was new. Clemmie leaned over from behind and took his empty plate away. He hadn't noticed he had eaten anything, or what it was. It wasn't nerves for what might or might not happen during his performance, but nerves about what had already happened and what was surely going to happen in a very short time over and above what he was presently going to do to Beethoven's Third. He pushed the plate away and stood up.

'You may leave us if you wish,' the Professor said smoothly, smiling.

Pat went out. He heard Backhaus chuckle in fatherly (fatherly!)

manner and caught his words, 'I know so well the feeling . . .'

How many bastards had the old buffer put into the world then? Pat wondered bitterly. Clemmie followed him out into the hall and said, 'Come into the kitchen and I'll give you something. They'll be chatting a while yet.'

He followed her and sat down at the kitchen table, amongst the pile of dirty dishes.

'What's the matter with you?' she said.

'Ruth's going to have a baby.'

'Oh, my Gawd!'

Clemmie set down her tray abruptly and gave Pat a shocked glance.

'That's a pretty kettle of fish! My word, Pat, you—' She could not think of the words, and stood shaking her head. 'The poor little thing! Poor little Ruth! She's just a child. Oh, dear me. And me thinking it was only the nerves. Oh, my word, Pat, but that's bad. Very bad.'

He could not disagree. Clemmie started laying out the coffee-cups, her plump face all puckered up and twitching with disapproval. Pat knew she wanted to rate him, but was held back— such was her years of grounding in such things—by knowing that in a few minutes he had to play for Herr Backhaus.

'You'd better have some strong coffee,' she said severely, as if it had the power to purge both mind and body. 'What a time to have this broken to us! Dear me! I don't know why you children don't *realize*—oh dear.' She pulled herself up short, clicking her tongue. 'Really, Pat, you . . .' She stopped herself by a great effort. But it was all in her pursed-up mouth and her censorious expression. Pat, taking his coffee, remembered Ruth's arms about him and the smell of the cold evening grass all bound up in their brief and beautiful and solitary moment of loving six weeks ago on the sea-wall, and wanted to shout at Clemmie, '*Poor* Ruth! *Poor* Ruth!' There had been nothing poor about Ruth then, and she would be the first to acknowledge it. But he said nothing and took his coffee into the music-room and sat down at the piano. The doors were closed, and he shook his wrists and his arms and his shoulders into a playing disposition and laid his fingers on the keys. Soon the Professor would come in and sit down at the other piano to play at being a sixty-strong orchestra, and the other man, the sharpest critic of any he was ever likely to meet in all his life, would lie back in his armchair and light up his cigar and roll his brandy in the Professor's expensive crystal brandy glass and say, 'Very well then, shall we start?' and he would have to do this thing, whether his life's course was shattered or not. The only thing he could think of, sitting there, was to remember Ruth as she had been, loving him, and would be again, God willing, when this monumental muddle was a thing of the past and then, with that to power him, hope that there was some remote and ailing chance that his soul might grope its way in Beethoven's direction and his fingers do its bidding.

# Chapter 3

Ruth's mother looked nervously out of the window for the umpteenth time and said to her husband, 'If they caught the four-fifteen bus they ought to be here any minute now.'

'Hmm.'

Mr. Hollis was reading the newspaper but was not concentrating very hard.

'It's they who ought to feel nervous,' he pointed out. 'Not us.'

'Yes. I know. But I feel awful. The whole thing is horrible.'

'Have I got to play the heavy father. I mean, get angry?'

'Of course! You're not pleased, are you?'

'I don't mind if they get married.'

'I'm not at all sure whether that's the best course. It would be if he were a decent, stable character. But he's a jail-bird. He hasn't even got a job—oh, we've been through all this! I wish they'd hurry up and we could get the wretched business over! I never dreamt I'd have to go through all this with Ruth! Ruth of all people—she's never been the slightest bit interested in boys. I still can't really believe it's happened.'

'Hmm.'

'I keep thinking I'll wake up and find out it's just a nightmare.'

'It's not the end of the world.'

'But such a mess! At that age, seventeen! And what's he—just twenty? He had his birthday in prison, I believe. What sort of a start is it? The coming of a child should be a lovely thing, not a great ghastly mistake with ructions all round.'

'Fifty per cent of the population are great ghastly mistakes, and always have been, all through history.'

'Oh!' Mrs. Hollis gave a great sniff of exasperation. The calm reasonableness of her husband had always exasperated her. He had always taken Ruth's part, ever since she was little. She was shattered by what had happened: he was philosophical. Mrs. Hollis knew that Ruth was quite aware of her basic security. In spite of what had happened, Ruth knew that she wouldn't be thrown out, and her mother was annoyed by the girl's acceptance of this fact. She could not stop voicing her own bitterness. She had been voicing it every day since she had found out. It had the effect of making Mr. Hollis stick up for Ruth. The whole family had talked itself round in circles, airing opinions but deciding nothing.

'Because it's not for us to decide,' Mr. Hollis had pointed out firmly to his wife. 'It's for the pair of them.'

'And if the lad decides he doesn't want to be involved, and Ruth is left with the baby, who is going to be lumbered with the job of looking after it? Tell me that! It will be me, of course! The universal doormat—'

'You like babies.'

'I won't *have* it! I don't want to start all that again at my age!'

The voice had verged on hysteria. It had railed spasmodically through all the grades from horror and grief to indignation for the last four days, and now, faced with the actual confrontation, to make the decision, it was taut with nervousness. Mrs. Hollis could hear her own voice, querulous and agitated, and was annoyed with herself. It was not for *her* to be nervous! It was for her to dictate, to take command, to make it go her way. But she felt defeated before it even started.

'The young today—they do just what they want,' she muttered. 'No morals, no standards . . .'

If the boy had been more suitable, she supposed she might have felt more optimistic. But what little she did know of him was daunting. The only opportunities she had had to observe him at length were during his playing of the Rachmaninov Piano Concerto in the Northend Pavilion a year ago, when he had appeared to her to be extraordinarily controlled, refined, and gifted; and during his appearance in the dock at the Northend Quarter Sessions a few weeks later when he had struck her as equally uncontrolled, unrefined and downright undesirable. Her last sight of him was of his being bundled into the back of a Black Maria, en route for Pentonville, handcuffed to a young man with long hair who had knocked out an old woman and stolen her handbag—while she coped with a weeping Ruth and her own mangled feelings, having aged another year or so during the day. It was not entirely surprising that she felt apprehensive about meeting him in the present circumstances, not knowing which of his Jekyll and Hyde faces to expect. Nobody she had ever come across was quite such a paradox. And Ruth not only in love with him, but irrevocably pregnant . . . 'Oh!' Mrs. Hollis could not suppress another groan at the prospect.

'Here they are now,' said Mr. Hollis from his armchair.

Mrs. Hollis flounced round, tight-lipped. 'Huh!' She went to the door, her hands shaking.

It was going dusk, the smell of frost in the air, the elms gold and baring across the lawn. Ruth was in front, almost running, laughing, her face bright with cold. Her mother had never seen her look so healthy and happy, so *unsuitably* carefree—it made her almost snort with rage. Pat was behind, not looking nearly so carefree, Mrs. Hollis was gratified to note, but not particularly apprehensive either. It was his old expression, the look he always wore when he had been the baker's boy, and which had annoyed her then, not polite and helpful and how-are-you-today, but slightly hostile and impatient—his normal expression, she supposed. She had thought of him in the past as ominous, and had no reason now to change her opinion; his movements were not politely contained in a nice public-school manner, but brought to her mind the ridiculous simile of a tiger in a cage. He had always given her this unease, she realized, even when he had been a mere baker's boy. There was this feeling of restrained energy about him, a total lack of the normal human conditions of boredom, indifference and relaxation: he was large and taut and disturbing, even when he was just standing there doing nothing, and Mrs. Hollis had always wanted a *nice* boy for a son-in-law, a kind, well-bred, soft-voiced, *normal* boy. Pat was none of these things. She suppressed another groan, looking up at him, and said in a tight voice, 'Do come in. We guessed you would be on that bus.'

He came in. He was wearing, Mrs. Hollis noticed with distaste, patched jeans and a black polo-necked jersey, and his hair was fast losing its neat government appearance. She nodded to him curtly, and he nodded coldly back. It was not an auspicious start to what was likely to be a long, intimate relationship. 'Son-in-law,' Mrs. Hollis thought; the title stuck in her brain, meaningless. More like out-of-law—there was nothing lawful about what he had done to Ruth. Mr. Hollis got out of his armchair and advanced slowly, holding out his hand.

'How do you do.' He was perfectly right, his wife thought with surprise, cordial but rather aloof, only the faintest smile. Very civilized. Pat shook hands and muttered something under his breath. Mrs. Hollis realized then that he certainly must feel worse than she did, whatever sort of a face he was putting on it, and immediately she felt better.

Ruth, flinging off her coat, her face positively beaming light and joy, said, 'It's all right, we're going to be married!'

Her father turned to her, as flinty as Mrs. Hollis had ever seen him, and said, 'Surely the decision has still to be made? Isn't this what we are all meeting for?'

Ruth's mouth dropped open in astonishment.

'But—'

'Old-fashioned as it may seem to you,' Mr. Hollis continued, 'your mother and I are still the ones to decide on your future.'

Mrs. Hollis was almost as amazed as Ruth at the unprecedented sternness in the voice of this carpet-slipper man whose mildness they had taken for granted all their lives. She saw Ruth's face, white and blasted, and felt a most unusual stab of triumph go through her. '*Yes*,' she thought, 'why must it always be *we* who are the manipulated, the pitied, the derided?' The arrogance of the young was so total that their elders could be quite unkeeled by it, their own scraps of wisdom, garnered by hard experience, quite tossed away by sheer, bursting confidence. What, for heaven's sake, had Ruth to be laughing about, shackling herself for life to a jobless young jail-bird, with the child to tie her freedom right from the very first moment? And yet, apart from her momentary surprise at her father's attitude, she was obviously over the moon with excitement and pure joy. Her confidence was, to her mother's eyes, quite maniacal. And yet, of course, to the young quite normal.

'I'll put the kettle on,' she said flatly. She could not help noticing that Pat did not appear to be sharing quite the same confidence. Or if he was, it wasn't quite so evident. 'Poor young devil,' she thought, with a quite irrelevant and completely out of place pang of sympathy. He was going to pay for his seduction with a vengeance! Ruth had assured her that they had only made love on the one occasion. There was, if you were dispassionate enough to stand back and appreciate it, a distinctly ironic and funny side to most of the common human dilemmas. With all this philosophy swilling unusually and somewhat disjointedly through her mind, Mrs. Hollis went to make a pot of tea.

'Go and sit in the other room,' she said. 'I'll bring it in.'

Mr. Hollis led the way and sat in his usual chair opposite the television set, wondering if Pat was as acutely aware as he was that Arsenal were playing Spurs and they only had to turn the knob to enjoy themselves, instead of ploughing through the agenda before them.

'Interested in soccer?' he said.

'Yeah, I played a lot once.' Pat then looked at the blank television set in such a way that Mr. Hollis knew that he knew very well what was on.

'Years since I played it,' Mr. Hollis said. 'I still follow Ipswich, though. That's still the home team, as far as I'm concerned. It's had its moments.'

'Yes, it has. I used to train evenings sometimes with some of the Northend United reserves. Before I left school. I thought of doing it sometimes, but then so did a lot of others.'

'Easier than what you *are* doing, I'd have thought.'

Pat shrugged. 'I got the opportunity.'

'Ever regretted it?'

'Not yet.'

'It's very competitive, as jobs go.'

'Yes. Like soccer.'

'How did it come about?'

'Professor Hampton heard me, when I was still at school. It was a coincidence, really—that he heard me, I mean. And he offered me a scholarship, talked me into it.'

'Is he the man whose place you're at now?'

'Yes.'

'Does he know—about—what's happened?'

'Not yet.'

'Your parents?'

'No. I don't see them much.'

'You've no brothers and sisters?'

'No.'

'Not really any family life at all?'

Pat shook his head, frowning. Mr. Hollis could see that he

hated being questioned, yet knew that he had put himself in a position that made it inevitable. For his own money he preferred Pat to the boys that his wife would have considered suitable as son-in-laws, but he could not help agreeing with her doubts as to whether this taciturn lad was actually going to make Ruth happy. He could see the romance part of it, yes . . . the physical desirability of the boy he could acknowledge without any difficulty; his particular talent was impressive and persuasive and by its very nature far more attractive than bank-clerkery, motor-car selling or hod-carrying . . . but when it came to the brass facts, shorn of romance, the boy was insecure, aggressive, penniless, jobless, temperamental, irresponsible and without prospects—except possibly long-term prospects. Mr. Hollis sighed. His glance went again to the blank screen of the television set. Mrs. Hollis brought the tea in on a tray and Ruth pulled up a small table.

'You must be cold,' Mrs. Hollis said to her. 'Out all day in just that thin jacket. It's turned quite sharp.'

'I wasn't cold.'

'There's a meal in the oven we can have a little later. I didn't know what time you'd be back.'

She sat down and poured out the tea. They all took their cups, passed round the sugar, stirred, and sat back in the easy chairs. Nobody said anything. Mrs. Hollis sent an angry, impatient glance in her husband's direction. He intercepted it, resisted.

'Put the box on, Ruth. We'll just get the end of that match, I'd like to know—'

Ruth grinned, and got up and switched on the television. She dared not look at her mother. The commentator's voice came through, taut, clipped, and the picture followed slowly, the ant-like figures running across the screen. Pat's eyes flicked up.

'Three minutes to go, and two minutes' injury time . . . Spurs will really have to pull something out of the bag if they're to equalize now!'

'Arsenal. That means they'll be playing the winner of the Ipswich—Colchester match next.' Mr. Hollis looked deeply contented.

'Ipswich,' Pat said.

'You reckon? Five minutes to play . . .'

They all watched the television until the match was over and spectators spilled out over the screen, making faces and waving.

Mrs. Hollis got up and turned off the set pointedly and Mr. Hollis said, 'Any more tea?'

She took his cup and refilled it, her face grim. He got up and sugared it and took it back to his chair again.

'Well?' Mrs. Hollis put the tea-pot down firmly. 'What—'

'Yes,' said Mr. Hollis. 'Let's see what these two have got to say for yourselves. The object of the exercise.'

'We're going to get married,' Ruth said.

'You mean you would like to get married?'

'Yes.'

'Pat would like to get married too?' Mr. Hollis turned and looked at him.

'Yes.' Pat was still looking at the blank television screen.

'Because you've got to?'

Pat's head jerked up. 'No. I didn't say that.'

'You don't feel you've got to, then? You don't feel any responsibility for what's happened?' Mrs. Hollis cut in.

Pat glared at her. 'I am responsible. I never said I wasn't.'

'And what can you offer her, if you get married? Are you in a position to offer to marry her?'

'I will be soon enough if I put my mind to it. I'll get a job, and we'll find a room somewhere, and then we'll get married.'

'A room!' Mrs. Hollis snorted.

'It's all we want,' Ruth said.

'What, with a baby and the washing and nappies and—'

'Oh, Mother! It will be all right!'

'Oh!' Mrs. Hollis positively snorted. 'When will you ever, *ever*, come down to earth! I—' She choked, her face working. She turned to Pat. 'And you! You've nothing! Nothing to offer! And yet you take her, and you do this to her without any thought for the consequences, and then you have the arrogance to—'

'Mary, don't—it doesn't—'

'Oh, she is such a child! She's no idea—'

Pat was looking white, stricken. 'After a slow start,' Mr. Hollis was thinking, 'we're in with a vengeance.'

'Mother, we're not stupid,' Ruth said. 'Of course we'll manage! You're making it sound as if we're imbeciles.'

'Well, sometimes I wonder—'

'Let's be practical,' said Mr. Hollis. 'What will you do, Pat? What sort of a job will you get? You mean with your music?'

'No. Any job to start off with. Just anything, to pay for some-where to live.'

'And the music will—'

'It will fit in. I've done it before. I've often had to get jobs. You do the job, and then when you've finished you get the practice in. And then I'll start getting engagements and eventually I shall make money that way and then I can give up the other.'

'Have you any money of your own, now?'

'No.'

'Well, I suggest the first thing you do is get this job and some wages and find somewhere to live and then we'll talk about your getting married. How does that strike you?'

'That's all right.'

'You're quite prepared to do that? I understand that you'll be giving up a good deal if you part ways with this teacher of yours?'

'Yes. But it's time I got by on my own.'

'He's been very good to you, I understand?'

'Well, yes. He has.'

'And you've yet to tell him about these present developments?'

'I haven't told him yet. I will now.'

'I don't know how much influence he has over you. I imagine he won't want you to get married—he might try very hard to talk you out of this course. You're prepared for that?'

'Yes. He'll go berserk. I've had it before.'

Mrs. Hollis said tautly, 'You repay him well for all he's done!'

'He knew what he was taking on. I've never asked him for anything, ever.' Pat was looking at the carpet, as if trying to memorize the pattern.

'Why I'm saying this,' Mr. Hollis went on rapidly, 'is so that we all know exactly what the situation is. You might have decided a certain course now, but when all parties are brought into it—your parents as well—you might well be prevailed upon to take some other action. I don't think you ought to feel bound to go ahead with this marriage, until you've talked to these other people concerned. Ruth's mother and I are not forcing you to marry Ruth, you understand. In fact we aren't sure whether it is the best solution at all. For all we know, you might have said you'll do it because you thought you had no alternative. But you're still a free agent. You understand this?'

Pat was silent, the carpet absorbing him. Ruth said nothing, looking petrified.

'You understand?'

'Yes.'

'Well, shall we leave it at that for the time being? You can come back when you've had more time to consider your situation and we'll talk again.'

'In other words, he can get off scot-free if he so wishes, as men always have done and always will do!' Mrs. Hollis's voice shook.

'We both agreed on this, Mary,' Mr. Hollis reminded her.

'Oh!' It was an explosion of despair and disgust, choked with hopeless anger. Ruth looked from her father to her mother and said, 'One thing, I'm not giving up the baby, whatever happens.'

'We can talk about that later,' her mother said.

'No,' Ruth said.

Her mother turned to her, eyes flashing, but Mr. Hollis said sharply, 'How about that meal, Mary?'

Mrs. Hollis slumped, the tears coming up into her eyes.

'I'll help you,' Ruth said, aghast.

'I can manage by myself, thank you!' She got up and walked out to the kitchen, slamming the door behind her. Mr. Hollis leaned back in his chair, gazing at the ceiling, silent. The atmosphere was lacerated, the clock's ticking unfamiliarly loud in the sudden strained silence of shock and embarrassment. In the Hollis household emotional upsets were rare: it was as if the very house was surprised. Ruth could feel it painfully, and wondered if it was as sharp to Pat, who was well-grounded in emotional upsets in a great variety of situations, and might consider this a very minor example. He looked heavily, angrily miserable, not at all like a lover looking forward to marriage. Ruth did not know now where she stood. She could feel the tears rising up from so deep inside her that it was almost a physical pain. She looked desperately at her father, who had gone half-way to rejecting Pat, and he, as if feeling her pain, half got up from his chair and said to Pat:

'How about playing something for us? It's time our piano knew what it was all about.'

Ruth said, 'Oh, Father, really! He surely doesn't feel like—'

'Well, if he's a professional, that's where the difference lies.

Isn't that right, Pat? You play to order, not when the muse stirs?'

Pat sighed. 'I suppose so.'

'I feel that something soothing could be very beneficial just at the moment. Come on now! Did you know that Ruth has acquired a piano and is trying to teach herself to play?

'No, I didn't.' Pat got slowly to his feet.

'Only to learn turning over,' Ruth said hurriedly. 'Pottering. I can't do it at all. I'm useless.'

'She made us get a piano. An old lady down the road was throwing it out, and she got Ted to bring it down here on his breakdown lorry. It's only done hymns all its life, and then Ruth's efforts—'

'Bobby Shafto with one finger.'

'Come on. Give it a surprise.'

Pat smiled, looking as if it was an effort. He crossed over to the piano, sat down and looked at the keys, not saying anything. He played some chords and arpeggios to see what it sounded like, then stared into space some more, bit his thumb-nail thoughtfully —presumably adjusting from thoughts of a shotgun marriage to consideration of a work in suitable mood—then launched into a piece so melting and poignant that Ruth's painful efforts to cool her feelings were sabotaged in the first ten bars. If only it had been brisk and knotty and extrovert like some of the pieces she had heard him play! But it was quiet and flowing, a quite heart-stopping piece, familiar enough to know what was coming and to anticipate the exquisite, hanging crescendoes of the melody, almost held back, to savour the poignancy to the full, then falling down soft and fast to catch up, in such a way that Ruth had consciously to steel herself against it, not to be drowned. She almost hated him, for making it so hard—one had no defence against music, this great mainspring of pure emotion—and she was in emotional disarray already, without Chopin to add to it. She was torn, the music shredding her, and she resisting manfully, because she still did not know where she was with him; she could not allow herself to give in. She watched him angrily, the absorbed tenderness of his expression which she had noted long ago when he played, inspired by his work, needling her with such a mixture of jealousy, despair and downright adoration that she felt quite overwhelmed. She lay back in the armchair and shut her eyes so that she couldn't see him any more, but the music—it seemed to her—got in under her very eyelids, crumbling all her defences.

When it stopped, there was a long silence.

'Ah.' Mr. Hollis broke it with a satisfied sigh. 'The very thing. Very soothing. What was it?'

'Chopin.'

'What's its name?'

'Nocturne in B-flat Minor.'

'Oh.' He sounded disappointed. Ruth remembered she had asked, long ago, the same thing about the Brahms, and found that it was only a waltz, with numbers. It was very precise, the cataloguing of music: there was no clue in the title 'Number one in B-flat Minor, Opus 9, number one' to suggest what a passion it had the power to evoke in a susceptible breast. Ruth sniffed.

Mrs. Hollis put her head round the door and said, 'If you've done, the macaroni-cheese is on the table.'

Pat's thoughts after the interview were in equal disarray. They were unworthy, self-centred and completely materialistic, and he knew it. His heart kept whizzing up with relief that the old man had given him *carte blanche* to scarper, but, ironically, the release had come too late, for he had spent the last week forcing himself to think of all the advantages of marrying Ruth, instead of the whole calamity of the situation which had been his earlier reaction. And he had talked himself into a very real readiness to leave the Professor, so much so that the sudden thought of not leaving him made him feel incredibly restricted again, like a child.

And now the piano! During the very first bars of the Chopin piece he knew he would be happy to marry Ruth for her piano. It was only an upright, but quite the nicest upright he had ever come across. His lack of a piano, if he moved out of the Professor's, had been something of a stopper to his plans. At least if he got Ruth's as a dowry, it was something to keep going on. The unworthiness of this sentiment made him feel somewhat guilty, but he could not quell it. It wasn't, in any case, as unworthy as that instinctive surge of utter relief that had shaken him when Ruth's old man had told him he needn't marry her. This door suddenly opening again, restoring the status quo, knocked all his planning for six. Cripes, there was nothing to stop him, if he really wanted, to get shot of the lot of them, ship himself off somewhere

42

where no one had ever set eyes on him, get a job and start again from scratch!

He sat in the train going back staring out at the racing lights that were the back bedrooms of all the tens of thousands of married couples in the suburbs of London, and tried to think of himself as one of them, and then he thought of himself playing a pub piano in St. Ives, hitching to Afghanistan or Tangier, or even stealing a car and going to Birmingham or Manchester or Clacton-on-Sea. He had only to *choose*. There was no one to stop him. But freedom on such a scale was as frightening as all the other prospects, and he knew himself so well—he had had the opportunity to do all this before, when he had been in equally tight corners, and he had never taken advantage of it. The possibilities had flowered in his head, as they were doing now, but they were as insubstantial as candy-floss. He had no faith. He had learned from an early age that, for him, nothing was easy.

And then, the nub of the whole thing, which ought to provide the answer, did he truly love Ruth? He ought to know, after Clarissa, what love was, but sometimes he thought that she had merely taught him what it wasn't. What he felt for Ruth was such a tangle of affection, guilt, desire, resentment, tenderness, anger and pure confusion that there was no knowing what the real answer was. He peered out of the window, scowling. The bright windows were still flashing past, miles and miles of evidence of married life. One more window, what difference did it make? What a drop in the ocean! He couldn't draw any conclusions at all.

The old man had been all right, but her mother—there was an old cow if you like. . . .

# Chapter 4

'What did he say when you told him?'

'Don't talk about it! I don't want to discuss it—I want to *forget*—'

'Do you, Patrick Edward, take this woman, Ruth Margaret, to be your lawfully wedded wife . . .'

'I want to forget—'

'He plays the C Minor as if his mind is elsewhere . . .'

*Forget*!

Pat opened his eyes, as if aware in semi-consciousness that present reality must be better than what he was dreaming about. He had this feeling of panic which was now almost familiar, and the feeling of having to struggle up to some mythical surface, as if he were in very deep water, swimming up, and the panic to be kept down, drowned, under his feet. He was in a sweat, and groaned as he awoke. The sun fell across the pillow, a pigeon crooned on the window-sill outside.

He shifted, stretching under the sheet, putting his arms up and linking his fingers under his head. The sun dazzled him, making a live spark of the little gold medal of Beethoven round his neck which was all he wore. Morning sun had been the chief attraction of the small room—its only attraction, a cynic might have said, but Pat, his eyes roving round slowly, found comfort in it. He liked it. 'You'll feel at home here, after Pentonville.' Ruth's mother hadn't actually said those words, but Pat had sensed them in her look. He smiled at the ceiling. It was yellow and homely; the wallpaper was so old that the walls were just a pink blur; Ruth, looking very closely, said it wasn't William Morris reproduction, which was the 'in' thing, but original William Morris if they wanted something to boast about. There was actually a jug and basin too, that antique shops sold to smart people.

44

The water tap was four floors down in the café kitchen and the jug and basin were for real, not ornaments. 'I suppose that's for bathing the baby in,' Ruth's mother had said in her scathing voice. Afterwards they had rolled about laughing. There were times when they couldn't stop laughing and Pat, who wasn't used to laughing, had found himself wondering sometimes what it was all about. Everything had gone wrong; all the events that he had just been dreaming about had actually happened, and each one had been exceedingly painful at the time, but lumped together, put behind him, they had liberated him to a degree that was still a pure astonishment every time he thought about it. It had its panics, the deep-water feeling—he could scare the living daylights out of himself if he thought about it hard enough—but on the surface it was a magical relief, a rebirth. He was answerable to no one for the first time in his life, and Ruth didn't count, for weren't they, in the extraordinarily quaint words that had been used by the Northend registrar to marry them, now 'one person'? On their tod together. And he loved Ruth dearly now for being so happy with the absolute nil he had to offer her. They were at rock-bottom. They could only rise up. Awake he liked it, but asleep he got the panics sometimes, the underwater feeling, which was because he knew it couldn't last long, the status quo—he would in fact, *have* to rise up, for the arrangement was strictly for the moment. It didn't include his work, nor the baby. When he started thinking about that, he stopped laughing.

His work . . . that was the crunch, that was what really gave him bad dreams, not the baby, which must take pot-luck like all human beings. But the baby decided the time-factor. By the time it was born he must have got somewhere. This was where, if he was wise, he stopped thinking, and turned his mind back to the ceiling, blank and warm above his head. He did so now, scowling. He concentrated on the ceiling. It was completely unmusical, flat and abstract. 'A cup of tea,' he thought. That meant going down four floors to fill the jug, which had been empty last night and was no doubt still empty now. The thought put him off. 'Ruth,' he thought. That was much better. He turned and looked at her, still asleep. 'Ruth, Ruth . . .' Better than ceilings. Better than work, and better than thinking.

'I love you.' He had put her before his work so it must be true. He could say it now. His new freedom had released all sorts of inhibitions, including his tongue. He felt the flowering of this strange, lovely happiness which was the antidote to the darker thoughts, the ceiling thoughts, the drowning panics . . . it was what made sense of the whole thing. . . .

It was Sunday. Nothing to get up for. Pat had got the room through a Pentonville connection: the brother-in-law of its owner had been in the next cell, was still there in fact. 'The old-boy network,' Pat had called it. Luigi, the owner of the cafe, had remembered Pat from visiting day, and had offered him the room in exchange for a 'spot of washing-up and the little wife as a waitress, eh?' Pat had put the proposition to Ruth somewhat doubtfully, but she had been thrilled at the idea of being a waitress. (Pat could not help thinking of Clarissa at this juncture, although he thought of her very rarely now. The thought made him laugh.) Luigi considered Pat's prison-record a commendation for the job. 'You in ze keetchen, very 'andy if we 'ave ze drunk man in ze café. We 'ave ze bouncer then. Me not beeg enough.' Pat washed up from eight in the evening until two in the morning, and all the rest of the time he was free to pursue his musical career. His musical career, it seemed to him, was now centred on a small landing half-way up the stairs, which was as high as they had managed to get Ruth's piano without getting stuck. Ruth's brother, Ted, had brought the instrument up to London on a borrowed lorry, but the combined efforts of Pat, Ted, Luigi, Luigi's father and Luigi's brother, could not get it past a particular part of the banisters three floors up. It was Luigi's idea to leave it on the landing.

'You play it 'ere. There is room for ze seat. And you 'ave ze electric light. Mama is deaf, she do not worry.'

'Cripes,' Pat thought, when he had extended the light-flex and got the bulb hanging in the right spot over the music-rack— if the Professor could see him at work! If anyone came up the stairs he had to get up and move his seat out of the way. From below, warm smells of spaghetti and risotto and coffee came up to tickle his nostrils, and above him the sagging, fly-spotted ceiling rained gentle flakes of distemper during forte passages. The sound of the ancient plumbing and the flushing of the lavatory pipes punctuated his pianissimos. Carmen, Luigi's wife, brought him cups of coffee at hourly intervals but, otherwise, surrounded by the bare damp-stained walls, threadbare lino underfoot (the acoustics were unnerving at times, after the Professor's music-room) there was absolutely nothing to distract. Not even a window to look out of. His exercises resounded up and down the stairs in both directions and amongst the crashing of china, the explosions of the espresso-coffee machine and the loud Italian conversation from below, he could play unremarked. He missed his lessons with the Professor desperately but kept telling himself that—if he was the musician he hoped he was—it was high time he managed without his mentor and started to work it all out his own way. When it sounded terrible he told himself it was the conditions. Sometimes the panics would get him and he thought he was useless, but he had had those feelings at times ever since he had started studying. It was just a part of the whole business. But now there was no one to get him on a level keel again, only himself. He had to do it all by himself. It was terribly hard.

'What are you thinking about?' Ruth asked him.

He had got up and was shaving, scowling into the mirror over the marble wash-stand with such ferocity that Ruth was prompted to ask the question. She was in bed, watching him. She could watch him by the hour, still trying to convince herself that it was true that she was married to him. Sometimes she thought it was just a dream.

'Growing a beard,' he said. Actually he had been thinking about trying to get some engagements and where to start knocking on doors. He had a repertory that was good enough, a proper mixture of the fashionables with the warhorses and enough to suit it to most audiences—it was just a matter of finding an agent, the right person . . . Now the Liszt sonata was coming together—if anyone wanted that it could be ready, God willing and the stars kindly, not to mention quite a lot of Schumann, the Beethoven sonatas that mattered, three of Prokofiev's and two of Scriabin's, and if it was Tory ladies in Kingston-on-Thames or a musical evening in Steeple Bumstead, he had all the right Chopin and the Moonlight and the Golliwog's Cakewalk, not to mention the Air on a G-string and several Hungarian rhapsodies to boot. 'Blast!'

'You've cut yourself,' Ruth said.

'Blunt blade.'

But Pat had to admit that he was happier shaving with blunt blades over a chipped china basin with roses round the rim than he had been borrowing the Professor's expensive machine in the plushy bathroom in S.W.1. With the kettle boiling on the ring in the hearth, the gas-fire popping in homely fashion and Ruth, decorative as well as useful, groping herself into her dressing-gown and preparing to make toast, there was a good deal to be said for the squalor of bed-sit life. If some agent could only be persuaded to think he could play half as well as Ruth assured him he did, life would be pretty well perfect.

'Do you think a beard would make me look a better pianist? Older, more impressive?'

'Oh, you impress me no end as you are, and who wants to look old before their time?'

She did say some extraordinary things at times, Pat thought. He thought that, considering they were a married couple, they didn't really know each other very well. There had been a bare three months before Pentonville, with not very frequent meetings, then nine months of seeing each other for half an hour once a month, then bang: they were married. He liked it. It was interesting, finding her out.

'What are we going to do today?' She fetched the loaf from its bin on the landing and started to cut some slices for toast. 'I like Sundays. I like every day. But Sundays best.'

'I must do an hour or so on the Liszt first.'

'I'll do the housework then, with the door open, and tell you when you go wrong. Is that the one full of great swooning bits, and then all maniacal? Starts as if he's dropped something and is looking for it in the dark?'

'Yes.'

'I like that. I wish I could play a bit. Couldn't you teach me?'

'Only for money.'

'All I have is yours!'

They had twenty-two pounds and sixty-one pence exactly. Ruth sat down on the hearth with the bread stuck out to the gas-fire on the end of a fork.

'Isn't giving lessons a quite easy way to earn money?' she asked.

'It might be for some people.'

'You could practise on me.'

'Yes. But I don't want to be a teacher.'

'Oh.' That seemed fair. Nor did she. 'What a pity I can't do something frightfully lucrative.' One year at an art school had taught her how lovely life was, but nothing about earning money. Her only qualification, after seventeen years, was her Pony Club B test.

'How do you like your toast? Striped?'

'Of course. Shall I make the tea?' He reached for the tea-packet on the mantelpiece and shook some into the tea-pot. He poured water from the kettle into it, put it in the hearth, and sat down in front of the fire beside Ruth.

'It's nice, isn't it?'

'Yes.'

'You know, Pat, you ought to tell your parents you've got married. It's three weeks now.'

'Why? They won't mind.'

'They ought to know.'

'Why?'

'Parents like to know things like that. You could write to them. You haven't got to actually see them.'

'Well, I might do that.'

'It would be thoughtful.'

Pat grinned. He took the buttered toast she was offering him, and poured out the tea. 'After breakfast I'll practise the Liszt. Then I'll write a letter and tell my parents that a scheming little bitch got her claws into me and I had to marry her, then we'll go for a walk up to Hyde Park and post the letter. Then we'll go to Luigi's cousin's place and get some chips for lunch, and then we'll go to the South Bank and see if we can get a couple of seats for John Ogdon; we'll have some tea and come back here and work the rest of the day. Then tomorrow I'm going to put my best suit on and go and call on all the people I can think of who might get me an engagement. Every morning next week I'll go out looking for work—I mean music, not more washing-up.'

'Concerts?'

'Anything. Don't expect me to come back with a recital at the Q.E. hall in the bag . . . don't expect anything at all. There are thousands of pianists as good as me, all looking for work.'

'Oh, rubbish. You're by far the best.'

'Backhaus didn't think so.'

'He didn't say you were no good! He said you needed more time.'

'Who doesn't? He couldn't very well say I was out-and-out lousy after the meal Hampton gave him, could he?'

'It was my fault, telling you all that just before!'

'No, it was my fault.'

'Oh, that time—' It had been dreadful—Ruth's face went stark. They had had their bad bits, more than their share, right up to getting married, facing up to the Professor . . . but the bits her mother had prophesied would be bad, having no money and living in squalor, had not turned out bad at all. She loved this funny little room, with its battered window looking out over a yardful of dustbins, walls, roofs and—if one nearly broke one's neck craning—the corner of the church in Hanover Square where all the best people got married—and she loved sitting on the floor (the only chair was down on the next landing with the piano) with Pat beside her, drinking tea and making toast. When the baby came . . . well, they would have to have got a bit by then, she supposed, but she didn't think ahead. She had implicit faith in Pat to provide. Thinking about providing had caused Pat to lapse into a heavy silence, staring into the puttering, expensive flame. He was given to long periods of silence; after telling the Professor, one had lasted for three days. He had gone down to stay with Mrs. Bates, and had taken Ruth out, but he had scarcely spoken at all, except for necessities, and Ruth, aware that she was the whole cause of this dreadful condition, had been steeped in such reciprocal despair that the memory of it could still freeze her in her tracks. She had never heard exactly what had taken place. It was like Pentonville: some things Pat would not discuss.

'Oh, well.' Pat got up, slowly. 'This won't get us anywhere. I'll get started.'

'Leave the door open.'

'You can go back to bed,' Pat said, looking down at her. He wished he could too. There were times when he wished he didn't have to be a pianist. He could have been a waiter, like Luigi, with no worries.

Ruth went back to bed, and lay curled in the hollow left by Pat's weight on the sagging springs. Luigi and his family had gone to mass, and the house was unfamiliarly quiet. Somewhere in a technical magazine Pat had left lying about she had read that Liszt's B Minor sonata was 'one of the most technically daunting in the repertoire', so when its great tirades started flooding up the staircase she could lie in her warm hollow in this strange state of complete relaxation, basking in the marvellous noise that was as taxing to make, presumably, as the hardest work one could care to think of, and which by its very essence was relaxing and entrancing to the listener in a way that was the very antithesis of hard work. Not for the first time Ruth was drawn to ponder on the strange case of music, what it was and why. And how it drove Pat, stretching him with all this effort and worry, when he could quite easily have earned enough money by being a bus-driver. It possessed him completely. She knew perfectly well that, with the house to himself and no distractions, he wouldn't be ready in an hour—more likely three—but she was quite happy to lie and wait, listening, the music driving her thoughts, the content inside her so strong, so impregnable that it was almost frightening. She loved living with Pat.

The music broke off and Pat came back, scowling.

'Where did I leave the music—the Liszt? I had it by the bed.'

'It's on top of the wardrobe, on the top of the pile. I dusted them all yesterday. The brown one—is that it?'

Pat groped about, muttering, 'It's not right, that ruddy bit right near the end, just when you think you're nearly there, home and dry—it's *unkind* . . . this is it . . .'

He retreated and after a long silence from below, as if gathering strength, the wild climax broke out again, funnelling up the staircase and into the room almost like a physical presence, culminating in a torrent of double octaves—then cut off in mid-bar and repeated again, and again . . . and again . . . Ruth opened her eyes and looked at the clock. It was one o'clock, the letter to write . . . 'Dear Mother and Father, Just to let you know I got married a week or two back. Hope you are well . . .'

'Oh, cripes,' Pat was saying. 'Is that the time?'

He got back into bed beside her and put his arms round her. He was all hot and sweaty and Ruth laughed.

'Do you like my lovely sonata? Would you pay a whole pound to hear me play it, if you were a proper connoisseur of good music?'

'Not when I can have it free, in bed, with cups of coffee. I thought sonatas were little after-tea sort of things, not to make you all sweaty and smelly . . .'

'No, no. You don't know anything.'

'Oh, I do! I do know! I do know I love you—'

'Tomorrow,' Pat said, 'I shall start looking for a job. It'll work out. It'll have to.'

'Of course,' Ruth said. And laughed.

# Chapter 5

There was a man who knew a girl whose mother ran a music club in South London who said they were looking for a pianist. 'We won't be having another audition until March, but if you want to give us your name . . .'

'That big fat contralto with the teeth—what's her name?— Ingrid something—she was looking for an accompanist a week or so back—'

'Where does she live?'

'You've got me there, mate . . .'

'Haven't I seen you playing somewhere? I know your face.'

Pat lost track of faces. It was impossible, dunning all these people and bashing on all these doors, to get the practice in *and* wash up. The big fat contralto offered him a pound a morning which he turned down; he could have played for a ballroom-dancing class in Croydon if he could have had the evenings off. But the evening spent washing up was their home. He went to all the agents and they were very polite. They had heard of him. They would take his name. There was a stocky, brooding young man with a pockmarked face and a foreign complexion and a lot of golden-brown hair who followed him out of one of the agencies and said, 'Didn't you used to play with a violinist, a girl?'

'Yes.'

'What was her name?'

'Clarissa Cargill-Smith.'

'That's it. I remember you. You were a lot better than she was, but she looked good. Very striking looking. A striking looking pair, people said.'

'You don't get engagements by what you look like.'

'You'd be surprised. Why not a pleasure to the eye as well as to the ear? After all, people come to see you. They could stay at home with their records if they preferred it that way.'

'Well, girls perhaps.'

'Her father, I take it, is *the* Cargill-Smith?'

'Yes.'

'Why are you looking for work, if you know him?'

'I fell out with them.'

'Unwise.'

Pat shrugged.

The young man followed up: 'Are you the guy that played that concert with Backhaus and then went to prison?'

Pat looked at the man curiously. He seemed to know a lot about him.

'What if I am?'

'Just for the record, I might be able to help you some time. Where are you living?'

Pat wrote it down for him and the young man put the piece of paper in his wallet.

'Cheers then.'

Pat did not reply, and the man walked off. The agent's place was in a narrow street off the Strand, heavy with the smells of the market. Pat stood, indeterminate, shrugged down into the collar of his hairy jacket. He had known what it was going to be like, but to feel optimistic was asking too much. He had the address of a woman in Hammersmith who wanted a pianist for a ballet class. What a haul, after the life's blood he had expended on his craft! Being ruddy good just didn't come into it. He kicked an orange viciously into the gutter.

'That bloke you were talking to—'

He looked up, and saw someone he had known vaguely at College, a woodwind man. He had been in the agent's, talking engagements.

'What about him?'

'He's useful to know. I mean, if you're looking so suicidal, take heart.'

'Thank you very much.' Pat was sarcastic, unconvinced. The woodwind man looked very affluent. Pat remembered that his name was Wilfred.

'Don't mention it. They're open. Fancy a beer?' Wilfred was a friendly youth, and Pat needed a friend.

'Okay.'

They drifted towards the nearest pub. 'That bloke, Mick he's called, Mick Something Unpronounceable, from Bulgaria or Armenia or the Ural mountains or somewhere, he's supposed to be branching out on his own as an agent. They say he's got a nose for new talent. Like a terrier for rats. Instinct.'

'Who says?'

'Well, the old boys who do the job nicely. They don't like him. They've just given him the sack.'

'That's typical. If he's good, don't promote him, give him the sack.'

'Yes.'

'He seemed to know what I've been doing.'

'I tell you, he knows everything.'

Pat tried to feel a bit more cheerful.

Wilfred said, 'I thought you'd have got by with Hampton behind you. You always seemed to impress the right people.'

'Not any longer. I fall out with all the right people as fast as I impress them. What are you doing?'

'I play with an Early English consort. That keeps me pretty busy. Teach the recorder in an infants' school. And play sax in a rock group.'

Wilfred's indelible aura of success depressed Pat. Wilfred was one of the world's favoured; even without his full time-table of desirable work, he had well-off parents and that cheerful insouciance that Pat always envied, grown of confidence and a good education. He was successful by birth. His woodwind playing was competent and workmanlike, but he could just as well have been a good bank-manager.

'Drink up! You'll soon be dead.' Wilfred ordered two more pints.

'Do you know a piano anywhere—needs playing—?'

'Got one myself.'

'Yeh, but I couldn't practise in your place. Not with you fluting.'

'I flute upstairs. The piano's downstairs.'

'Just standing there doing nothing?'

'That's right.'

'What is it?'

'Steinway grand. Came from my mother's place.'

Pat couldn't believe it was going to happen.

'Your mother—would she mind—if no one's using it—?'

'She's past playing now. She's harping. If you want to use it for practising, you go ahead. Move in if you like. There's room. Have to pay rent, mind you.'

'Where is it?'

'Off Finchley Road, Hampstead way.'

Pat stared into his beer. It was the opportunity of a lifetime. A Steinway! Just lying around. Rent.

'I'm married,' he said.

'Oh.' Wilfred was surprised. 'Well, it's a big house.'

'What would the rent be?'

'Last chap paid twenty quid.'

He couldn't afford twenty quid. He'd *have* to afford twenty quid.


'Twenty pounds!' Ruth said, frightened. 'But if we leave here we won't have any money at all!'

'There'll never be a chance like this again!'

'Did you go there? What's it like?'

'It's a Steinway, I told you. A grand—'

'Yes, but the rest of the place. Is it a flat?'

'I don't know. It was a big room, downstairs. Great big house. There was a garden too.'

'It would be all right when the baby comes? Did you ask him?'

'No. But it would be all right. Bound to be.'

'Why? He might hate babies. Crying and all that. If he plays the flute. Does he live there all alone?'

'No. There was a female. His sister, I think.'

'What was she like?'

'I don't know. I didn't notice. The piano is perfect. I *must* find a job—nights perhaps. I'll go and see him again.'

Wilfred said he could play the piano whenever he liked, and move into the room when he could afford it.

Ruth went to see it. It was raining. Ruth had a strange impression that she had been there before; the atmosphere of the road was familiar. She was trying to place it without success as she walked along, sniffing the odours that the rain brought out of the worn pavements, the earth smells crushed by drains and car exhausts and oil and cats. But she hadn't been to this exact place before—

there was nothing evocative about the house itself, an ugly early Victorian house standing back, shabby, hung about by a lot of dripping overgrown trees. The path to the front door was made of patterned tiles. On one side there were similar houses, on the other a high wall blanking it in, garages and a workshop, a few shops and then the main road going by at the bottom with a ceaseless hum and swish of wet tyres, the tired acceleration of buses from the bus-stop. There was a front door filled with stained-glass panes and a note hanging on the knocker saying 'Two pints please'. Wilfred had said his sister was usually in, so Ruth rang the bell and after a while someone shouted from inside, 'Half a mo!' There was a long wait and then the door opened.

'Wilfred said I could come and see the room.' Ruth spoke nervously. She was nervous. It all meant so much, that Pat should have his piano, and that they could have the baby here. It was a baby place—she could see that already, with a garden and room in the hall for a pram.

'Oh, yes, come in. I'm Rosemary. Are you the wife of the fellow who's got his eye on the piano?'

'Yes.'

'Plays Liszt? That piano's not met Liszt before. I hope it's man enough. I'm on the top floor luckily so it won't worry me. I paint for a living. You have a look round, just as you please— I'll go back to work. There's some friends of Wilf's staying—I think they've been sleeping in there, but they're only temporary.'

The hall was dark and Rosemary disappeared before Ruth got more than an impression of her looks, but she seemed cheerful enough, rather plump and blonde and about twenty, Ruth supposed. She wore a black smock and smelt of linseed oil. Encouraging, Ruth thought. Not at all snooty and smart. Ruth didn't like smart girls.

The hall was as big as a room in itself, with mahogany stairs going out of it and doors opening off. The doors were painted a deep purple. Ruth opened the nearest one and found a curtained bedroom with two men asleep in the beds. She shut the door hurriedly and tried the next one. This was the room with the piano: it was very large, shabby, gracious and cold, with a high corniced ceiling, faded rugs on the parquet and faded curtains at the windows. It had a double divan in it, and the enormous piano which was parked like a car across the French windows. Ruth stood looking, feeling. It was quite quiet, save for the sound of the rain outside, trickling in the gutters and dripping off the bare winter trees. She could see the small square of garden outside, bowed down by the rain, dark and secret, feel the damp and the dust in the big room, sense all the questions, all the possibilities harboured: she knew that if they had this room it could see them happy and successful, or it could see them in debt, or ill, or in despair; it could be warm and kind and happy, or it could tax them beyond their means. It could see Pat to the concert platform, applauded and smiling, or it could watch him work and sweat in vain. The piano, silent, dusty and neglected, was like a key to their future, to let them in or shut them out. Ruth did not want to be aware of all this, but it was as if, standing there, the realization came at her, cobwebs of feelings, half-sensed, touching her. It was not like Luigi's, smelly and cheerful and temporary: this place was serious, where it must all be worked out, for better or for worse as it said in the marriage service. Ruth had no idea why she felt so solemn about just looking at a room, but she could not help herself. She thought it must be the weather and her condition, and yet, far inside herself, she knew that the feelings were the real truth. It wasn't just a great coincidence that she had married Pat; it was all part of something that had a pattern yet to be worked out. For the first time, it seemed, she was aware of the dangers. She was frightened. She could have ruined Pat, if it didn't work out right. His path with the Professor would have been smooth and clear and inevitable. With her it had obstacles as big as double-decker buses.

'Oh God,' she said to the piano. 'Make it be all right! Make it work!'

If she had had an abortion she could have married him just the same and gone out to work and kept him while he got started, and there would have been no worries. He never mentioned the baby; he had no interest in it at all.

'But I couldn't have done that . . .' She could never have done it. She started to cry, standing there, and all the time she knew she was being absolutely stupid. She had only come to look at a room.

'I say, it's not as bad as all that, is it?'

Ruth almost choked, jumped round and found Rosemary looking at her curiously.

'Oh, heavens, no! I'm— I'm sorry—' She wanted to die. She felt terrible.

'It's a devil to keep warm, it's so big. But much nicer in the summer. Are you all right?'

'Yes, I am. Really! It—it's just things—I was thinking of—'

'Oh, don't. It all comes out in the wash. Come and have a cup of coffee. You must be frozen. Come up to my department.'

Ruth followed her up flights and flights of stairs, feeling sick and awful and demoralized. She didn't know what had come over her. It was the thought of Pat not making it . . . looking at the piano . . . and all the things her mother had said rising up to haunt her. She felt very tired. She had to go and be a waitress in less than an hour.

'I have to go to work—'

'It's all ready. Don't worry. Sit by the fire for a minute or two. Are you going to have a baby?'

'Yes.'

Rosemary's room was a riotous jumble of painting things, large cardboard boxes of bits of material, an unmade bed and piles of books. It was brightly lit by neon strips, and a large gas-fire roared in the hearth. It was so different from the silent room downstairs that it did not seem to Ruth she could be in the same house. It was cheerful, lived-in chaos. It occurred to Ruth that, should she and Pat ever move in downstairs, that room too could easily become as chaotic, Liszt and a baby's bawling contributing.

'He didn't say you were pregnant.'

'No.'

Ruth tried to pull herself together, sensing that Rosemary's remark was perhaps a rebuke. Perhaps they didn't want a baby in the house. Wilfred's invitation, after all, had only been for Pat to play the piano.

'I'm sorry. I only came—to see. I—I don't suppose we could— I don't know. If we move from our present place, Pat would have to get a job first. I don't know if we can afford it. And you probably wouldn't want people with a baby.'

'It would be ideal for a baby, with the garden,' Rosemary said. 'We wouldn't mind. We can't make the rent any less, though.

The house belongs to our father and he says it has to be economic. He lives in the next road—'

She mentioned the address, and Ruth then realized why the area had seemed familiar. Clarissa lived there, in the same road as Rosemary's father; they had walked this way the day Pat had come to practise with Clarissa, the awful day that had ended with his being taken into custody. If they came to live here now, Clarissa would be just up the road.

She shivered, huddled over the gas-fire.

'Are you sure you're all right?'

'Yes.'

Rosemary was kind, but Ruth had got herself into such a state that she couldn't really take Rosemary in. Their situation was so difficult now: why ever hadn't she realized before! The baby was only three months away and Luigi's place was no home for three. She hurried away from Rosemary, excusing herself awkwardly, and ran to the tube-station. Rosemary had noticed her condition, and when she ran she was uncomfortably aware of it herself; she couldn't manage far, lumbering and out of breath. When she sat in the train, she could feel the child moving inside her. Usually she loved to feel this movement, but now it only emphasized the problems she had suddenly awoken to. She went back to Luigi's and found Pat just in himself after a visit to the ballet class in Hammersmith. He was in the kitchen, helping himself to a plateful of chips. Ruth tried not to go hysterical on him, but felt shaky and queer.

'What's the matter?' he said. 'Did you go up to Wilfred's place?'

'Yes.'

'What do you think of it?'

'It's—it's nice. It would be marvellous—'

'There'll never be another piano like that again,' Pat said. 'Even finding a place where we could take yours—it would take a lifetime. We must go there—'

'But the rent?'

'I can have this job in Hammersmith if I want it. I told her I'd let her know. It's real hack—just thumping away for a dancing class, but it's something. Then if I can get something else near home—any ruddy thing—I'll go and have a nose round this afternoon—we might be able to manage the rent. I doubt if we'll eat—have some chips, make the most of it. You all right? You look funny.'

'Worried.'

'Here, sit down. That makes two of us. It'll be all right. Nobody actually starves these days.'

They were in a corner of the café kitchen, with Carmen and Luigi and Carmella jostling and shrieking through the hatch and the sizzle of beefburgers and chips drowning their conversation. The smell of the food made Ruth feel sick.

'You look awful,' Pat said. 'Why don't you go up and get into bed? I'll do the waiting.'

'But you've got enough to do.'

'No, not this minute. Go on. I'll bring you a cup of tea. I'll do the lunch stretch, then I'll go and look for a job Finchley Road way.'

Ruth gave in. She had never really suspected Pat of being kind, in a solicitous sense, but there were times when he surprised her.

She lay on the bed and Pat put the eiderdown over her and put the cup of tea where she could reach it.

'It's all right?' he said, frowning down at her. 'Nothing's going—going wrong?'

'I don't think so.' She had no idea really, knowing very little about the process.

'I wouldn't like—now—' He hesitated, and turned away. 'I wouldn't like it not to happen, in spite of everything.'

After he had gone Ruth wondered if she had heard him right. She thought she had, and wept a little more, but not for despair and fear, only for relief.

Five days later he came home at tea-time and said he thought he'd got a job which would see them through.

'Doing what?'

'Driving. Car-hire firm, mostly weddings.'

'Good heavens!'

'The big advantage is that most people get married between lunchtime and about four o'clock, which is the time of day that I can spare best.'

'You mean a big smart car with white ribbons on the bonnet?'

'Yeh, a Rolls, like the Queen's.' Pat grinned.

'You've really got the job?'

'I've got to see the boss's partner tomorrow, but it sounds hopeful. It's right near Wilf's place too. If I get it, I'll go and tell Wilf we'll move in.'

'What about the ballet class?'

'With luck, I'm hoping I can do that as well. She starts at eight-thirty. Depends what time I have to start driving. I'm supposed to start the ballet class on Monday.'

'When will you practise?'

'I'll get up early and do it, and when I get home.'

'Suppose—' Ruth hesitated. Suppose anything. It was all fluid and tricky and nothing to make real plans on, only hope. She was frightened of leaving the security of Luigi's. But she was nearly past waitressing as it was, getting more cumbersome day by day.

That evening she was clearing tables when a man touched her shoulder and said, 'Someone called Patrick Pennington work here?'

'Yes,' she said. The man looked foreign, dark-skinned, although his mane of hair was curiously fair, a reddish-gold colour. 'He's in the kitchen.'

They were very busy and she hesitated to say that she would ask Pat to come out, but this man was obviously a man of action for he took the laden tray from her with a charming continental courtesy and said, 'Lead on.' The kitchen was such an inferno of activity that she didn't think anyone would notice an extra waiter, so she took him across to the sink where he could unload the tray and talk to Pat at the same time. Judging from the state of the draining-boards, there was not much prospect of Pat taking time off for a chat.

'This man was asking for you.'

Pat looked up and saw the visitor. A nervous suspicion came into his eyes. He straightened up slowly.

'We can talk here?'

What was his name? Pat was trying to remember. Mick Something-Unpronounceable from points East of Europe. 'Yes, if it's okay by you. I can't knock off for a couple of hours yet.'

'I'll wipe,' Mick said.

He unloaded his tray into Pat's washing-up water and Ruth took it off him. She had no idea who he was and could not spare the time to listen-in. When she came back with the next load, he was diligently drying plates, and Pat, reaching for the wire wool with one of Carmen's pie-dishes in his hand, was saying, 'The

Scriabin four is all right. I can do that now. I'd need at least a week to work up the Handel Variations.'·

'The Chopin sonatas?'

'Yes, but I'd rather do the Liszt.'

Ruth thought it must all be coming true and went off with one Spanish omelette and chips and two egg, sausage, and bacon, feeling so agitated that she gave them to the wrong people. She did not dare believe it, but the temptation was so strong that it was hard to stop her imagination from running away with her. At these times it was nothing less than the Festival Hall, and everyone standing up shouting 'Bravo!' and clapping with their hands held out to the platform where Pat would be taking his bows, and the orchestra would be clapping as well and one of the most eminent conductors in the world would be smiling, and she would be standing in the wings in a long elegant dress, and talking to a member of the Royal Family. She took another pile of plates back and Pat was aiming a squirt of detergent absently into a fresh sinkful of water and saying, 'I'll get the music tomorrow and go through it. How often do they rehearse?'

'They'd probably step it up a bit for this. Usually they do two or three evenings at Albert's house. I'll give you his phone number and when you're ready you can give him a ring.'

Pat was wearing denims and plimsolls and Carmella's apron with roses all over it, but the stranger was in a soft suède jacket and a silk tie and had a rich but shabby look which Ruth had always thought the ideal to aim at, as if you didn't care but it wasn't money that was stopping you. She wished they had enough money for Pat to look like that. He only had his concert suit and his evening dress wrapped up in plastic bags in the wardrobe, which were tools of the trade and never to be worn for ordinary life, and otherwise the uniform old rubbish that most students wore, only the patches on his were not merely for decoration. The stranger appeared to have finished his interview, for he hung the tea-towel on the rack and said, 'I can find you here then? In case anything crops up—'

'No,' Pat said. 'We're moving tomorrow.' He gave the man Wilfred's address.

'You know where to find me,' the man said. 'I'll see you on Wednesday afternoon.'

'Okay.'

He gave Ruth a charming smile. He had gold stoppings, she noticed. He was attractive in a very peculiar, slightly sinister way. Luigi was shouting at her, waving a plate of risotto in the air, and she had to hurry back to the dining-room. When it was time for her to finish, she went straight up to her room to bed; she wanted to talk to Pat in bed, not in the kitchen. Something had happened; the man in the suède jacket had come to talk business. Tomorrow they were going to live in that great cold room with the acacia trees tapping at the windows. She knew she ought to feel pleased, but she felt terrified.

'What was it then? Who was that man?'

'I thought you'd be asleep.' Pat put the light on and came and sat on the bed. 'He was an agent. He's got me a recital.'

'Oh, Pat, that's marvellous!'

'It might be.'

He started undressing, dropping his clothes in a heap on the floor. Ruth could see that he was excited, but trying not to be.

'What do you mean? "Might be"? It must be!'

'Yes—well—if I do it all right. Someone else was going to do it, but now he wants to do something else that night. They want mostly the same programme, because they've gone to a lot of trouble doing programme notes. I'm just a stand-in, playing someone else's programme. Like an understudy.'

'Is it your sort of stuff?'

'Yes, fairly. I wouldn't have accepted otherwise. The Scriabin four and the Brahms Variations and the Liszt sonata—the other bloke was going to do Chopin, but Mick said the Liszt would be all right.'

'Mick?'

'His name's Mick Zawad—something—don't know how you say it—ends in ski, all ks and zs—he gave me his card—Wilfred knows him, said he was useful to know. This recital—don't get excited. It's only a music club in the outer suburbs—some school hall and an old beat-up piano and an audience of old ladies. You'll have to come and be polite. I hate that part, before you can do it now—it's what wives are for.'

'To talk to old ladies?'

'To help their husbands. Have you seen Brahms' Handel Variations?'

'Brahms is on top of the wardrobe.'

'And Schubert?'

'Schubert's under the bed. Up to M is on the wardrobe and M to Z under the bed.'

'I'll look in the morning.' He put the light off and got into bed. 'Cripes, I can't believe it's really happened!'

'But it has.'

'And yet it's nothing really. To play to people like that—they're only there for the coffee. Ninety per cent of them don't know Brahms from Liszt anyway, whatever you were to play. And yet it matters terribly when you're sat up there. To yourself.'

Pat rarely spoke about feelings, and most of what he thought about his work Ruth had gathered merely from his silences, which were at times almost impregnable—she knew how much it meant by how much it occupied his mind, and that was as near totally as the particular exigencies of their way of living allowed. Whether he was really good or not she had no way of knowing. She had heard him play so often now that she knew when he was playing well by his own standards, or badly, but how these standards compared to the general standard she had no idea. He had told her that the general standard got higher and higher every year—she supposed like the time for running a mile and the record for the single-handed Trans-Atlantic yacht race and how many sausages could be eaten at one sitting—and that to prove you were merely capable at your craft it was necessary to be able to perform pieces that once had been considered too taxing for all but the supreme virtuoso to manage. And even when one could perform these incredible technical feats, one could still be damned as 'a mere pianist' and not a real musician, which apparently still mattered even more. And how Pat stood in the hierarchy she had no idea.

'Are you good?'

He was lying beside her in his characteristic attitude, hands linked behind his head, staring at the ceiling. The back alley lamp through the window gave their little room the perfect Bohemian touch, softening its dereliction into a desirable homeliness, and Pat's face in the same improving light was grave and thoughtful and turned in Ruth such a turmoil of passion for him that she was almost afraid.

'Yes,' he said in answer to her question. 'If I didn't think so, I wouldn't go on.'

'Mick must think you're good.'

'I've got to go and play for him on Wednesday.'

'But this engagement is for sure?'

'Yes. But there are other things as well. Enough to go and live in the other place. I'll tell Luigi tomorrow.'

In the other room the rain ran down the windows like Chopin's prelude, full of a great sadness of spirit. Ruth remembered her panic, and wondered why she didn't think of what a good place it was to have a baby in—how big, and how jolly with Rosemary upstairs and the shops just round the corner and a clinic nearby with orange-juice and advice, but all she thought of was how happy they had been in this little room with the William Morris wallpaper. She had never been a great optimist in her life, always fearing the worst, even when it had just been riding ponies, and now she could not learn to look ahead with great confidence and gusto, even when Mick had come with all his promises. Real happiness, when it depended on other people, was very vulnerable, she thought.

'What are the other things?' she asked.

Pat did not reply at once. He was frowning, still watching the ceiling. Then he turned over towards her and put his hand over her shoulder, caressing her long hair.

'You mustn't mind,' he said. 'You've never exactly said, but I've always thought—you minded—'

'Minded what?'

'Clarissa.'

'What do you mean?'

'This Mick wants me to play with her. She's in a quartet, and they want a pianist to do "The Trout" with them. He asked me if I'd like to try it.'

'It's not Clarissa alone?'

'Not this time.'

'Would it ever be?'

'I doubt it. She's not good enough.'

What could she say? Clarissa just up the road, Clarissa in the quartet . . . It was inevitable that she should crop up again some time, but *already*—Ruth turned her head, touching Pat's cheek with her own.

'I hate Clarissa.'

'Yes.'

But how could she tell him why? Because Clarissa could approach him through his work, which she never could; because he had loved her 'desperately' (his own word) and she had let him down when he most needed her; and, mostly, because she still wanted him, and she was clever and beautiful and fantastically well placed to help him in his career, while she herself was an encumbrance, a liability, with an ever-thickening figure, soon to be housebound by the child.

'I'll tell you what,' he said softly.

'What?'

'You can come too. To turn the pages. Like you did before.'

'To warn her off.'

'That's right.'

'Transfix her with dagger-like glances.'

'Yes. Exactly.'

'I hate her.'

'Yes. But don't mind about it. Because we want the money. And I would love to play Schubert with a string quartet.'

She supposed, if she had to be jealous, it was his work that ought to spear her: even now, it was Schubert before Clarissa. But Schubert was dead and buried and Clarissa was still queening it in West Hampstead, and Ruth knew that she was jealous, even without cause. She could not help herself. If Clarissa had grown indifferent towards Pat—then it would be all right. Perhaps Clarissa was infatuated with a new lover and when she saw Pat she would just shrug and be perfectly normal, and nice to his new wife—that would be all right. But Ruth, with such an infatuation for Pat herself, could not imagine Clarissa having fallen out of love with him.

# Chapter 6

It was hard to tell, when they met again, what Clarissa was thinking. Ruth, all geared up to hate her, was considerably shaken when Clarissa came up to her and kissed her and said without any discernible trace of malice, 'How lovely about the baby! I'm so pleased for you!' And to Pat, 'It's lovely to see you again! What are you doing now? I hear you've left old Hampton?' She made no attempt to kiss *him*, Ruth was pleased to note.

She looked rather plumper and less imperious than Ruth remembered her, but she was still eligible for the description 'gorgeous', with a natural elegance and flair for clothes in addition to the handsome, sensuous features and gold-and-tawny colouring already endowed by nature. Nobody, male or female, could help but look at her twice. And she had this fantastic poise and confidence of the extrovert, attractive girl which Ruth always felt that she herself conspicuously lacked, being quiet by nature. And now, not only quiet but tired and heavy and lumbersome—a state she was perfectly happy to accept except when faced with Clarissa's lissom grace. But Clarissa's warmth towards her, as well as to Pat, rather disarmed her.

They were introduced to Albert, Pongo and Richard, the other players of the Schubert quintet. Albert, the leader of the group, was an affable middle-aged man, bald on top and wearing a fawn cardigan like a man in a knitting pattern. It was his house they were rehearsing in, a comfortably casual, rambling old house but with the blessing of central heating, Ruth was quick to notice, unlike Wilfred's (one thing about being pregnant, one did keep warmer than usual, and at Wilfred's that was now a great advantage). Pongo and Richard were younger and hairier, Pongo rather earnest-looking with spectacles which he kept pushing at, and Richard more dashing and forthcoming in a bright orange shirt and black cords falling to bits. They played the cello and double bass respectively; Clarissa was playing the viola part. There was a radio playing pop-music in the room next door and the sounds of small children doing evil to each other.

'The wife is bringing coffee in a moment,' Albert said. 'Get you warmed up! We've been playing for an hour already. If you want to try the piano . . . Here's a chair for Ruth.' Albert moved his violin off it and put it at the piano.

There were aspects of Pat's work, Ruth decided as the evening progressed, that were very nice; this was one of them. She could see that it was very hard work, but it was lovely hard work, and practising with a group seemed to Ruth far more fun than the hours of grinding practice alone with no one to discuss and joke with, which was Pat's normal lot. Her mother had come to visit for the day to see what she thought of the new abode, and Pat had played nearly the entire day, not whole pieces, but endless repetitions of furious passages full of diabolical fingerwork, and her mother had retired into the kitchen in a rage and said, 'I don't know how you can stand it! In one room—it's enough to drive any ordinary mortal crazy! And what when the baby comes and it has to live with it and sleep through it—!' The kitchen was minute and Wilfred's two friends wanted to make breakfast (at three o'clock in the afternoon) so her mother was driven back into the living-room again, and sat crouched by the gas-fire, knitting baby clothes that were a whole generation out of date. Ruth had been very hurt by her disapproval—'So cold! And so un-healthy doing everything in one room. I admit it's a big room, but with that monstrous piano taking up three-quarters of it there's not much room for—' Ruth hadn't listened, but she had been bitterly angry. If Pat had played Schubert, things might have been a bit better, but, as if for spite, he had played nothing but Scriabin and Liszt in his darker moments. Even her mother, Ruth thought, would have been melted by 'The Trout' music, which was like sunshine after Scriabin; it was like coming back to earth from some outer, mystic and terrifying firmament, and finding fields and cows and streams and stones and the fish in the cool shadows and lovely simple things—'Schubert for sunshine,' Ruth thought, and she taxed Pat with his dark choices, and he had smiled and played her a melting 'Impromptu'. This was after her mother had gone, and when he had finished, he got up from the piano and flung himself down on the bed. The room still bathed in Schubert, Ruth had gone over to him and put her arms round him and he had grinned and said, '—to your mother!' very rudely, and pulled her down beside him. They had then laughed themselves stupid, and toasted some buns at the gas-fire, still lying on the bed, and Pat had said, 'Living in one room is full of advantages, like cooking in bed. Your mother doesn't know anything!'

According to how 'The Trout' went, Pat might get himself another engagement. Ruth, turning the pages, thought he was acquitting himself very well. She had only heard the piano bits, on their own, and threading them into all the other parts seemed to her a very complex task, but Pat made no mistakes. Mick had said he thought he could get him an engagement in Manchester playing the Rachmaninov two with a newly formed orchestra, and there was the recital in the outer suburbs to take place the following day, which would pay the rent for a week or two. They had so little behind them that the engagements were essential, to keep them in bread. If she ever stopped to think about it really seriously, Ruth thought she would run screaming back to her parents. The driving job started the following week but it remained to find out how that would suit; Pat had accepted it in preference to the ballet class, which he had only done for two weeks. He would have liked to do them both, but the timings had overlapped. The driving job would be a certain security, if it worked out all right, but it wouldn't keep them entirely. Ruth preferred not to dwell too closely on the situation. There was a chance she could do some work at the garage too, but Pat hadn't sorted it out yet.

'Wait till I start. I might drive into a brick wall the first day. How do we know?'

The first hurdle was the music-club engagement, which was a demanding programme and, in spite of the total insignificance of the occasion, important because it was Pat's first real solo recital— solo in a complete sense, apart from his erstwhile musical mentors —also because Mick was going to be there 'to assess his impact'. Ruth didn't like the sound of that, but apparently Pat was used to having his impact assessed.

His impact on Albert, the leader of the group, seemed satisfactory, for they finished the rehearsal in very good spirits and Albert made a date for another meeting.

'We—I mean the regular quartet—generally have two or three engagements a month, at a hundred pounds a time. If you're interested, we share it equally—expenses on top. We all have other jobs—in the profession, of course. This doesn't pay much, considering the rehearsal time, but we like doing it, so nothing's lost. How are you fixed?'

'I want everything I can get,' Pat said. 'I'll play with you any time. Through Mick—I have to do it through him. He's my agent.'

When they went out, Clarissa said, 'I'll walk with you. I go your way.'

Pat said nothing. It was raining slightly, but not cold, a few stars coming and going faintly beyond the radiance of the street lights. Ruth thought of her old home and the lane thick and muddy underfoot, sludgy with dead leaves—the quick, instant pain of homesickness, and her father's face, kind and content; it would come without warning, and tear her. She had last been home on Christmas Day, with Pat—a day of dreadful tensions mixed with a strange traditional bonhomie, saved by the normality of Ted and Barbara and the antics of their eight-month-old daughter. She rarely thought of home consciously, only when this unaccountable nostalgia came at her without warning.

Clarissa said to Pat, carefully, 'If I get any engagements, would you play with me again?'

Pat said, 'Surely you've found someone else after all this time?'

'I've been playing with Arnold Patience, but he's not as good as you, and he's moving to Southampton shortly.'

'How many engagements do you get? I thought it was just a hobby for you?'

'Yes—but Daddy gets me recitals. He likes me to do it. I get quite a lot.'

'For money?'

'Oh, yes. Unless it's a charity.'

'I'm not playing for charity. We're our own charity at the moment.'

'You'd play with me if you got enough money out of it?'

'I'd play with Felix the cat if I got enough money.'

'You will then?'

'You'll have to see Mick about it.'

'Would you like to come over and go through a few pieces

some time? Ruth too, of course. Mummy would like to see you again. Would you like to come for dinner?'

Pat shrugged.

Clarissa said smoothly, 'Or would you have to ask Mick first?'

Ruth looked across at her, and saw the way she was watching Pat. Her malice was provoked by his rudeness; because he did not respond, she had to try and needle him. Ruth was not sure whether his extreme coldness expressed his genuine feeling for her, or whether it was because he had a wife listening to the conversation. After Clarissa had left them, without an answer to her invitation, Ruth asked him: 'Would you play with her?'

He shrugged again.

'She's improved a lot. I would for money.'

Ruth was silent, unhappy with the answer, but acknowledging its sentiment. Pat went on, 'She knows all the right people. It would help to keep in with her—her father and all that . . . But in this business—I mean, I don't approve of it, but it helps—it helps to know somebody like her father. If we didn't *need* it—but for God's sake, we do—'

He sounded angry and pressed, and Ruth did not say any more. They did need it. But the thought of his playing with Clarissa disturbed her considerably.

The next day he hardly spoke at all; he looked white and gloomy, and wouldn't eat anything. He played all morning and went out in the afternoon to get his hair cut while Ruth brushed his evening suit and tried to fold it up to fit into the disreputable old grip which was all they had in the way of a suitcase. She brushed his one and only pair of black shoes and wrapped them up in newspaper. Outside it was foggy and drizzling and almost dark by half-past three, and the gas-fire had no pressure, puttering feebly in the great hearth designed for an uneconomic Victorian blaze, to be fed by the footman and polished every morning by the kitchen-maid. Ruth crouched by it with a mug of tea, worried and miserable. Pat came back but the tea was cold; she went to make another pot, and Pat lay on the bed staring at the ceiling, silent.

'Your hair looks nice,' Ruth said, bringing a fresh pot and another mug.

'Should do, what it cost.'

She poured out the tea and put it by him, but he just lay there and it went cold too. She didn't like to say anything.

'Did you put the music in the bag?' he asked.

'But you don't use it. No, I didn't.'

'I want it in. I like to know it's there.'

Ruth wondered what possible use it could be in the tatty old bag, if he was out on the stage playing and forgot what came next, but she pulled the books out of the piles on the floor under the piano and obediently put them in the bag. The Liszt was twenty-five pages long, the Brahms not much better. 'Heavens, why does he do it?' she wondered. How to *remember*, let alone get ten fingers on the right notes at the right moment . . . when you could be a farmer, or a mechanic in a garage with a radio going and blokes to lark about with. It didn't make sense sometimes. She sat crouched on the hearth-rug in the dark, listening to the wind in the bare trees outside, the twigs scraping on the windows.

They went in plenty of time, the journey awkward on the underground and two buses. Everyone else was going home, squashed together in wet mackintoshes reading the evening papers, bound for lamb chops and chips and a nice evening watching the telly in their warm, bright houses. 'Why do we have to be so different?' Ruth wondered. 'Going the other way.' She had to carry the bag because Pat had to keep his hands unused, unstretched, warm in his pockets. When they arrived at the school they were met by a little posse of well-dressed ladies and two teacher-looking men. Ruth remembered that this is what she was for, to deflect them from Pat, who had not said a word since setting off and didn't look as if he was going to say anything now, apart from, 'How do you do,' at introductions. They stood in the school hallway where it was warm and bright and smelt of new polish and plimsolls, the eternal smell of school, and Ruth had to make her great effort, taking on the members of the Committee unaided.

'. . . so pleased you could come, so pleased you managed to get here nice and early—'

'Do come in—mind the step . . . we'll take you to the staff-room . . . a cup of tea?'

'We are very keen, you know—we have a very enthusiastic group . . . meet here every Friday evening . . .'

'. . . try to have four or five recitals each winter—as many as we can afford . . .'

'. . . generally a full hall. You would be surprised. People do like the *real* thing, don't they, after records . . .'

They were so kind, and fussing—Ruth could see how Pat could not possibly cope with such attention in his present mood; he had known what it would be like. How useful that she had a part in the performance—she was pleased to be so important to him, saying the right things and smiling and doing all the conversation, while he quickly drank his tea and went out to try the piano before any of the audience turned up. When the early-comers started to dribble into the hall he retired to a piano in the gymnasium where he did five-finger exercises until it was time to change. Ruth went to fetch him. The gym gave her an extraordinary sensation, as if she had never left school at all. 'Ten minutes,' she said. 'Are you ready?'

He changed and came and stood beside her in the wings of the stage, while the chairman of the music committee gave out the month's notices and the last comers settled into their seats. The greetings, coat-shifting, umbrella-shaking, laughing and talking had settled into an expectant tension which Ruth, in her sharpened awareness, could feel reaching out from the corners of the hall. She found she was sweating and trembling, yet all she had to do was listen. Pat was silent, so far removed both in spirit and appearance that he might have been someone she had never even met. She had no idea at all what he was thinking. He might have been the man in the moon.


Pat had not realized, until the few hours before the concert, how much he had lost during the last year. Until it happened, he had persuaded himself that nothing was any different from the last time he had played in public. He had always felt bad beforehand, that was nothing new, but it was quite new to feel so utterly *alone* as he did this time, walking across to the piano. The feeling was quite terrifying. His *own* concert, the pieces entirely his own concern, worked over entirely without advice from anybody, the interpretation his own, the success or failure his alone, credit to no one. He had thought himself ready for it, kicked out of the Professor's nest but the wings ready, the feathers formed; sitting down at the piano, he was not sure at all. The isolation was terrible. In his misplaced arrogance, he had set himself a formidable programme; he had never supposed that he might lack confidence, given an audience and a platform to himself. Afterwards it occurred to him that the whole of his nine months in Pentonville had been designed to flatten the aggressive ego that had got him in there in the first place, and the aggressive ego was exactly what he now felt the need of, the stiffening of mere confidence, to do justice to his composers. Their stuff could not be played by a flattened man.

It was always the worst moment, starting, the sound of the first bars reacting on unknown acoustics, the unfamiliarity of the instrument surprising his own ear, but, 'Cripes!' he thought. 'If I'm not *into* it by the time I start Scriabin, I might as well pack it in!' The introductory Schumann pieces were the only charming works of the evening, and it was upon himself that the charm must work. It was like an examination: if he didn't pass tonight, he wouldn't be able to go on with it. There were no excuses allowed: that the piano had a sticky A flat in the lower registers, that the hall smelt of damp tweed, that he felt constricted in these ridiculous clothes . . . but the first fragment was finished: he had played no wrong notes, muffed no runs, no one was booing—indeed, he felt a cordiality in the atmosphere, a sense that—although they knew it was not the place to clap—they would have liked to. He edged the stool back a fraction. Ruth was standing behind the curtains watching him, monumental in her seven months' shape, but delicate about the face and neck, her ears showing where she had pushed her hair back, giving her the look of a child. He had heard people say about her, 'But she's only a child,' which he always took as an accusation towards himself, but he knew that in her strength she was no child. Seeing her there helped. She smiled at him. He played the Schumann for her, deceptively simple stuff with a warm, sad melody, feeling it now, the hands growing happier. By the third piece, more glittery, he was enjoying it, beginning to look forward to the hard work to come—even, fleetingly, mischievously sorry for wooing them with Schumann only to prepare them for the metallic shocks of Scriabin—God, he must have been a fool to say he would do that thing! Just to impress Mick the Unpronounceable, and merely as an *hors-d'oeuvres* for the mountains beyond . . . But now he *wanted* to—he was all wound up and raring to go, bowing to the applause and having to walk off and on again twice because they were so easily pleased . . . Oh, come on! There is so much to do and we must get out before closing time . . .

Ruth sat down. It was no good standing there like a piece of furniture all the evening because she was too nervous to relax. Pat had smiled at her when he came off, the first smile for twenty-four hours, and it was still all to come, so something must have defused the tensions that had wound him up all day: he must have realized that he really could play the piano without the Professor to hold his hand. She sat down and let herself unwind too, letting the first spooky bars of the Scriabin, deceptively muted, flicker through her brain. He was all right if he was smiling, she didn't have to worry; he could do the worrying, flinging all those peculiar jazzy rhythms and nervous staccato hammerings into the warm receptive hall, to make the comfortable ladies frown and raise their eyebrows and think how advanced they were, paying to listen to such stuff. He was away, she could see now; she could lean back and shut her eyes and think of all the lovely money, resisting the music because she didn't like it very much, but still able to appreciate that it was shaping as well as she had ever heard it. Its splitting climax was irresistible, through sheer force, and the applause came with it in great waves of appreciation. How lovely the afterwards was, compared with the before!

After that it was all right. She knew he was playing well. Did they know? she wondered. All the tricky bits which she had heard practised to distraction now took their rightful place so smoothly that, even to her, who had sat in on the labour, the illusion of the whole thing being easily within his compass was complete. And not only the technical side—there was no sense of the Brahms fugue being merely well practised: it was compelling in a way which she, who had not come in any sense to receive the music as an experience like the people in the audience, found moving beyond her expectations. It was monumental, inexorable, a performance so intense that Ruth herself was knocked out of all her petty preoccupations by its sheer power.

It was the first time she had heard Pat play in public since she had become so familiar with the music, and it reminded her of the Professor's remark that Pat had the luck—was that the word he had used?—to possess the rare and valuable temperament that rose to the occasion. She had not been prepared, now, to listen in any other than a strictly critical, personal way, to comprehend Pat rather than Brahms, but Pat had compelled her into Brahms. When it was finished, and Pat was making his bow, she felt for the first time since they were married that she need no longer endure her nightmare that Pat might never make it to the concert platform.

Having found his old confidence and concentration, Pat then gave a passionate performance of the Liszt sonata. The Professor, Ruth remembered Pat's saying, had advised him against putting this work in his repertory; Pat had since worked at it more ardently than at any other work. There was nothing half-hearted about the Liszt—it required total emotional involvement. Played badly it could sound a decadent, self-indulgent thing, full of moonlit melodies and manic frenzies; played well it was a compulsive, all-embracing experience. Ruth, not sure whether she was carried away by the music itself or by the pure excitement of having Pat's ability so plainly exhibited in public, went to meet him as he came off the platform, and hugged him rapturously. He was sweating, smiling.

'We made it!'

'Oh, it was lovely! You did it beautifully!'

'It went all right. It all worked. God, I feel pulverised!'

He was normal again, exhausted but human. The audience was clapping with enormous gusto and it sounded to Ruth as if it was for everything, not just the music, but for her being married to Pat, and for the baby and all the hopes and aspirations that kept leaping about in her breast when she was in an excited state— which she was at this moment.

'Oh, Pat, it was *all right*!'

He was wiping his face with a handkerchief. She kissed him again and he laughed and said, 'Go and bow for me—you look marvellous! Like a great big bus.'

'I can't bow. It's in the way.'

'I love you.' He was smiling at her and combing his hair, making himself tidy to go and bow. The audience kept on clapping. He had to go out three times and they wouldn't stop, so he had to sit down again to do an encore.

'Three waltzes from Brahms' Opus 39, numbers thirteen, fourteen and fifteen.' His public speaking was not up to the standard of his playing; Ruth doubted if anyone beyond the first three rows had heard him. But it didn't matter. It was a perfect ending, the dash and vigour of the first two and then the tenderness of number fifteen—'our tune', Ruth thought—and Pat was looking at her as he played, smiling again, and she knew it was for her, as it had been the day he came out of prison. Beneath his thorny hide, a tiny vein of sentiment lurked. Once or twice in a lifetime he had let it show.

Mick Zawadzki met them in the pub afterwards. Ruth had forgotten all about him. He was in a very good mood. Pat bought him a pint.

'I reckon I owe *you* one,' Mick said. 'That was a splendid night's work. I enjoyed it. I wasn't sure what to expect, you know. The public performance isn't always the same thing as the private performance. I don't have to tell you that.'

'No.'

'You come over very strongly, you have a very positive presence. That's the show-biz side of it, and it helps—it helps enormously. There is the excitement and the fire—but as well the playing is terrifically accurate, scrupulous. I like that—the two things together—one cannot ask for more. I feel very optimistic about getting you work.'

'Yes, well—the way we're placed just now—I'd do anything. Solo, accompanying, I don't mind. Just as long as I get paid.'

'How much modern work do you play? After Liszt—do you do any Ravel? Debussy?'

'Some of the Debussy preludes—yes, quite a few . . . Ravel's "Jeux d'eau". I've worked on "Gaspard"—I can play the "Tombeau de Couperin" but I wouldn't want to do them in public yet. A couple of Prokofiev sonatas . . .'

'What do you like?'

'It changes. At the moment, Liszt and Schumann. Before Liszt, Schubert. It's too soon not to want to do everything. I suppose later you find what you're really best at. There just isn't enough time, though.'

'Too much fodder. You've chosen the wrong instrument.'

'Yes. I often think that. Too much competition.'

'I don't think you need fear the competition.'

'Easy to say! You only keep up with it by doing it, thinking it full-time. And yet without the engagements you've got to earn some cash other ways, wasting time. Next week I start being a chauffeur.'

'Hell! Who for?'

'Car-hire firm. Weddings and suchlike. I've been on a dummy run without denting anything, and they start me on Monday. I have to take a bloke to Heathrow before lunch and a bride to church after lunch.'

'God, we must deliver you from that as soon as possible!'

'That's why I said I'd do anything. Hack-work, not just being a virtuoso. I only want the money, not the glory.'

'Accompanying you said?'

'Yes.'

'That girl, what's her name—Vanessa?—'

'Clarissa?'

'Yes. The girl with the father. She came to see me. She said she wanted you to play with her. She could get an engagement but her pianist has left for foreign parts, she said. Southampton or somewhere. Would I instruct you—her word—to do a Brahms sonata with her at Hemel Hempstead on April the tenth. Also give you permission to go to dinner at her house. She said you told her to arrange everything through me.'

'I was giving her the brush-off—I was bloody rude to her. What a nerve! She actually called on you and told you that?'

'This morning!' Mick was grinning. 'I thought she was rather a peach myself. I didn't take her very seriously, but I think *she* was serious. At least about the engagement. She said you could have half the fee and expenses and what she called "practice facilities" whenever you wanted them. I was going to pass it on to you in any case—I told you earlier I thought you made a good pair— musically, of course—' he gave Ruth his small continental bow and his charming smile—'but you said she wasn't good enough. I think she passes muster myself, but it's up to you. Half the fee is twenty-five pounds, less my ten per cent, of course.'

'Well, it's a week's rent,' Pat said. He looked at Ruth dubiously. He was glowering characteristically. 'She's got a flaming cheek. About the dinner—'

'I thought it was rather funny,' Mick said. 'I told her I'd like to come myself, and got an invitation straight away. I was a bit bowled over—thought she might think me a bit pushing, so I changed it to a dinner on me, tomorrow night. I'm rather looking forward to it.'

'Good luck, that's all I can say.'

'Shall I tell her you'll accept the engagement?'

'Yes. But the practising will be done at my place, not hers.' He looked at Ruth, slightly nervous, she thought. 'You don't really mind? Not for the money?'

'No.' She did mind, but it wouldn't help to say so. She thought of them going to Hemel Hempstead together. She'd have the baby by then and have to stay behind. The thought made her feel quite sick with jealousy. She knew that Pat was reading this in her expression. She thought that it was genuine that he didn't want to do it with her. But the money was what mattered. Pat put his hand up and squeezed her shoulder. She knew too that Mick wanted to ask Pat about Clarissa, but was polite enough not to in front of her. He must have guessed—or had Pat told him?— that they had been lovers. The evening, having run the gamut through nervous foreboding, dry-mouthed fright, excitement, joy, triumph and—now—nervous foreboding again—was beginning to pall. Ruth felt very tired.

'Come on,' Pat said to her gently. 'I'll take you home.'

'My pleasure,' Mick said. 'I've got my car.'

'Thank goodness,' Ruth thought.

# Chapter 7

Pat duly drove the Iranian oil magnate to Heathrow and Miss Priscilla Mainwaring to St. Martin-in-the-Fields—to get married, with a copy of Brahms' music in the glove locker of the Rolls, and Ruth went to the hospital for an examination and was told that her baby was the wrong way round and if it didn't turn of its own accord they would have to try to do something about it. She didn't ask what, not particularly wanting to know. She didn't like the clinical side of having a baby; the other mothers made her feel as if she was only playing at it, all being so much older, worldlier and worn out than she was. She felt guilty about Pat having to work so hard and having nothing to do herself; she wished desperately that she could play the piano too and be able to talk to him intelligently about it, in the same way that Clarissa could talk music to him. She asked him to teach her, and he sat her down at the piano and sat next to her and showed her how to play the notes of the scale of C major, with her thumb going under to the fourth note, and how to play 'Twinkle, twinkle, little star'.

'Mozart composed a set of variations on it, did you know? No, fourth finger. Lift it up. Holy Moses, you're paralyzed.'

'It won't go on its own.'

'Do this.'

His fingers went up and down quite separately, like pistons.

'Exercises?'

'You've got fingers like duck's feet.'

'You wouldn't make a very good teacher. If I was paying you, I mean. I'd be insulted.'

'I'm no good at teaching. I just can't see how you can be so bad at anything so simple.'

'Well, you've been taught often enough. I don't see how you

can be so stupid as to not understand how hard it is if you don't know how to do it.'

'Come again?'

'I mean, the Professor must have thought you were stupid quite often.'

'He used to get cross. And yet he was a good teacher.'

'How do you know he was?'

'Because I learned so much so fast with him. If I start earning money, I would like to have lessons again—not with him, but with—well, there are one or two, if I could get accepted. It's too soon for me to do without lessons.'

Ruth was amazed. 'But you—'

'I thought it was all right—well, it is, really, but there are things you want to work out. You don't always know if you're doing it the best way—you want someone else to—to just be there, to work it out with, just talk about it. You can't always *hear* what you're doing as well as you ought. You want someone to tell you.'

'If you went to see the Professor, would he—'

'I wouldn't go back to him. Not after what he said.'

'It was my fault.'

'*It's* fault.' He put his hand on her bulge. 'What's this about it being the wrong way up?'

'Feet first.'

'Sounds sensible to me. Landing on your feet.'

'Well, it's wrong apparently.'

'So what are they going to do?'

'Shove the poor little thing round.'

'How?'

'Ugh! I can guess! I didn't ask. I never did like biology.'

'God, I'm glad it's not me.'

'You aren't a very keen father! Lots of them go to classes about it at the hospital, and they're going to be there when it's born. The hospital encourages it. They've already asked about you.'

'Cripes, I'd faint! You're not serious? You don't really want—you didn't tell them—'

'No, I didn't, don't worry! I don't want you there. Only afterwards . . . you have to come with flowers and a box of chocolates, properly, and be nice about what it looks like.'

'That's all right. I can do that. But the other—' He looked worried. 'You don't—'

Ruth was amused. 'No, honestly! I don't.'

'I don't like hospital things.'

'Well, that's not surprising. But having a baby isn't being ill.'

'No, but I'm still glad it's the female department.'

'We're all happy then. I wouldn't want to do what you do.'

'I thought you wanted to learn?'

'Enough to understand.'

'All right. Thumb on C . . . twin - kle, twin - kle, G with the fourth finger and A with the fifth.'

'Where's G?'

'The dominant, five up. There. No, with the fourth finger, else you haven't got a finger left for A.'

The lesson ended with Ruth sitting on Pat's lap concentrating hard on the melody, and having enough fingers required, and Pat playing an accompaniment on either side of her bulk. They were engaged in this when the doorbell rang with three rings, which meant it was for them. Ruth went out to answer it and found Mick and Clarissa standing on the doorstep. Clarissa had her violin with her.

'Okay to come in? We were just passing—'

'Do! Business or pleasure?'

'A bit of both,' Mick said. 'Some good news for Pat—work, I mean, and Clarissa wants to see how the sonata sounds—'

It was dark and raining outside and they both looked wind-tossed and breathless and glowing in a way that made Ruth wonder if they had fallen for each other. Clarissa was in a nature-girl guise, her hair loose, her clothes flowing and billowing in the draught. It occurred to Ruth to wonder if Mick was married. Pat came out into the hall and Clarissa turned to him and said, 'Mick says you've agreed to do the Brahms with me at Hemel Hempstead. I'm so pleased.'

Pat stood looking at her with a strange expression on his face. Ruth had the impression that so many conflicting thoughts were going through his head at the prospect that he was unable to remark on any one of them. In the end he smiled politely and said nothing at all.

'Perhaps we could try it out, if you're not busy?'

'Perhaps we could.'

'Do come in,' Ruth said, wondering if covering up for Pat's bluntness was going to be one of her major roles in life.

'I've come to ask you how are you on the concertos?' Mick asked. 'Could you knock off the Brahms two if requested? Not entirely a hypothetical question. There's a possibility I might get you an engagement—'

'You *are* joking?'

'No.'

'I played it with the College orchestra.'

'Ah! Splendid! Just work on it, in case.'

'In my spare time?' Pat gave him a scornful smile.

Ruth turned the gas-fire up and put the kettle on the ring. She didn't ask them if they had eaten, for there were only two eggs in the pantry and that was their breakfast. They only had four pounds to last until Friday, when Pat got his garage money. She knew, suddenly, that if Clarissa asked Pat to give her piano lessons at fifty pence a time he would agree. Mick sprawled himself on the divan and Clarissa sat down on the hearth-rug. The firelight shone on her coppery hair.

'Apart from the hypothetical Brahms, Mick's really got you a job, Pat. From someone who wants more.'

'He heard you at the recital last Tuesday. Wants the same again —the Liszt sonata, anyway—at an Arts Group in Guildford, end of March. He suggested some Debussy or similar, said they were prepared to be "stretched". I said yes, you would. Then this Oswaldtwistle Philharmonic—Ramsbottom Symphony—or whatever, is all set to play the Rach. two with you if you're game. I suggested a rehearsal the same day—it seems a lot of time if you go up any more. They say they know their way around it so I presume it'll be okay. That's short notice, three weeks. You'll have to get an engagement diary.'

'We'll write the dates on the calendar,' Ruth said, glowing. 'Great red rings round them! I'll get a diary at Boots tomorrow.'

'One of those big ones,' Mick said, 'with lots of room. When is the Music Societies' competition? That's a date in March some time. You told me you'd entered for that.'

'Yes, I have. The London heats—the finals are to be in Scotland.'

'You'll have to get a car at this rate,' Clarissa said.

'I'll tell you what—at the rate we're getting people interested, you might have to pack in your driving job. The Brahms concerto is a definite possibility, probably for the late summer. As your personal manager, I'd like you to be able to play it, put it that way.' He smiled, but not light-heartedly. Ruth recognized that he was as serious about his work as Pat himself. He was one of these people who never relaxed, who always had to be driving, building, achieving.

Pat said, 'There's no question of my packing in the driving job until these engagements are regular. Unless, as my personal manager, you're prepared to advance me some wherewithal to live on.' He smiled too. Another entirely serious smile. 'I imagine it's a bit soon.'

'At the moment, yes. But as soon as I see my way to it, I would agree to that. You've got to have the repertoire. I don't know your rate of learning as yet, but if I go out and get the work, it's no good if you haven't the time to prepare it.'

'Even with the driving job, I do five hours a day. I've done two hours before breakfast.'

It was true. At six o'clock he got out of bed, flung on several layers of clothes, put on the kettle and sat down at the piano. The room was deathly cold and dark, the music-rack illuminated by a lamp with a sinister green shade. Ruth, putting her nose out of the blankets, would watch Pat's green-flushed face scowling over the sheets of music, his new work, which he reckoned 'softened' more easily at the start of the day than at the end. He would warm his hands on the tea-mug, do ten minutes of cascading scales in all directions and then start on the difficult bits, muttering and swearing at the composer and the world in general until brief moments of accomplishment and the first glimmers of daylight mellowed him.

'Yes, it's true,' Ruth said, loyally. 'It's all he does when he's at home.'

Clarissa gave her a strange look, almost sympathetic.

'He learns very fast,' Clarissa said to Mick. 'Prodigious memory.'

'Not for telephone numbers or names or what happened last Saturday,' Pat said.

'For notes. Unfair advantage.'

'My luck,' Pat said.

'Well, I'm glad to hear it,' Mick said happily. 'Carry on with the good work. What are you on now?'

'Schumann mostly. Fantasy in C. Lots of lesser Liszt. Did you say Debussy for Guildford?'

'Yes.'

'Preludes?'

'Very suitable.'

'Three or four? I'd rather just do the ones I'm happy with now, not work up the dicey ones—not by then. It would mean dropping the other things. I can do them a very nice Brahms rhapsody—how about that? Does he want the Scriabin again? A drop of Beethoven to start with?'

'Well, you work it out, and we can let them know. I could ask him to telephone you and you can discuss it with him. Would that be the best thing?'

'Yes, any evening. But not me telephone him, because I can't afford it.'

'Not yet.'

'No. Unless he pays for his concert in advance.'

Mick grinned. Ruth fetched coffee things out of the cupboard and set the mugs out in the hearth, hoping the firelight was doing for her what it was doing for Clarissa. She felt breathless and heavy; she *was* breathless and heavy. On the strength of one recital behind them and one ahead, Mick and Pat were concocting concerto schedules.

'The Brahms two by August. You can have the Rach. two, Liszt one, and Grieg now and the Beethoven three, four or five if you give me a reasonable warning . . .'

'Clarissa's only given me Mendelssohn and Brahms.'

'Are you her personal manager too?'

'Yes. I've finalized Hemel Hempstead. Are you going to go through it tonight? I ought to have a preview.'

'You might cancel it. Better not.'

'No, you must,' Clarissa said. 'It's ages since we played together. I've forgotten—with you—Arnold didn't annoy me half so much. With you it was quite different. Harder.'

'He covered up your mistakes? She makes a lot of mistakes,' Pat said to Mick, 'but the audience is so fascinated watching to see if she'll get her hair caught up in her bow that they don't notice.'

'You're exaggerating!'

'Your time-keeping is eccentric, to put it mildly. She expects the piano to keep up with her, even if it means the pianist having to leave out a few bars here and there, or put some in while he's waiting. Perhaps Arnold was better at it than I was.'

'He didn't get nearly so cross.'

'That's what I mean. He humoured you. I'd rather humour the composer.'

Clarissa said to Mick, 'I told you Pat was appallingly rude. Haven't you got any polite pianists on your books?'

'None as good as him. I don't care what happens in rehearsal as long as the result is okay.'

'I do,' Ruth thought. She hated Pat talking music with Clarissa. The news of the engagements had put him in a good mood and although he was being insulting, his manner was kindly, not spiteful. He was obviously quite prepared now to play in public with Clarissa, in spite of what he had said earlier.

'Coffee?' she said abruptly, looking up from the mugs. Pat was actually smiling and Clarissa was looking up at him with her glowing, inviting expression which made Ruth's fingers on the coffee-mug twitch with irrepressible rage. She knew she was being ridiculous, but she couldn't help it, any more than Clarissa could help being so attractive. Clarissa was in fact being charming, not only to Pat but to herself as well.

'Lovely!' she said, taking her coffee. 'Just a moment—I must go to the loo first! Which direction? No, don't get up—I'll find it—'

'Across the hall, the door on the right,' Ruth said. 'I left the light on.'

'Fine.'

As soon as she had left the room Mick said to Pat, 'You're not being very intelligent if you don't accept an invitation to dinner at her place. You know perfectly well that you and I can work like beavers getting you engagements, and yet one word in the right place from her old man is worth three months of toil on my part. That's why I want you to play this recital with her. For your own good, not hers. She's adequate, but no more. You can't afford to miss chances like this. Not when you're starting. Afterwards, you can snap your fingers at the lot of them, I won't care. But this is my work as much as yours. If you want it that way, that is.'

Pat was frowning.

'You can't afford temperament,' Mick said. 'Not yet.'

'I don't want favours.'

'God, man, I'm not talking about favours! An opening, a way in, isn't a favour!' Mick looked almost angry, his mane of hair standing up in leonine vigour round his bony face. Ruth thought suddenly that he really did look like an impresario. She could see that Pat needed him, and that he was talking sense.

Pat said, slowly, painfully, 'It's not a question of—of work. I've told Ruth this—when I first started in London, I went there a lot, they were kind—to suit themselves. But when I got into trouble, and I really needed some help, they didn't want to know. I suppose I embarrassed them. They went potty, dropped me like a red-hot brick. You can't, afterwards—go to people like that as if nothing's happened. I was so green—now, it wouldn't worry me the same way, but at the time I thought people like that—you know, educated, rich—I suppose I thought they were different. That's when I found out they weren't. Even Clarissa . . .' His voice trailed off and he shrugged.

Even Clarissa what? Ruth wanted to ask. But didn't.

'Yes, well,' Mick said, all fatherly. 'That's past history now. You're in no danger of repeating the antics that got you into trouble, surely? You can forget all the differences.'

'Yes, I can forget all that happened but I can't change how it made me feel about certain people. That's all I'm saying.'

What he really meant, Ruth was thinking, was that when he landed in court the first time, Clarissa's mother decided that he was unsuitable for her daughter, and Clarissa, dominated by mother, gave him the brush-off. Afterwards she was sorry. The second time it happened, Ruth, defying *her* mother, visited him every visiting day and was rewarded for her fidelity by getting him as a husband. The only cloud in this lovely sky was the fact that he had married her out of a surprising kindness, because of what he had done to her, and not at all out of the consuming passion which he had once, on his own admission, felt for Clarissa. Ruth minded this very much when faced with Clarissa, although she had felt secure enough before.

Mick said, 'No, that's reasonable. But don't throw away opportunities when they arise except for fantastically convincing reasons—which you haven't got now. Or I'll go and find someone else to personally manage.'

'If you say so.'

Ruth handed Pat his coffee. He looked quite amiable, and Clarissa returned to a conversation on the bugbears of Brahms in general and the concerto in particular, on which Pat could wax quite eloquently.

'The sonata Clarissa has chosen, of course, being one of those in which the piano is definitely the inferior instrument,' he pointed out.

'Of course,' Clarissa said. 'It's my recital, after all. I don't want to be outplayed.'

'This time last year you wouldn't have admitted the possibility,' Pat said.

'I don't work hard enough,' Clarissa admitted.

'Ah, that's very unwise admission to make in front of your personal manager,' Mick said. 'If you worked as hard as Pat then—'

'I'd be playing Brahms' violin concerto by now, instead of having to sweat over a mere sonata.'

'It's not all that mere.'

'Come and sweat then. Ruth will turn over—you don't want me music-less for this recital, I hope?'

'Not necessary, no.'

'I'm not turning over at any concerts,' Ruth said hastily. 'I don't mind now, but—'

She followed Pat to the piano to take up her lowly role, while Clarissa tuned her violin and flung her long hair back out of the way.

'Which one?' Ruth asked, hunting through the dog-eared heaps.

'A Major,' Pat said.

He sat down and started to play Brahms' piano concerto while Ruth hunted out the music.

'*Do* you mind?' Clarissa shouted at him. Ruth hastily opened the sonata on the rack and Pat switched to a gentle introductory melody. 'Allegro am-a-a-a-bile,' he said to Clarissa.

'What does that mean?' Ruth asked.

'Amiably fast. Smile as you quickly play. Come, Clarissa, you've missed the gun. And again.' He started again. Clarissa said something rude and played a few notes. Pat's face became absorbed, eyes on the music. Ruth, watching him, thought painfully of 'Twinkle, twinkle, little star'. He was taken up totally with Clarissa, through playing the music, committed entirely to her efforts. When Ruth turned over two pages by mistake and he had to come to a halt, she got sworn at, but when Clarissa went wrong he laughed, and when she repeated the tricky bit nicely he said, 'Good girl!' and smiled as if she had done him a favour. Afterwards they worked at the harder bits, with lots of repetitions, and she didn't have to turn over any more, but sat staring into the fire. Mick was lying on the bed. Once she looked up and found him staring at her, and was distracted. She thought his eyes were for Clarissa. She heard Pat say, 'God, you can't even *read* it. It's not—' demonstration on the piano—'it's—' — another demonstration. She was pleased. Clarissa called him a big-headed anti-feminist pig, and they started to play a fast bit together, full of spite, but then, into their stride, it started to come together—even Ruth could feel the difference—and they were entirely serious and tender, and Brahms in his grave could rest in peace, it was all as he intended. Ruth hated Clarissa then more than ever, basking in Pat's approval.

'But listen to this,' he said when she laid down her violin. 'This is lovely. Are you going to let me do a piece on my own at your recital? I'll play them this.' He started to play the Schumann Fantasy, which at six o'clock every morning Ruth had never heard him describe as lovely.

'No. It's much too long,' Clarissa said. 'You can play a little short piece.'

'You can't have enough of this.'

'Oh, the conceit—' Clarissa shook her head and sat down beside Ruth on the hearth-rug, and Pat went on playing. It was true, Ruth thought, when he played it properly, that one couldn't have enough. It was the flowing, romantic music that she loved, and now, played to friends, uninterrupted by repetitions, curses, one monotonous phrase done sixty times to the metronome and coffee between movements, it was magical. This, in the firelight, playing for pure pleasure for friends, was the rare essence of music, better than concerts, far better than lonely practice, with all the warts showing. The conditions exactly right, Pat played superbly, and no one tried to stop him.

At the end Mick said, 'We ought to have had a tape going. How about that for the Guildford recital?'

'It's not ready yet,' Pat said. 'Not the second movement. And anyway not with the Liszt. You can't give them two king-sized romantics in one evening. I'd like to try the "Waldstein" on them, but that's a bit hefty with the Liszt as well. It's just that I'd like to try it out in public. "Les Adieux" is shorter, might be better.'

'See what the bloke says when you ring him—he rings you, I mean. Often they have ideas of their own—they don't always know much about programme balance. I wouldn't bother so much about balance at the moment as playing what you want to try out on them. You want the experience.'

'You mean it's me that wants stretching, not this audience you mentioned earlier?'

'You get all you can out of it. Keep the niceties for when you appear on the South Bank.'

'Thank *you*,' Pat said drily.

'With me,' Clarissa said, smiling.

After they had gone, Pat said to Ruth, 'Her father is on the administration of the Royal Festival Hall.'

'That's what Mick meant about keeping in with them?'

Pat shrugged.

'I take it. He's as bad as the Professor, keeping me up to the mark. I must say, though, he doesn't let the grass grow. It all sounds quite hopeful.' He yawned, stretching in front of the fire. 'We might even make some money.' He smiled. He looked tired. 'Brahms' two is worth more than peanuts.'

He didn't say anything about Clarissa.

# Chapter 8

'Well, look, are you sure?' Rosemary's face was crumpled with anxiety. 'How long have you been like it?'

'No, I'm not sure, that's the trouble,' Ruth said. 'I've been like it for two days. Not really pains, but a sort of—ugh—low-down, heavy feeling. It's not really enough to go to hospital on.'

'No, but going to Guildford with Pat tonight is a bit potty. Have you told him?'

'I mentioned it but he—oh, you know what he's like when it's a concert—at least, he was like it before. He just said, "Oh, you must come", as if it was nothing. The baby's not due for a fortnight so I suppose it's all right. And if I tell him it's coming, it's not very good for his playing tonight, is it? I mean, it might put him off and we can't afford that.'

'Yes, but you can't let that stand in your way. Heavens, it'll put him off if you have it on the train on the way to Guildford.'

'Oh, I'm sure it's not as close as that. I'm a bit worried, that doesn't help. I only came up to see you because I've got the fidgets. Pat should have been home half an hour ago. If he doesn't buck up we'll be cutting it pretty fine. The concert starts at eight.'

'Is he out driving?'

'Yes. He had a wedding at half past three. I thought he'd have been home by now. I've put all his things together. We shall have to hurry.'

'I still don't see why you have to go.'

'I want to go, and he likes me there. It saves him having to make polite conversation.'

'You spoil him!'

'Yes, but he works terribly hard and I don't do anything.'

'You will soon. Have you got everything ready you want? Nappies and things? A pram? A cot?'

'No, not yet. Until Pat gets paid for tonight we haven't any money. I've tried to save but it always has to go on something. And the Rachmaninov people haven't paid yet as apparently they've got to have a committee meeting or something. Pat was fed up after hitch-hiking there and back and no actual money to show for it.'

'Yes, that's not good enough. I don't blame him. Here, sit on this box. I'm afraid the place is in a bit of a mess.'

'I must keep an ear out for Pat.'

Ruth sat on the box, pale and anxious.

'If the baby's coming you'll want those things,' Rosemary said. 'Have you looked in the adverts for a pram?'

'Yes, I looked in the paper but every time I said I'd go and look at one, Pat hadn't any money.'

'You can use the pram for a cot as well for a bit. I'll find you one, if you like. I mean, if the baby's really on the way—'

'Oh, don't say that, for heaven's sake! It can't be. I wish Pat would hurry. We're supposed to be at Waterloo at half past six. What's the time now?'

'Half past six.'

'Oh, God! Whatever's happened to him?'

'Don't worry! He might go straight there if he's running late.'

'But his clothes are here. He can't play in his chauffeur's suit.'

'Oh, no. Well, he'll be here in a minute. I think you ought to stop worrying about him and think about yourself. He only thinks about *himself*. I don't think you ought to go.'

'I *want* to go. It won't come yet, I'm sure. Don't say anything to him, for goodness' sake. The time I told him about it in the first place, he played so badly afterwards that he missed the chance of a lifetime doing Beethoven's Third in Edinburgh.'

'Poor lad—I'd love to have seen his face! At least he can't say he's not expecting it this time.'

'No, but all the same, don't say anything.'

'All right. We'll all be nice to him. Because you need the money for the pram. Talk about cutting it fine!'

'He's been ever so bad-tempered the last week or so. Too much work to do—he hates the driving, because it takes up so much time. I'm hoping I'll be able to go out and earn something—somewhere I can take the baby with me. Golly, I wish he'd come!'

'I'll make a cup of tea. Have you eaten? There are some crumpets in a bag. If we do **something, it's much** better than just waiting.'

He came at ten past seven. Ruth heard the front door go, and thundered downstairs.

'For God's sake, where's my suit? I'll change here. Get it out! We're going in the Rolls—Paddy's given me permission. Otherwise we'll never make it. That ruddy bride—changed her mind—I had to wait while they all talked her into it—an hour and a half—'

He was flinging off his clothes, while Ruth feverishly unpacked the suitcase, shaking out the folds that had taken her such agony to get right earlier.

'Here you are—'

'Cripes, I ought to shave—Wilf's got an electric razor—go and nab it—'

'I'll get it!' Rosemary, hovering on the stairs, galloped back up.

'Shirt! Where are the braces? This flaming clobber, for God's sake—'

It was made for more leisurely times, for a man with a valet to do up the studs, tie the tie. Ruth didn't know how it went.

'This coat *smells*!' she discovered, horrified. 'I should have taken it to the cleaner's.'

'Yeh, what do you expect? You sweat like a pig—should play in a track-suit. Are you ready? Only the first few rows will smell it. Where's the other cuff-link?'

Rosemary came down with the razor; Ruth scrambled for her coat, gathered up the music.

'Have I got the right ones? I don't know why on earth you take it—'

' "Les Adieux" ', Debussy's preludes . . .'

Rosemary saw them to the door. The Rolls-Royce stood outside, white satin ribbons on its bonnet, the inside a mass of confetti.

Rosemary shrieked with laughter.

'Can I be a bridesmaid? Have a lovely honeymoon!'

Pat was scowling furiously.

'Forty minutes! Jesus!'

Ruth didn't dare say, 'Do drive carefully.' She felt fragile although she couldn't honestly say she was experiencing pains. It was quite impossible to say anything to Pat about her condition The Rolls was beautiful, a warm palace purring through the dusk Ruth looked out of the window at the drivers of old vans and

Minis, her long hair picking up the glittery confetti. They gave strange looks back, trying to beat them away from the lights and failing. A lot of people smiled at them, presumably because of the white ribbons. Ruth thought of the bride who changed her mind, and was 'persuaded' into it, while Pat sat outside drumming his fingers. What was she thinking now? How terrible not to be sure; how terrible for her now, wondering if she had done the right thing! 'I have done the right thing,' Ruth thought, even if it had only been her father's old Anglia and the Northend registry office, and Maxwell popping out of the motor showroom for ten minutes to be best man. No Rolls, no white ribbons, not even any confetti. If anyone had doubted, it had been Pat, although he had not actually said so, only looked—rather as he did now—pale and screwed-up and silent. There was a lot of traffic, and he kept swearing dreadfully. When they got out on to wider, more business-like roads, the Rolls swept along, its needle obediently on seventy, no more, no less. The last time Pat had 'borrowed' a car he had landed in prison for it; this time Ruth presumed it was all right. He said Paddy had given him permission. One day, when Pat was a famous concert pianist, perhaps they would have their own Rolls and going to recitals would always be like this, only without the white ribbons. Pat did not say a word, concentrating hard. Ruth knew better than to disturb him. They reached the hall where the concert was to take place at seven minutes past eight. Ruth knew it was for her to do the explaining, the apologizing, the gushing, for Pat had to think himself into Beethoven's Opus 81, the first piece on his programme and concerned with far higher things than traffic difficulties and brides who changed their minds at the last moment. He was already in his withdrawn, absent state when they stepped out of the car; Ruth thought he looked positively ill, but she didn't feel very marvellous herself.

The welcoming posse this time received them with exclamations of relief and delight. Ruth did all the explaining very rapidly and excitedly while Pat locked himself away in the lavatory in order to think himself into Beethoven.

'I'll go and explain to the audience. They'll wait another five minutes while he composes himself, as long as they know he's here. Far better than if he rushes straight on immediately.' The committee-man understood the situation, and was sympathetic.

His wife said to Ruth, 'Do have a chair, my dear. I do hope the rush didn't upset you. It's very difficult for a performer when things like this happen. But he'll find it's a very appreciative audience, a fairly knowledgeable one too, as these club meetings go. He should find it worth while. We were very impressed when we heard him last month. He has such a range for one so young—he gets you right *into* the music, such an involvement, besides the technique—'

Ruth was hoping that it was money she meant when she said he would find it worth while. She went to root him out of the lavatory, not sure whether he was being sick or merely thinking. He looked like she felt. When does a "feeling" become a pain? she wondered. It was a pain now, holding her, and relaxing. 'God in heaven, it can't happen here!' she thought. Pat walked straight past her, not even looking at her, down the corridor and on to the stage. She heard the applause break out, and stopped bothering about him. He was there; it was his pigeon now, her part done, and she had her own plight to cope with, her own act of creation to control. There was no doubt now that the baby was on the way. She must have been daft, coming, so wrapped up in Pat's artistic temperament! If she were just to sit down, quietly, and think about something else, it would surely not bother her for an hour or two . . . first babies never came very fast. Did they? She suddenly felt the sweat breaking out—pure fright! Whatever was it going to be like? She had heard such stories . . . oh heavens, and no pram, no nappies, no money . . . Pat! She wanted him, sitting on her hard chair alone. The whole building was wrapped in silence, save for the distant piano going like the clappers, and a scuffle of starlings in the chimney above her head. Rosemary . . . she wished Rosemary was there; she could have come. She wanted her mother. The pain came again, far off in a curious way, but quite adamant. She got up and walked about slowly. She mustn't let Pat see it, whatever happened, which meant not letting anyone know, not for just the hour and a half of his recital. Nobody had a first baby that fast. They could be back in London in an hour, straight to the hospital, and everything would be all right. Barbara, her sister-in-law, had been fourteen hours from the first pain. Time enough for Pat to go through his Beethoven and his Scriabin and his Debussy and his Liszt . . . they needed the money, for heaven's sake!

She walked down the corridor towards the back of the stage. Beethoven, having lamented the departure of his friend, had just received him back with a forte of joy, and Pat had embarked on the frantic bit marked 'vivacissimamente'. Ruth was so familiar with all Pat's concert work that—knowing nothing of music—she yet knew these particular pieces bar by bar. If he were to go wrong, she would know instantly, even if he covered it up. She thought, 'The baby will know them too, living in one room.' It already knew them. She sat down on another handy chair, where she could see Pat through the wings, and thought about the baby. It seemed quite extraordinary that in a few hours it would be *there*, a boy or a girl, a human being on its own. It was a quite terrifying thought, what they had done: created another human being. Not even meaning to. A whole, living, breathing human being with its life entirely in their hands, to make happy or to make sad. And yet it was the most common-place incident in the world, a birth. The thought of actually holding the baby, having to look after it, was quite terrifying to her. She supposed a sort of instinct might tell her what to do, or a magazine. She thought there was a Penguin book, Dr. Spock or somebody . . . or had she got muddled up with 'Star Trek' on the television? The man with pointed ears. Everything was in books, if you knew where to look. But mares knew what to do with their foals, even the first one . . . she had seen one of the hunters at MacNairs, doing everything right the first time, and no one to tell her.

There was suddenly a most tremendous crashing of applause. Ruth came to with a jerk, and the ridiculous footnote out of the sonata book concerning the last seven bars came into her mind, quite unbidden: 'In case the player is technically incapable of mastering the difficulty of this passage with the requisite rapidity, the following facilitation is allowable, or at least preferable to an involuntary dragging . . .' Why ever should she remember that? Pat was standing beside her, presumably having managed the requisite rapidity—and she had never even heard him. She stumbled to her feet.

'All right?'

He looked anguished. Who was asking who? She wasn't sure.

'It ought to have been better,' he said.

'Well—' The applause didn't suggest so. '*They* aren't complaining.'

'They're just relieved they got anything at all,' he said.

He went out to bow again and came back. Ruth stood there wondering if he had *learned* bowing as a student. She imagined a whole class of them with a teacher, bowing. He came back and combed his hair, which she suddenly noticed was rather long. It looked longer, somehow, with a suit, than with his usual scruffy rags.

'What now?'

'The two Debussy. Then Scriabin . . .' He was what she thought of as 'going into' the first Debussy even while he spoke, his mind disengaging from her presence almost before the words faded away. He just stood there, and she thought that, if a pain came *now*, badly, he wouldn't notice. He could be looking at her and not notice. But fortunately the next pain didn't come until three-quarters of the way through the Scriabin four, when the music was becoming so violent that she could let out a small moan of apprehension undetected. When he came off the stage she was all right. She kept telling herself it was nothing to worry about, only the very beginning; she had to hold out through the interval, and then after that they would be on the home run. She thought perhaps it was her imagination, and not really birth-pangs at all, just a sort of cramp, because of being nervous about Pat. The committee-man and his wife came back-stage bringing a coffee for Ruth, very kind and tactful, understanding about not bothering Pat, who was staring out of the window on to an asphalt car-park.

'We kept a seat for you in the front. If you want to come out after the interval . . . or do you prefer it here? I should have brought a more comfortable chair. Do sit down. You must be having your baby quite soon? How lovely—'

Ruth wondered what would happen if she said, 'Yes, now actually.' But she smiled hopefully, and the man said, glancing at his watch, 'We'll keep the interval as short as we can. He's obviously wanting to get on.' He nodded in Pat's direction. 'Afterwards you must come for a drink, and meet some of our friends . . .'

To Ruth's intense relief she got through the interval without giving anything away, and Pat played the Brahms Rhapsody and was half-way through the Liszt before another pain came. It wasn't her imagination at all. She felt quite sick with fright. She got up and walked about and hung over the hot pipes. The Liszt was nearly through, coming up to the wild octave bit before it all went quiet for the end. Something was wrong with it. Ruth straightened up with a jerk, the shock as bad as the last pain. Wrong notes in the left hand and then, not a smooth professional cover-up as if no mistakes had sounded, but a sudden ringing silence, abrupt and awful. Ruth couldn't believe it. No applause, like a proper ending, but a murmuring in the hall, a buzz of speculation and surprise. Pat was still sitting there, looking at the keys without any expression. He lifted his hands, then gave a slight shrug, got up and came off the stage. Ruth stood and stared at him. She thought if she hadn't got the radiator to hold on to she would have fallen over. The murmur in the hall was a frenzy of excitement, as if a physical accident had occurred.

'Pat! Whatever—!'

'I couldn't do it.'

'You forgot it?'

'No.'

'But you can do it. You've done it hundreds of times.'

'I couldn't do it then. I just couldn't. That's why I came off. If I'd forgotten, I'd have stopped and gone back.'

Ruth couldn't believe it had happened. It was even worse than having the baby here in the hall. Pat was standing there looking white and stunned, his arms hanging loosely down and his wrists turning, his fingers playing against his thighs.

'You've got to,' Ruth said. 'You can't just leave it. You've got to do it.'

He didn't answer.

The committee-man came out from the hall, his face all screwed up with anxiety.

'Are you all right? A lapse of memory? Don't let it throw you. It happens to the best people. Can I get you a drink?'

'He's all right,' Ruth said. She felt suddenly as hard as nails, thinking of the money. 'I'll get the music,' she said. 'You can have it with you. There's no law about it.' She wanted to say, 'Get on with it. I'm having the baby.' She wasn't in the mood to pander to temperament. Pat had always said it was a job like any other. She fetched the sonata and opened it where he had stopped. It looked terrible. No wonder he had lost heart.

'There.' She thrust it at him. 'Take it with you. It's your memory at fault, your concentration. Not that you can't do it.

For heaven's sake, go back and play it. You can't leave them in the middle of it. They've *paid* to hear it.'

The committee-man was shocked at her nagging.

'There's no hurry,' he said. 'Have a few minutes to collect yourself.'

'There is, there is,' Ruth thought. She felt quite desperate. 'Don't be so damned stupid!' she said sharply to Pat. 'Go back and get on with it! You know you've got to. The longer you leave it the worse you'll feel.'

What he actually felt like just at that moment she had no way of knowing, but he turned round and went back on to the stage. The committee-man, throwing Ruth a hurt and disapproving look, hurried after him. The audience started clapping madly as if he had done something marvellous instead of miserably failing. Pat sat down and said something to the committee-man, and the hall went suddenly silent. Ruth felt sick again, and slightly hysterical. The committee-man came tiptoeing off, still with the music, and Pat said into the hush, 'I shall start at the fugue, half-way through,' and started to play. It sounded perfectly all right. Ruth felt another pain coming, a great eager, awful pain.

The committee-man stared at her.

'It's all right,' she said. 'The baby,' she added, by way of explanation, when she got her breath back.

He looked horrified, terrified.

'Oh, my dear!'

Through all the alarms and excursions of the evening, Ruth—seeing the man's face—saw, faintly, a very funny side to it. She hadn't time to pursue the thought, but she thought, afterwards, when she told Rosemary, Rosemary would appreciate it. The man was not knowing whether to give his whole attention to her or to Pat.

'It's all right,' she reassured him. 'Plenty of time.'

'Does your husband know?' he whispered. 'Is that why—?'

Ruth, with a flash of inspiration, nodded her head. What a marvellous let-out for Pat's lapse! No one, in those circumstances, could possibly hold the breakdown against him. The man looked pale, obviously convinced she was going to give birth before the end of the sonata.

'Don't worry,' she whispered. 'Truly, it's all right. Only just started.'

Even she, in her predicament, was now more intent upon Pat's safe delivery of the B Minor sonata than of her own child. There was a tenseness in the atmosphere that suggested that everyone in the audience was feeling the same. Because he had stopped before, the same place was going to be his testing-ground. Ruth knew that he was playing very well now; she thought it would be all right, but she could feel her skin pricking with nervousness when he came to the great majestic theme which heralded the finale and all its rigours. The committee-man was nervously rubbing the side of his nose with a forefinger. Was everybody in the audience, Ruth wondered, feeling the same? It was all wrong, to be tensed up for the middleman instead of drowning in the composer's glorious imagination. Pat would be furious when he came to, however well he might play it the second time. Ruth could picture his self-disgust, and was thankful that she could give him the baby for distraction, and keep safely out of his way in hospital. If he failed a second time, she did not dare . . . she couldn't contemplate it. Whatever had happened to him? Was it the upset at the start, being late, his state of mind? No proper concert pianist ever did it, did they? Did they? She didn't know. His playing now was completely assured. He went through the crisis part without a falter, both hands thundering up and down the octaves without a single blurring, boldly up to tempo, magnificently controlled: Ruth had never heard it played better. The relief was so great she wanted to lie down on the floor; her knees were trembling. She felt terrible. The sonata drew to its strange, breathless close, with a pulsating silence after the final bottom single note which Ruth felt she was interrupting by her very breathing. Then the applause broke out, clapping and cheering, and the committee-man was beaming. 'Splendid! Splendid!'

Pat came off looking exhausted and nervous. Ruth went to intercept him. She put an arm round his neck and said into his ear, 'The baby's on its way. We ought to go home.' She didn't want him not to know, when the committee-man opened the conversation. He looked at her as if she had gone out of her mind. He looked terrified, just like the committee-man. The audience was going mad, cheering and stamping and shouting. Pat said, 'Cripes, *now*? It's coming now?'

'Yes.'

'God Almighty.'

He looked completely demolished. He groaned. The audience went on shouting and clapping. Ruth said briskly, 'Go and bow, for heaven's sake. Wake up, you look ghastly!' Nag, nag, nag. She wanted him to look after her, and it was all the other way round: she wanted to scream. She gave him a handkerchief to wipe his face, and a push to get him back on to the stage, and the audience went on with its cheering and stamping. Pat came back.

'They *like* it when you fail. It's ridiculous.' He was looking angry, which was an improvement. He looked closely at Ruth. 'We'd better go. I'm dropping. I suppose we can't.'

The audience wouldn't stop clapping. The committee-man came over and shook Pat's hand. He had to shout to make himself heard. 'You'll have to go back!' He looked dubiously at Ruth and said, 'They want an encore. If you could possibly—? Something very short? I don't want to hold you up in the circumstances. Oh dear, it's very difficult.'

Pat shrugged. He looked at Ruth.

'Oh, go on. You'll have to. I'll go and wait in the car.' She was past making polite conversation. She could see that Pat couldn't just walk out. He had created a situation, and had to see it through. The committee-man escorted her anxiously outside. When he saw the Rolls with its white ribbons, his eyes opened wide and he gave Ruth a strange look. Ruth felt sorry for him, his evening being full of shocks, right from the start when they hadn't turned up in time. But she didn't want to talk any more. She wanted the lovely elegant peace of the silent car. But Pat had the key in his pocket. She had to lean against the Rolls in the cool darkness.

'I'm quite all right. You must go back. I'd rather stay here until he comes.'

'I'll get him away as soon as possible.' He started to walk back and Ruth remembered something terribly important, that she was sure was going to get forgotten. She hurried after him.

'Please—'

He turned back, anxious to please.

'Please don't—' —the embarrassment caught her, flushing her face—'Don't let him come away without the—without the cheque.' They were going to want the pram, and the nappies, and whatever else it was Rosemary had said. It was no good being polite and waiting for the money. The committee-man gave her yet another surprised look. 'No, of course not.'

By the time Pat came, at last, she felt close to tears. He opened the car up and she got in, curling up in the roomy seat. She wanted to be looked after.

'Have you got the money?'

'Yes. He gave it to me.' Pat got in and started the engine. 'Are you okay? Have I got to hurry, I mean? Blue light flashing?'

'No. Just ordinary.'

'You're sure it's coming?'

'Yes.' He heard the note of panic which she could not prevent, and started the engine immediately.

'It's all happening tonight.' His voice sounded quite normal. Ruth had expected him to be in a terrible mood because of the mistake.

'Franz Ludwig von Pennington,' she said. It's what they called the baby, after Liszt and Beethoven. 'He's ready. Sending messages.'

'Did you know, when we set out?'

'No. I felt peculiar, but no pains. It started when you were playing.'

'Enough to give anyone pains, how I played tonight. It might not be the baby at all.'

'*They* liked it.'

'Huh.'

He drove in silence for a bit and then said, 'It's like your show-jumping thing. The horse that knocks everything down—they clap like mad.'

'It's not like that at all, but after you went back, and did the Liszt again, you played it as well as you've ever played it. If you'd made a hash of it then—*then* you'd have something to worry about.'

He didn't answer. Ruth could see that he was going to go through an agonizing post-mortem on why he couldn't complete the Liszt, but she would have her own problems, and he would have to work it out on his own. She had timed things worse than she knew. But she was too far gone now to carry his troubles. She couldn't help feeling frightened about what was happening to her; she couldn't really think about anything else.

He drove fast, in silence, concentrating. Whether he was

thinking about her or about the concert she had no way of know-ing. She had to make herself be very calm, holding her breath, terrified for the next pain. They weren't very close together; she wasn't afraid of not getting there in time, only for the pain itself, which threatened this precarious calm. She could feel the sweat gathering. You had to relax, she remembered. They said that part of the pain was because of being tensed up and frightened. Take deep relaxing breaths.

'Are you all right?' Pat asked suspiciously.

'Yes.'

The deep relaxing breaths were frightening him. She stopped, and felt a bit giggly.

'It's not going to—?'

'No. It's all right.'

'We'll go straight to the hospital? Or have you got to go home for anything?'

'I think straight there. You can bring my nightdress and things when you come.'

It was strange, but she wanted to get there now, to be looked after. She wanted people who knew about these things; she wanted to be told it was all right. She wanted her mother. She started to cry. She couldn't help it.

'Cripes!' Pat was pale as a ghost. He jumped the lights on amber and the Rolls went down the Bayswater Road at sixty miles an hour.

# Chapter 9

Pat couldn't get the page of the sonata out of his mind, where he had faltered. The feeling of his fingers actually stopping, the numbness of his mind, not actually forgetting—which would have been forgivable—but seeing the notes in his mind and somehow not being able to make them happen. It was inexplicable, a kind of spastic refusal of the nerves to work the fingers. It appalled him. Just to recall the moment made him come out in a cold sweat. It had been a great weariness, as if, when it got very difficult, he just hadn't the pure energy of spirit to see it through. Trying to think of it logically, he supposed it was in fact caused by fatigue, by the day's frustrations, the lateness, the lack of opportunity to concentrate beforehand. And yet he had been so sure that he was professional enough now to surmount those sort of obstacles—not play well, perhaps, under adverse circumstances, but at least to see it through in such a way that an undemanding audience would accept it as a reasonable performance. But he hadn't. Even a moronic audience could not have failed to see that something had gone wrong, that he wasn't capable. The fact that he had played well afterwards, which he knew he had, and given a stunning performance of a taxing Chopin étude for an encore—to prove to himself, not only to *them*, that he was good, in spite of such a bungle—could not erase the awfulness of the moment. He needed confidence, he needed to know that he was good, to make all the incredible difficulties of the whole business worth persevering with. And to do this—fall flat on your face in public—was enough to undermine anybody's ego, let alone as nervous a one as his.

He wasn't in a state of mind to accept it and forget it, as in normal circumstances—with Ruth and his friends to reassure him and a good stiff whisky to drown his sorrows in, he would have managed. By the time he got home, having walked from the garage up a cold, midnight Finchley Road clutching his useless music, he felt abandoned, gibbering, suicidal. He knew he ought to be thinking about Ruth, but all he could think about was the damned music. He felt that Ruth had left him just when he most needed her, and in fact from henceforth would be taken up with the wretched brat that he had no money to support. The cheque in his pocket would just about pay last week's rent, next week's rent, and buy the list of baby equipment that he could put off no longer, and then they were back to normal—penniless. And if he made another mistake like the one he had made tonight, there wouldn't be any more cheques to come either.

He now felt very restless, not at all tired. Walking up the road, some drunken youths jeered at him and his evening clothes, and he could easily have waded in and banged their heads together. He wanted to do it, and had consciously to stop himself, keep his hands in his pockets. He felt aggressive and angry. It was how he had felt many times in the past, when things had gone wrong, but since marrying Ruth he realized that the feeling had become quite rare. It came as quite a surprise, realizing this. 'An old married man,' he thought. And he felt abandoned again. And angry because he wasn't thinking of Ruth. Angry with himself. He had delivered her to the hospital, followed her down some antiseptic corridors, heard a woman somewhere screaming, and departed at a rate of knots, sweating and sick. The car-parking attendant and the maternity receptionist gave him extraordinary looks, which he could not fathom until his mind had surfaced farther down the road, and he was able to picture Ruth's arrival as they had actually seen it, getting out of the Rolls with its white ribbons and confetti, straight into the door marked 'Maternity'.

Ordinarily this would have been good for a laugh, but nothing was funny tonight. When he got home, he wanted to talk to Wilf or Rosemary, but the house was deserted. They had gone away for the week-end; even Wilf's two friends had gone. He rang up Mick, but there was no reply. He stood in the hall, having banged down the receiver, and the whole house seemed to him balefully empty, spiting him. There were draughts under the door, the net curtains bulging, the laburnum eternally tapping, a soft March wind outside with the smell of spring in it, but rain in the air and the clouds dark as hell. The dim electric light was hostile. Their big room was cold and untidy, his clothes strewn about, a mat askew in their haste, tea-mugs in the hearth. It was nothing without Ruth in it. Just a sort of barn. It was shabby and poor-looking, not a penny spent for comfort. Normally he never noticed, but without Ruth it somehow all showed. Apart from his night away playing the Rachmaninov it was the first night he had been without Ruth. He resented it bitterly. It was the first time the baby was putting itself in the way, deflecting her from his needs, and he had a strong feeling that it was not the last. He didn't like it. He could feel himself being petty and ridiculous, and it didn't make any difference. He ought to be feeling tender and excited and full of sympathy for Ruth, but he was angry with her, and full of a pig-headed self-pity. He didn't care a damn about the baby.

He flung off his clothes and pulled on his old ones, decided to have a bath, and went to start running it. The condition of the pipes made this a long-drawn-out business, and the water-heater, eating coins, was unreliable. He left it mulishly spluttering and spewing and went to raid the house for a drink which he badly needed and which he doubted whether he would find. Wilf had two gallon cans of beer, unopened, which he was dubious about broaching, Rosemary a sour bottle of milk and two bottles of tonic water. There was nothing in the kitchen, but the room of Wilf's two dubious friends yielded six half-pints of bitter. He took two of the cans back to the bathroom. This was the sort of occasion when a joint wouldn't have been out of place; to go clean out of his mind for a few hours would have been no bad thing. But he knew from past experience that it solved nothing. It was all just that much worse coming back. No friend of ambition. Just an emotional procrastination. A pint of beer would cool his physical thirst; the bath would clean the stale sweat of pure funk from his body, but the old brain would be at square one, on the straight and narrow, with a fresh disaster to chew over. He had never stopped in public before. He had made mistakes; he had forgotten once or twice, but covered up quickly enough to bluff an amateur into thinking nothing had happened at all, but he had never experienced this quite shattering blank before. Remembering the feel of it, sitting there, made the flesh creep. Suppose . . . He had the competition next week, and the Liszt sonata was his centre-piece, the one he had asked to be judged on. The way he felt now, this minute, it wasn't possible to contemplate . . .

He plunged out of the bath, wrapped himself in a towel and went back to his room. The house was like a great ghoul, empty and cold and heartless, creaking and tapping and gurgling, unconcerned, an asthmatic old pile, home of lost causes, dead ambitions. The gas-fire flickered blue and hopeless. He pulled on his old clothes. The dress-shirt was lying on the floor, in disgrace; he made no move to put it away. He wanted to go to bed but he didn't feel tired. It was a quarter to one. Was it too late to change his choice for the competition? He could ring them up on Monday, see what they said. Get a job as a bricklayer.

He walked about the room, kicking at the rugs, the patch where coffee had been spilt, noticing the chipped paint, the flaky walls, the sagging armchair. He had never really noticed them before. His poverty depressed him utterly. There was only the piano, the lovely, ruddy piano, like fate itself, a confection of strings and hammers, a meaningless piece of furniture. He walked up and down, the damp bath-towel draped round his neck, looking at the piano, hating it. Paddy would take him on full-time, if he wanted. Driving to Heathrow every day, a sort of drugged existence, bound up in the traffic, learning patience, cunning, deceit and more patience. Being polite. A nice wedding every afternoon. He sat down at the piano and stared at its grubby yellow keys. It was nothing, without the person to play it. And the person to play it was nothing without the person who had written the music. He started to play the music that came into his head, the first variation of Beethoven's Opus 109, and whether it had come into his head because it suited the moment, or whether, having come into his head, it changed the moment, he did not know, only that it was suddenly very desirable to be a piano-player, impossible not to be one, Beethoven in the soul, to be his medium, his ghost, realizing his incredibly perfect, hesitant, melancholy, haunting tune, so that one was moved all by oneself to a rare and ecstatic state of communication. All the labour was for this, the distillation of the composer's genius delivered as intended, no more, no less. For Beethoven to nod his head and say, 'Yes, that's what I meant.' Nothing else. For Liszt, from the shades of his life's tempest, to say, 'Yes, that's what I meant.' Not retch with frustration in his afterlife. Not to have people clap because *you* were good, but because you showed them the composer's intention. Not to be big-headed, self-opinionated, a jumped-up finger-gymnast. 'Oh, God,' Pat said to the piano. 'If only it was easier.'

After all he had done, to *stop*! . . . He ought to play the Liszt, but it was impossible. He kept to Beethoven, the daddy of them all, to calm, to inspire. After three-quarters of an hour he felt very cold. It was getting on for two o'clock and he remembered Ruth was having a baby. The bath-towel was clammy and heavy. He flung it off and marched out into the hall and rang the hospital.

'Maternity.'

A wait of ages. They were all in bed. Surely women had babies all night?

'Yes?' Slightly breathless and cross.

'Has she got a baby yet? Ruth Pennington?'

'Good grief, it's two o'clock in the morning. Take some aspirins and go to bed.'

'I'm entitled to know, aren't I?' He wanted to crash the silly woman's head against the wall.

'What, at this time of night? Yes, I suppose you are, but you'd be far better off in bed. What's the name?'

'Pennington.'

Long, long silence. Distant voices, clatter of tin things. Feet coming back.

'Pennington? Are you Mr. John Pennington? Twin boys, six pounds each.'

Pat felt sick. 'I'm *Patrick*. Patrick Pennington! She's Ruth.'

Cripes, it was a common enough name! She wasn't—she couldn't have—

'Hang on a minute. When did she come in?'

'Tonight. Elevenish.'

'You're sure you're not John? I haven't got her name. I'd better go and . . .' The voice faded. Feet going away.

Pat found he was shaking. He was freezing cold and his teeth were chattering. The stupid, silly b—

'Ruth Pennington?'

'Yes.'

'Oh, you'll have to ring in the morning. Nothing to report.'

'You mean—she—isn't she having it?'

'Yes, but you're too soon. Ring in the morning.'

He put the receiver down. The shock of John Pennington's twins had made him feel disintegrated. He stumbled back to their room and crawled into bed. It was freezing cold without Ruth. He had got accustomed to her big hummock against his hip and her mass of hair on the pillow getting in his face, making him sneeze. He felt abandoned again. What on earth were they doing to her in that awful incompetent place where they got all the names mixed up? Suppose, with two Penningtons, they got the babies mixed up and he got one of John Pennington's twins instead of his own? A woman like that could easily get them muddled up. The panic he felt was akin to the Liszt panic; he was trembling. It was that woman saying twins. He threshed about, trying to get comfortable, longing for Ruth. How long would she be? He couldn't do without her. Baby or no baby, he wanted her back. He wanted her hair in his face and her arms round his neck. He couldn't sleep without her.

He dreamt he was back in Pentonville. He dreamt he was in his cell and three screws came in to beat him up; he was up against the wall and he was all tied up, he couldn't get his arms out to protect himself. Struggling frantically, he started to shout for help. He woke himself up, and found that he was all wrapped up in the sheet like a mummy, with the eiderdown on the floor and his bare feet sticking out in the cold. It was seven o'clock, icy cold and grey. He could still smell Pentonville in his dream; it was so vivid. It made him feel deathly, remembering it. It was so awful, as if he really had been back. He lay still, remembering slowly about being alone, and Ruth, and Liszt, and having no money. None of it seemed very awful after the dream. It was extraordinary how he had gone through all that, known it was going to happen from the very minute he had hit Mitchell, and yet not been in any way sorry that he had brought it on himself. Even the night in the police-station, like something out of 'Z-Cars', only far more real and painful and elemental, refusing to admit that he had stolen the car, not making it any easier in spite of knowing he was quite defeated . . . he could not believe it now. The dream had reminded him more fiercely than anything he could have conjured up in consciousness. He must have changed since then. He could not imagine being so bloody-minded any more. He unwound himself from the sheet, chastened, shivering. It had been terrible, the dip back into his past. He felt he could face anything now, knowing that all that had been only a dream. He wrapped the eiderdown round him and went out to the telephone.

'Ruth Pennington? Just a moment. I'll go and see.'

Long, long wait. Prickling with excitement. Was he a father—had he got a son, a daughter? It didn't seem to make sense. He felt quite faint at the thought of a child looking like himself. He had never really thought about it before, that it was a real person coming. He just hadn't thought about it as anything but a worry and a nuisance, because of the money—the lack of it—

'Ring up at lunchtime, dear. Nothing to report.'

'Nothing? But—' He didn't understand. 'Is she having it?'

'Yes. She's in the labour ward now.'

'Well—' Cripes, how long did it take, for goodness' sake? He had no idea. He thought it was just . . . well, he hadn't ever thought what it was like. Was she still having pains like those she had in the car? Had she been having them all night?

'Is she all right?'

'Yes, quite all right.'

He couldn't understand it. The woman rang off. He went back to the room. How could she be quite all right? He wished there were someone he could ask. He wished Rosemary had been there. But she hadn't ever had a baby. God, it was only seven o'clock. Ring up at lunchtime, she had said. That was *hours* away. Whatever was he going to do all that time? He put the kettle on and when it was hot took it into the bathroom so he could shave. The bathroom was freezing, with bits of mould clinging to the damp walls and hairs in the wash-basin. Ruth's one pathetic tin of talcum powder, a Christmas present, sat on the cracked glass shelf, and made him feel bereft. He smelt it, to be reminded of her smell. Whatever was happening to her now? He didn't trust those confused people in the hospital. Perhaps he ought to go and see. But he didn't want to see. He was a coward. He wanted her to have it without bothering him. Woman's work. And thank God for it. He shaved, scowling into the mirror. He had long sideburns and his hair was down to his shoulders again. It grew very fast; he didn't want it any longer, but not much shorter either. It was thick and handsome and reminded him of the Professor who hadn't liked it and who had given him money for haircuts at regular intervals. But there was no joy in remembering the Professor, he knew from past experience; it was all pain in that department. He tried to sheer his mind away, wondering if he was getting too heavy—not fat, because it was all hard muscle. His shoulders, thanks to Liszt and co, could have belonged to a coal-heaver. Who was it who had worked out that playing Rachmaninov's Third required as much effort as moving ten tons of coal?—and that in forty minutes was going some. He had read it somewhere. It felt like it, no argument there. But however hard his muscles he doubted whether he could *run* far, not like in the old soccer school days. Soccer reminded him of the hospital again. Ugh. Driving there with that funny young sports master, Matthews, the one who had stuck up for him . . . He had waited for him in Casualty, taken him home again afterwards with a broken arm and been amazed because the house was empty— 'What time will your mother be home? I can't leave you like this in an empty house—' His mother had come home at midnight, and Matthews had been asleep on the sofa. He needn't have stayed. But he had. Asking him questions. 'Why are you so bloody-minded all the time?' There had been nothing to eat in the house save half a stale sliced loaf and three rashers of bacon. No butter, no milk. Matthews had gone out to the pub and come back with some cheese rolls for him, but he had felt too sick to eat anything. His mother was drunk when she came home. When he had gone back to school, a few days later, Matthews had said to him, 'I know why you're bloody-minded now. I shouldn't have asked.' That had been worse, he remembered, than anything else, Matthews saying that. And yet it had been his way of saying that he would still stick up for him. And Matthews, that time after the swimming gala . . . thinking of that, an idea came.

'I'll go to the swimming-baths.' Sunday morning early, it was the best time. He got dressed and found his trunks and a towel and let himself out. It was warmer out than in, grey and greasy and still raining. Funny how, being alone, you thought about all these things. No one to talk to. He missed Ruth dreadfully. He didn't really feel all there without her. And yet when she was there he often didn't say anything to her for days. He wasn't always very nice to her. It was rough, not having any money, but she never complained. 'God,' he thought, 'I'll work like a maniac and make her some money. We'll have a good time, it'll come right.' He'd win that ruddy competition next week. If he won that, and the finals in Scotland, he would be assured of a dozen recitals—it was part of the prize. Tomorrow he'd ring up the organizers and see if he could get his entry-form changed, not to play the Liszt. He'd do the Schumann Fantasy, and if it wasn't quite ready—well, it might be all the better for not being over-worked. He'd have to get stuck into the Brahms too, for Mick. That was weeks of solid work.

He swam countless lengths of the municipal baths, imagining that he was successful and what sort of a house they'd have, and a car, one each, and a Steinway of his own. It was a good way of killing time, and proved he was still fit enough. On the scales he weighed in at fourteen stone. No more, no less than he had been for years. 'I ought to walk more, that's all.' Get a dog. They could have two dogs, and a great big garden. And a gardener. Somewhere in Hampstead proper. Walk on the Heath. The baths were filling up with paunchy fathers bringing their young. He was dressed, going for a cup of tea. He'd never let himself get paunchy. A girl coming in stared at him, He could tell, from the way she looked, that she was wishing she had been a bit earlier, and seen him undressed, swimming. His instinct told him; he had no conceit. He got his cup of tea and sat where he could see her when she came out of the dressing-rooms. He had worked as a life-guard in the evenings for some months when he had been a student, and had always tried to see what a girl looked like dressed, after he had admired her swimming. It had nearly always been a disappointment. He still looked at girls, in spite of having Ruth. It was just a habit. This one was nothing special. He finished his tea and went out into the rain again.

He could not face going home to the empty, tatty, cold house. He could not work. He walked, not much caring where he was going. He was starving hungry, but daren't go anywhere to eat. There was only Paddy's money to last for the week, if the recital money was to get the baby gear and do the rent. The next recital bonanza was not for another fortnight, when he was playing with Clarissa, and that wouldn't be much. He must ring Mick up and see if he could get him anything else, playing for auditions or singers or something. Or any old music club, even for ten quid. Or he'd have to start giving lessons, God help him. He didn't notice much where he walked, but by opening time a pub loomed up and he decided to have a quick bitter, then go home and telephone again. Or telephone in the pub. He went in and went up to the bar. He was standing there, gazing into space, when a familiar voice brought him back to earth.

'Why, Pat, what are you doing here?'

It was Clarissa, with a smart-looking Guards officer type in tow. Pat came out of his trance, and realized that he was, in fact, quite close to Clarissa's home and that this was her local. He had been there before, in the old Clarissa days. It was full of glass fishermen's-floats and phoney fishing-nets and its clients were smart young executives and upper-class hairies like Clarissa. He hadn't noticed it was familiar, only that it had a telephone in the bar, which was what he wanted.

'Oh, hullo.' He should have asked her what she wanted to drink but was too poverty-stricken, knowing her expensive tastes.

'It's lovely to see you! This is Jeremy, Pat. Pat, Jeremy. Where's Ruth? What are you doing up here all on your own? Are you coming up to practise? I thought you spent all your time practising? Especially with the competition on Wednesday. I see you've entered.'

'Yes.'

'You're joint favourite with James Dupont, according to my information. Masses of entries.'

'How do you know?'

'Daddy's on the executive.'

Cripes, he might have known. 'Who's judging?'

'Oh, some Russian bod, and a French lady virtuoso, and Sir What's-his-name—' She mentioned an eminent conductor—the one Mick had told him to learn the Brahms concerto for. He ought to go home and do some work. Wasting time mooching around!

'Why are you on your own?'

He told her. She was full of female gush and concern.

'Oh, Pat, you poor thing! Why don't you come home and have lunch at our place, and you can ring up from there? Then we can drive over to the hospital this afternoon. You don't want to be on your own—do come! Mummy and Daddy would love to see you again.'

It occurred to Pat that Daddy, if he was on the executive, could probably smooth over his changing his programme for the competition. Also he was very hungry.

'Okay, I wouldn't mind.'

'Jeremy will drop us, won't you, darling? What a good thing we met you! If you're all on your own you can stay at our place, Pat. We could get some work in on the sonata—it's only the week-end after next, you know.'

Her effusiveness, and the thought of her plushy home and the traditional Sunday dinner groaning on the polished mahogany, was too much for Pat's scruples. He allowed himself to be swept back to her place in Jeremy's Mercedes, where Mummy and Daddy Cargill-Smith welcomed him with surprise and beautifully controlled curiosity.

'Why, Patrick!' Mrs. Cargill-Smith's elegant eyebrows shot up in the air. 'Well, fancy . . . and I'd been thinking you were avoiding us.' Her eyes took him all in in one practised swoop, from the scuffed toes of his shoes to the hair still drying from the baths. He gave her a cold stare in return. 'Still the same old Pat! What have you done with that charming girl Ruth?'

'That's the point, Mummy—she is actually at this moment producing *the heir*! Pat, do ring up.' Clarissa pushed him towards the telephone.

'Really? How very exciting . . .' Mrs. Cargill-Smith's voice was dry, with an edge of sarcasm. Pat could see her mind turning it over: out of prison end of June, sudden marriage end of September, birth of child end of March . . . he had seen his own mother at it, and even kindly Mrs. Bates on occasion. Did he think it was all he had married Ruth for, merely to do the right thing? Did she think? . . . And he knew she did. Standing there with the telephone receiver in his hand, he knew she thought that Ruth had caught him, and she was amused, sorry for him. Clarissa thought so too; Clarissa thought Ruth didn't count, that she was just his duty. Clarissa standing there, smiling at him, confident that she was highly desirable, as indeed she undeniably was, if one discounted all past experience. If one took her at face value, on the winning side, when she was generous and amusing and talented and pleased with herself, she was more desirable than anyone he had ever met. Close to her, the warmth of her personality was as positive as the smell of the scent she wore; the invitation in her golden-brown eyes was no figment of his imagination. Fixed to the telephone, while it burred nonsensically in his ear, he was aware of having fallen into a terrible temptation, coming back here to be fed and flattered and reminded what it was like to be comfortable and rich and in a position to claim attention for one's talents . . . It would do him no good to be seduced by the easy path, let alone by Clarissa. And he had a very uncomfortable feeling that that was what Clarissa was about; he knew her too well to mistake her intentions. All these thoughts ran through his head in the time it took for the hospital switchboard to put him through to Maternity; they were interrupted by the now familiar voice answering, 'Maternity. Can I help you?'

'Maternity' never seemed to know what was going on, without making the long journey into the hospital hinterland to inquire.

'You said Mrs. *Ruth* Pennington? Nothing as yet, dear. You're too early.'

'But—' Again, this feeling of complete helplessness. What on earth were they doing? 'It's—I mean—it's all right? She's—she's all right?'

'Yes, as well as can be expected. Ring up this evening and we might have some news for you.'

*Might* have! 'But—' But what? He didn't know what to ask. The woman had rung off. He appealed to Mrs. Cargill-Smith— after all the old hag had been in the same position as Ruth some twenty years ago, although one could not imagine her losing her mascara over the event.

'Why does it take so long? That's just what they said before— "You're too early." They keep *telling* me to ring and then all I get is, "You're too early." I don't think they know what they're doing—'

'Oh, Pat, don't worry! It's often pretty slow. She's in very good hands. Come and have a drink. We'll take you up there this evening and see what's happening. This is a classic situation, you know—nervous young father waiting for news.' She smiled, put a hand on his shoulder and pushed him gently towards the sitting-room where her husband was already pouring out the pre-luncheon sherry. Cripes, what a creep, what an evil smoothie she was—she had eyes like stones and yet a smile like royalty. Clarissa was sweetness and light beside her mother. The old man was a crisp, autocratic figure who had turned music into a business. He made money out of it; he couldn't play a note of any instrument, yet his knowledge was very deep and wide. He always had the effect on Pat of making him feel that his feet were smelling or he had a tidemark round his neck. Seeing him standing there, holding out the sherry and smiling quite amiably, Pat saw what enormous advantages lay in being friends with this family, just as Mick had pointedly reminded him, yet the whole set-up gave him the belly-ache. He knew perfectly well that Mrs. Cargill-Smith's patronage was offered purely on the gounds of his talent: she was laying her money on him to make the grade, and she wanted to be in on the ground floor when he made good. This was her hobby. He supposed it gave her a sense of power; there was no doubt that a lot of aspiring concert-players did in fact go out of their way to be very polite to her. She promoted a good many recitals, mostly for charity, but usually to discerning audiences, and to play for her was a good way of getting one's face known. Mick knew this perfectly well, also how the old boy had the power to promote anyone he favoured with one of the big orchestras—it could well be him, indirectly, that Mick was pushing the Brahms for: no wonder Mick had been so sharp over missed opportunities!

'Well, here's to your heir, Patrick!' Mr. Cargill-Smith lifted his glass. 'Very nice to see you again. Although I was expecting to see you on Wednesday in any case. I shall be listening, although I've no say in the voting.'

'Perhaps we might go along, Clarissa?' his wife put in, 'I'm free after lunch. You're looking tired, Pat. Are you working too hard? Or is it your present state of anxiety? What do you want, both of you—a boy or a girl?'

God, he only wanted Ruth! Clarissa's gold eyes were needling him. Why ever had he come?

'Lunch is served, madam,' said the maid at the door.

That is why he had come, of course. The great polished table, all laid with a mass of glass and silver, and the lovely roast beef breathing on a vast carving dish . . . he needn't tell Ruth. What was happening to her now, in that vague, complacent hospital, down the long white corridors? 'As well as might be expected . . .' What did that mean? As well as might be expected with those awful pains to contend with.

'Isn't it taking a long time?' he asked Mrs. Cargill-Smith. 'If she started last night—?'

'It's quite normal, for a first baby. And she's only a little thing.'

'Does that make it—?' He didn't really feel very hungry. 'Is it worse then?'

'It might be a bit longer. But I'm sure she's being very well looked after. When have you got to ring again?'

'This evening.'

'We'll distract you until then. You can play for us after lunch. It's a long time since we heard you. It will be most interesting to hear how you're progressing.'

'I came out because I didn't feel like doing any work.'

'Ah, well, I think you should sing for your supper, so to speak— play for your dinner—don't you think so, Julian? You'd like to hear him, darling, wouldn't you?' Ice-cold stare and stunning smile. 'You haven't changed a bit, Patrick. You really haven't.' Just as rude as ever, Pat knew she was thinking. He remembered that he wanted to change his piece for the competition. No good saying what he really thought.

'I meant to tell Mick,' Mr. Cargill-Smith said, 'there's an invitation in the office—a film company auditioning for someone to play Chopin. It might suit you, Pat. You might try it.'

'You mean play Chopin's music, or *be* Chopin?' Clarissa asked.

'I think they have a scene set in a Paris salon, and they want whoever they choose playing in the background—as Chopin. They stipulated the "Winter Wind" study, so I didn't think they'd get very many takers.'

'How far in the background?' Pat asked.

'Behind a pillar, if they choose you,' Clarissa said. 'Chopin was only six stone something.'

'Yes. You'll have to stop eating, Pat. The pay would be pretty good, though. The audition is at the end of April.'

Pat felt himself sinking under the load of his commitments. 'You could spend the whole month working it up, and then be thrown out for not looking like Chopin.'

'True, but all the young men who look like Chopin and can't play the "Winter Wind" study are just as likely to get thrown out too.'

'It's amazing what these make-up people can do these days,' Mrs. Cargill-Smith said.

'Dissolving seven stone or so might prove fatal, of course, but the money's good.' Clarissa, across the table, was giggling into her apple-pie.

'If I were you, I'd give it a try. Three hundred quid.'

Three hundred quid! He felt like work immediately. A few windfalls like that and life would take on a different complexion.

'You'll look lovely,' Clarissa said. 'Shrunk by the make-up department, dressed in knee-breeches and lace ruffles.'

He ignored her. For three hundred quid he'd do it in his underwear.

'More cream, Pat? You needn't start shrinking yet.'

After lunch they sat around in the music-room drinking coffee and liqueurs. Clarissa lay on the floor reading *The News of the World*. Mr. Cargill-Smith suggested that Pat should play some Schumann. 'Can you play "Carnaval"? Get the music, Clarissa. Do you need it?' Pat obliged. Clarissa turned the pages for the bits he wasn't sure of, leaning very close so that he got a faceful of her red hair and couldn't quite be unaware of her white breasts exposed by a low-cut blouse just below his eye-level . . . He played one or two wrong notes and heard her giggle softly. God, she was unscrupulous! He remembered that she always had been. He kicked her, accurately and hard, on the ankle and she sat down abruptly and left him to turn the next page himself. He was only flesh and blood and Clarissa knew him. He began to feel ill-used, very tired, the Schumann difficult to do justice to at the best of times, but the Cargill-Smiths needed to be shown. No good slacking. He was as sycophantic as all the rest of them, playing for a kindly pat on the head from the impresario-man. He shouldn't have come.

'What are you playing on Wednesday?' the great man asked, when he had finished.

This was his chance. This is what he had come for. Not to mention the reason why. . . . 'I think now I'll stand a better chance with the Fantasy . . .' It was worth it, for Cargill-Smith said, 'No great difficulty there, I think. In any case you might not be asked for your preferred piece. I'll see what I can do. What is your programme exactly?'

He told him, and Cargill-Smith asked to hear the Scriabin. Afterwards they went through the violin sonata. The grey afternoon darkened and the lamps were lit on the low tables; a maid brought tea. A blackbird was singing outside the window with the poignant urge of early spring that made Pat feel suicidal and optimistic at the same time, stirred up by his peculiar day in a very uneasy fashion; he didn't know if everything was starting for him with the birth of this child, or merely progressing into a deeper slough of debt, struggle and unremitting work. Walking up and down the deep-piled carpet listening to the blackbird, he ached for Ruth's ordeal. Evening, they had said, ring up in the evening. It was evening now, with cups of tea and the blackbird on the lawn. She might be dead.

'Can I ring up again?' His voice sounded quite desperate, even to himself. Mrs. Cargill-Smith looked up, startled.

'Of course, dear, but—'

He wasn't listening, on his way already.

'No news yet—'

'There *must* be! What are you *doing*? Can I come and see her?' He wanted to be with her quite desperately.

'Yes, well, I suggest you come and wait here, if you're worried. It shouldn't be long, and then you can see her straight away. Not much point before—she wouldn't know you from Father Christmas at the moment. Unless you want to see the baby born. She said you didn't.'

'Oh, heavens, no! I just want to see her.'

'We'll see what we can do then.' She rang off.

'What is it?' Clarissa asked.

'Will you take me to the hospital?'

'Yes, of course. What's happening?'

'Oh, that damned woman—she doesn't tell you a thing! I want to go. She said it shouldn't be long.'

'I'll fetch my coat. Mummy, have you got the keys of the Capri?'

'On the hall table, darling. Do let us know the news afterwards, Patrick. It's terribly thrilling for you. Do let us see you over here again, too. We've missed you.'

He must have played to her satisfaction, at least. He followed Clarissa out to the garage, and watched her shoot the bright yellow car out on to the driveway. He got in. She was a flashy driver; he didn't like driving with her. He sat slumped, staring into the dusk, feeling about ten years older in the space of twenty-four hours. Clarissa was silent, for which he was grateful, and delivered him promptly to the Maternity door.

'Would you like me to come with you?'

'No.'

'Shall I wait?'

'No. I might be ages.' He slammed the door and hurried up the steps. The building reared up into the sky, ablaze with lights against the singular electric blue of the spring dusk, a hive of living and dying in which he had a part whether he wanted it or not. Brisk, kindly nurses. 'This way.' Miles of corridors and stairs and baby-wailing, a sour-faced sister looking him up and down, needling out the patches on his denim knees.

'Mr. Pennington?'

'Yes.'

'You've got a son.'

'Ruth—Ruth's all right? Can I see her?'

'You may see her shortly. She's very tired. Just for a minute. It was a breech birth and she's had a hard time.'

He stared angrily at the disapproving sister. She thought it was all his fault. It *was* all his fault. He hated her.

'You can wait here and Nurse will call you when we're ready.' She walked tartly away. He leaned against the wall, feeling himself quivering. The younger nurse who had brought him up said, 'Don't mind her. She doesn't like fathers with long hair. Do you want to see the baby?'

He didn't particularly but the nurse obviously didn't expect him to say no, and said, 'I'll fetch him.' She went away and came back with a bundle. He tried to feel excited, but he felt numb. It was screaming furiously, and Pat's only emotion was sympathy— all these ruddy women—he could well have opened his mouth and screamed too; he would have felt a lot better for it. It was all red and bolshie, screwed-up, with black hair and squinting, scowling black eyes. 'Give 'em hell, mate, well done,' Pat thought.

'He's like you,' the nurse said, giggling. 'He hasn't been cleaned up yet. Five minutes old.'

It was just a noise, the cause of their trouble, Ruth's pain. He didn't feel like a father.

'What are you going to call him?'

'Ludwig.'

She rocked the baby kindly in her arms. 'Poor little darling. Poor little Ludwig.' She took it away, then came back.

'D'you want a cup of tea? There's one in the pot. Here, you can wait in the office.'

He went in and sat down. She poured him a cup of tea, then

sat at Sister's desk and wrote out 'Ludwig Pennington' on a piece of tape to tie round the baby's wrist. Pat hadn't the energy to say it wasn't true. At least it would distinguish it from John Pennington's six-pound twins.

'When can I see Ruth?'

'In a minute.'

It was nearly an hour before the nurse came back.

'You can see her just for five minutes. Come with me.'

Ruth was parked all by herself in what looked like a laundry room, lying on her back in a high white bed, her face as white as the sheets, her eyes shut. Pat thought she was dead. The nurse gave her shoulder a little shake and said, 'He's here, dear. Your hubby's here.' Ruth's eyes opened. Pat stood staring at her, transfixed. She smiled. Pat felt terrible, almost faint. She looked ghastly.

'*Ruth*!'

He didn't dare touch her, she looked so fragile. And that beastly baby, how it had screamed, all that energy at Ruth's expense, all that bawling rude male health.

'Have you seen him?' He had to strain to hear what she said.

'Yes. He's lovely,' he lied.

'Looks like you.'

'Poor little devil.'

'You—all right? Last night . . .'

'*I'm* all right. It's you—cripes, Ruth, I—I—' He wanted to say that she mustn't die because he couldn't do without her, and she looked so nearly dead, but the nurse didn't seem to be much worried. He felt quite desperate to tell her how important it was that she got better.

'You *must*—Ruth—Ruth, you *are* all right? It's awful without you.'

'Yes,' she whispered. She tried to say something else. He couldn't hear her.

'What? What is it?'

'My parents.'

'What about them?'

'Tell them.'

'Yes, yes, of course I will.'

Her eyes shut. He thought she had died. He touched her, put his hand on her cheek, and it was warm. He could feel her breath. She was breathing.

'Have you finished, Mr. Pennington?' It was the horrible sister.

'Is she all right?'

'Of course she's all right.' She sniffed, as if to add, no thanks to you. 'Very tired. Only to be expected. Come along now, we've work to do.'

He glowered at her, shrugging away. Bossy old bitch. She might know all about how babies arrived, but he doubted if she knew much about how they started.

'When can I see her again?'

'Tomorrow. Seven thirty.'

He went away, back down the endless corridors, in a trance. He felt battered, worse than Ruth. He needed a blood-transfusion. He let himself out into the cool darkness. Above the London roofs the sky was full of stars.

'Hullo. I waited.'

It was Clarissa. He glared at her.

'I'll run you home.'

His legs felt like water, so he nodded and followed her to the car-park. Past caring. What was she after?

'What have you got? A boy or a girl?'

'Boy.'

'Congratulations! How lovely! How's Ruth?'

She didn't really care how Ruth was, he thought. She was thinking it might have been her. Only she was cleverer than Ruth, on the pill. They'd have to think about all that now, not to have another. He couldn't stand another. Ask old boot-face, the sister, for advice. Old boot-face didn't believe they were married at all, from the look in her eyes. Clarissa ran him home and stopped outside the dark house.

He opened the door and she leaned forward and put a hand on his arm.

'May I come in with you?'

He remembered the awful empty room with the tea-mugs in the hearth and his clothes and the bath-towel lying on the floor and the piano waiting for the onslaught of the 'Winter Wind' study on its aristocratic keys. Clarissa was looking earnest and warm and comfortable and homely and incredibly beautiful.

'No,' he said. 'You can't,' and slammed the door.

She waited while he went up the steps and fumbled for the key. He let himself in and shut the door without looking back.

'Oh, heavens, what have I let myself in for? Picking up with her again, getting jobs off her old man, doing the duet in Hemel Hempstead. Don't think about it. It won't happen, only if you allow it to.' Let Ruth's parents know they were granny and grandpa. They weren't on the phone. Ring Ted, he could tell them. His mother-in-law would be over in a flash, organizing them, telling them what to do, cleaning everything madly, scouring the bath and pouring germ-killer down the lavatory pan. He wouldn't tell his own parents until the excitement was over. They didn't want them over as well, the grandparents clashing on their own hearth. They had enough to bear, without that ultimate horror.

# Chapter 10

'I don't know how you can bear it! It's enough to drive anyone demented. And heaven knows how it affects the baby!'

'I like it,' Ruth said.

'You must be mad.'

Pat couldn't hear, through the wild storms he was making at the piano, and would only have grinned if he had heard.

'Three hundred pounds,' Ruth said to her mother.

'Day and night! It's enough to turn the brain.'

'You're exaggerating. He's out half the day driving.' Ruth suspected that Pat was using the 'Winter Wind' study as a great cloak to shut himself away from his mother-in-law, a barrier of sound to shelter behind. True, the fiendish piece needed hours of practice, but when her mother pushed the baby out in the pram to do the shopping, Pat would stop and talk and come and sit on the bed. Ruth had to stay in bed for a week.

'I thought you'd died,' Pat said.

'Worried you'd have to cook your own meals.'

'Yes, I was.'

'I wish I hadn't missed the competition on Wednesday. I would have loved to have heard you!'

'Winning.'

'Yes, it's fantastic.'

'Except its only a semi-final. Three good ones still to beat.'

'I don't know why the final has to be in Scotland.'

'No. But I shall get expenses.'

'Enough to buy a white shirt?'

Pat smiled, then frowned. The financial situation was not at all funny. On the morning of the competition he had discovered he had no shirt to wear with his concert suit; the dress-shirt was no good, apart from which it had still been lying on the floor where he had left it the night after the Guildford concert. He had had to borrow one from Wilfred, and Rosemary had painted his heels with Indian ink where they showed through the holes in his black socks. Wilf had produced a tie which he reckoned would get him first prize and he had set off for the ordeal feeling disturbed and in the wrong frame of mind. One look at his fellow competitors in the hall, and the awful memory of his last performance in public, and he had gone to the lavatory to be sick. If he had had to play the Liszt, he thought that he would have packed up and gone home again.

'You should have played the Liszt, all the same,' Ruth had said. 'All that work you've put into learning it, and to be put off by such a little thing.'

'It wasn't a little thing to me.'

'If you'd played it, everything would be straight again. But by not playing it, you've been beaten.'

'You're exaggerating.'

'No. You're exaggerating—thinking the Saturday night thing was such a disgrace, letting it stop you from playing the sonata in the competition.'

'Oh, don't be stupid. I shall play it again soon enough.'

'In public?'

'Of course.'

'You can play it for the final.'

Pat did not reply. Ruth was right, in a way. It had been an admission of failure to change his programme. If he had played the Liszt sonata and still won, the incident would be closed. As it was, he knew he was now very reluctant to play it again in public.

'It's a waste, for no good reason, if you don't play it. You play it beautifully—and it's a terribly impressive piece, you know it is.'

'I can't help how I feel. When it matters very much, it's useless if you don't feel confident when you sit down to start. It's bad enough when you do.'

'Will you play it for the final?'

Pat didn't reply.

He was saved by his mother-in-law reappearing at this point and demanding some money.

'We really can't get by on only two dozen nappies, not without somewhere to dry them—this weather's hopeless, and you've nowhere to air them. You'll really have to get a spin-drier,

Ruth, and one of those electric airers. I don't see how you can possibly manage without.'

'She'll have to manage without,' Pat said shortly.

Mrs. Hollis rounded on him. 'If you'd get out and *earn* something—do some work for a change, instead of sitting there playing that wretched piano all day long, she might have—'

'Mother!' Ruth's voice was appalled.

'I've been doing the housekeeping out of my own money ever since I came here! I'm sure I don't want to starve, even if you're used to it! And cooking in that poky little kitchen with all the greasy washing-up dumped in the sink by those two lay-abouts next door—'

Mrs. Hollis, after three days of living in what were for her completely uncongenial conditions, knew perfectly well that she shouldn't speak to her son-in-law like that, but she was past caring. She disapproved strenuously of her daughter's living arrangements and, having cleaned the whole place out madly 'to make it fit for a baby to be brought up in', done the shopping, the washing, the cooking and everything else that needed to be done non-stop since she arrived, she was past caring about being tactful. She disapproved of the house and all its inmates, and longed to be back home in her clean, orderly box where every-thing was sane and tidy and as it should be. She was tired and desperate and the piano-playing was driving her mad.

'You can go home,' Pat said shortly. 'We don't need you. I didn't ask you to come.'

'And I suppose *you'll* look after Ruth and do all the baby-washing and the shopping and the cooking!' Mrs. Hollis rounded on him furiously. 'God help them, that's all I can say! You—you can't even pick your own clothes up off the floor and put them away. You can't even wash up your own teacup! You're totally and completely irresponsible—'

'Mother, stop it!' Ruth screamed from the bed, bolt upright and white-faced. 'You don't understand! It's not—'

'I understand your condition, my girl, which is more than he does!' her mother screamed back. 'It's not him I'm bothered with—it's you! If I go home now it's you that will suffer, not him. He won't lift a finger—I know his sort. He might be a genius at the piano but as a help about the house he's a pain in the neck—take, take, take—'

'Shut up!' Ruth sobbed. 'Shut up!'

Pat was sitting at the piano, rapidly considering which was the loudest and most violent piece in his repertoire. He started on some Brahms, and his mother-in-law gave a choking shriek and slammed out of the room. In his second-hand pram, the baby started to cry. Ruth wept. The doorbell rang, three rings for them. Pat swore violently, got up and crossed over to the bed.

'Don't cry,' he said to Ruth.

'I'm sorry! I'm sorry for what she said—'

'Well, it's true. But don't cry about it.'

'She—she said—"Do some work"—to *you*! I—' she knew that working on the 'Winter Wind' left him exhausted.

'Too tired to carry a teacup,' he said.

'Oh, *Pat*!'

'She's lucky I have to go out driving. Else I'd do ten hours, like Liszt.'

'Did he?'

'Yes. For years. She doesn't know anything.'

Their doorbell rang again.

'Mop up,' he said. 'We've got visitors. It might be Mick.'

'Give me Ludwig. He's hungry. Oh, I feel so dreary! So hideous. Don't expect me to make polite conversation.'

'You're beautiful. Get under the quilt and snore. He'll take the hint.'

'I've got to feed the noise. Push him over.'

Pat lifted the baby gingerly out of the pram. It never ceased to amaze him, every time he looked at it. Screaming with rage.

'Don't let his head roll about!' Ruth said anxiously.

'It won't fall off.'

'You're supposed to support it. Oh, poor Lud—give him to me!'

The baby was officially called Daniel, but seemed to have got stuck with Ludwig. Pat handed him over and went to answer the door. It was Clarissa.

'Oh, God,' he said, staring at her.

'I've come to make the arrangements for Saturday,' she said. 'The recital at Hemel Hempstead,' she added, to illumine Pat's blankness. 'They want to know what you're going to play for your solo.'

'Come in.'

A loud crashing of washing-up was coming from the small kitchen across the hall.

'How's Ruth?' Clarissa asked. 'If there's anything I can do to help . . . I meant to come down and offer earlier, but I've been so tied up.'

Pat looked at her dubiously. 'There is, as a matter of fact. Go and do the washing-up for my mother-in-law. Smooth her over. Go and show her what nice friends we've got.'

He pushed Clarissa bodily towards the kitchen. He didn't want her bursting in on Ruth without any warning; in fact he didn't want her bursting in at all. But if she wanted to be useful, charming people was the one thing she was quite phenomenal at. She looked surprised and amused, but unruffled.

'Mother-in-law trouble?'

'Yes.'

'My sympathy is all with her.'

'Go and tell her that then.'

He went back into the living-room, ignoring any meaningful looks Clarissa might be sending him under her chestnut eyelashes, cursing his luck. Anyone would think that the A Minor study was quite enough on its own, without weeping wives, irate mothers-in-law and tactless old flames to cope with. It demanded a great deal technically, as well as all the feeling that was being wasted on his domestic problems, and the fire of pure inspiration to boot. For the last item to make itself available, one needed to live a monastic, dedicated, untroubled and beautiful life, from which one could easily lift oneself into the required sphere of communication. At the moment, this last vision seemed to Pat as distant as a Himalayan peak in all its rare and impregnable beauty.

'Who is it?' Ruth asked. She was feeding the baby at her breast, an act that had a markedly pacifying effect on them both. Pat sat heavily on the bed.

'Clarissa.'

Ruth frowned. 'What have you done with her?'

'She's helping your mother.'

'Good heavens.'

'She's come to make the arrangements for Saturday.'

'That recital? If you get paid we could get those nappies.'

He shrugged. Brahms for nappies. 'Yes.' But Beethoven had written his heavenly sonatas and dispatched them with crochety letters to his publishers, complaining about money. Pat knew he was in good company. He went back to the piano.

'Does this practising worry you?' he asked. 'Really?'

'No. I'm used to it. I don't mind it.'

He wondered what he would have done if she had said yes, it did. The piano needed tuning. That was more important than nappies. The man was supposed to be coming tomorrow. The piano had a hard life too. Keeping back the money for the tuner was the reason he hadn't given any to his mother-in-law for food. It wasn't that he had forgotten. The tuner wouldn't do it until he actually got the money; he was wise to Victorian bed-sitters and student pianists. Pat shut his eyes and thought himself into starting on the Chopin study again. He felt very tired. It was like starting on a marathon race after a day's work. If he played it through just once, up to tempo, as well as he could, it took his whole day's strength. How could you begin to explain to anyone as thick as Ruth's mother? It was impossible. He started to play some gentle, soothing Schumann.

'That's nice,' Ruth said.

Feeding Ludwig at her breast and listening to Pat play gentle music was as rounded and restful a way to feel happy as Ruth knew she would ever experience. Even after the fireworks of ten minutes before. She had never dreamed how she would become so possessed by pure animal mother-love; it amazed her. She had instincts she had never guessed at; she was irrational, even hysterical, at times, and then cowlike, entranced, as she was at this moment, steeped in the fantastic content of regarding this astonishing child. By the time Clarissa made her appearance, carrying a tray of tea, she was no longer in a mood to resent her.

'Your mother's bringing poached eggs,' Clarissa said. 'Is there a table?'

Ruth and Pat had always eaten on the floor, but Ruth's mother had imported a table from the room next-door, appropriating it when the 'lay-abouts' were away, and even conjuring up a tablecloth from Ruth knew not where. It was all very civilized. Clarissa admired Ludwig, and Mrs. Hollis came in, obviously much soothed.

'Push it near the bed. I can sit by Ruth.' There were only two chairs. Pat brought his over from the piano and they all sat down.

'Clarissa tells me she's playing in a concert with you on

Saturday,' Mrs. Hollis said to Pat. Ruth suspected an effort to mollify him for what she had said earlier, this polite opening of the conversation. Pat muttered something incomprehensible through a mouthful of toast.

'They rang up to ask what you were playing for your solo,' Clarissa said to Pat.

'Play the Liszt,' Ruth said.

'No. The Schumann Fantasy. Or is it a very thick audience?'

'No. Apparently not. It's the distillation of culture from all Herts., Bucks. and Berks. from what I gather.'

'Why have they asked you then?'

'Because Daddy's on the committee.'

'Oh, God yes, I'd forgotten.'

Clarissa took Pat's rudeness in perfectly good part. Ruth could never guess whether she was so used to it from the past that she just didn't notice, or whether she was very coolly hiding what was surely a justified indignation. She was very good at it, if so. Ruth was full of a nervous suspicion where Clarissa was concerned. She didn't want to think about their day together in Hemel Hempstead.

'Or I can play some Chopin, if they'd prefer it. Or some pretty Schumann. Or a Beethoven sonata.'

'I'll try and sell him the Fantasy. Or why don't you ring him now? I've got his number.'

'Can't afford it.'

'I'll ring him tonight then, and let you know. Write down what you're offering. Mick says you're to be impressive because he's going to try to get you some club bookings for next season on the strength of it. There'll be a lot of music-club people there. It's a conference, and we're just for light relief, with the coffee.'

'If there are people worth impressing, I'll play the Fantasy.'

'Very well. Will you go through the sonata again after tea?'

'If you like.'

'There's something else I wanted to ask you. I've been talking it over with Daddy.'

Pat gave her a discouraging scowl and reached for another piece of toast. 'What's that?'

'I wondered if you'd give me piano lessons?'

'I don't teach.'

'Why not?'

Pat stared at her crossly. 'I've got enough to do.'

'I would have thought it a far less wearing way of making money than driving that taxi. You know I've been going to old Zippy-Thumbs? Do you know what I pay him?'

She mentioned a most impressive sum.

'But he's a renowned teacher,' Pat pointed out. 'He's got a waiting-list. He's like God.'

'Well, he bores me to tears. I said I wanted to give up, and Daddy said why didn't I try somebody else. Somebody with a completely different approach. He said ask you.'

'*He* said? Daddy said? He didn't say he'd pay me the same money?'

'Yes.'

Pat looked at Clarissa with scathing disbelief. 'Is your daddy a registered charity?'

Clarissa smiled. 'No.'

'Is there a catch in this?'

'No.'

'I don't believe you. You know I can't teach?'

'Do *you* know you can't teach? You might learn, if you try. You've never tried, have you?'

Pat shrugged. 'I can't—communicate, I suppose is the word—'

'In words, perhaps. But in music—surely that's what you can do superbly?'

'But you can't tell someone else how to do it. *I* can't. The best teachers very often aren't public performers at all. You know that. I suppose I could teach how to play notes.'

'Why don't you try? It's an opportunity you ought to take. Practise on me. If you *are* useless, I'll soon give up. And if you find you aren't, think how much easier life would be. You could take pupils instead of driving. It would pay as well.'

'At the rates your daddy pays it might. I don't know how many other people would think me worth it. Precious few.'

'But you don't know, do you? Unless you try.'

'You could certainly do with some extra money,' Mrs. Hollis put in pointedly.

Clarissa smiled at her sweetly, and Ruth saw Pat retract, almost like a tortoise, closing up. Ruth was wise enough not to say a word. She could not trust herself.

Clarissa said, 'Well, think about it. It's a perfectly genuine offer, and it would suit me down to the ground. Twice a week here. Save me trailing all the way over to Chelsea. Can we go through the sonata?'

Pat looked stunned, manoeuvered, frowning anxiously.

'Just once,' Clarissa said. 'I'd feel happier.'

'Mmm.' Pat looked at Ruth. She didn't say anything.

'Will you turn over for me?' he said to Ruth.

'If you want.'

Ruth reached for her dressing-gown and took Ludwig over to the piano with her. Pat brought the two chairs over.

'You can't do it with him.'

'Of course I can.'

Mrs. Hollis started banging the plates together with a lot of noise, her lips pursed together. Clarissa said, 'Let me help you carry them out,' and put her violin down and went to help. When she had disappeared briefly into the kitchen, Ruth said to Pat, 'Are you going to?' and Pat replied, 'She's mad. And so's Daddy.' It wasn't an answer. Ruth opened the Brahms music on the rack and sat waiting, holding the baby on her lap. He was asleep, frowning just like his father. Ruth looked out of the window beyond the faded velour curtain and saw the scraggy daffodils flowering at the foot of the laburnum and a thrush pecking about in the damp spring earth. There were leaves on the trees and the sun-shot speck of an air-liner high in the fading sky, very pure and distant. Ruth could sense all sorts of things stirring, looking at the garden, cradling the baby, waiting for Clarissa. It was that sort of moment when one had an intimation of the whole of life lying in wait, inscrutable, full of tricks and surprises and ecstasies: Ruth would not let her thoughts take charge, only fix her eyes on the music, the 'Allegro amabile' and feel the atmosphere, hold it in her mind, feel herself absorbing it, like a sponge, thinking nothing. She felt quite weak, not through anything post-natal, but through her possessive love of Pat.

'Are we ready then?'

Clarissa was back, standing in her boastful violinist's stance, head up and back, arm outstretched.

'Pat?'

Ruth looked up at her warily. It was the way she looked at Pat, warm, intimate, as if she was sharing with him all the memories of what happened long before she, Ruth, had come on the scene. Ruth dreaded Saturday, their going to Hemel Hempstead together. It wasn't that she didn't trust Pat, but it was hard to imagine that he was completely immune to Clarissa's scheming. And Ruth felt sure that the lesson idea was pure scheming. To sit at the piano with Pat as close to her as she was to Pat now; their thighs were touching . . . Pat would lean forward and put his hands on the keys by Clarissa's, and his face would be full of her mass of red hair . . . Ruth turned the page for him. She wanted to put her head on his shoulder while he played. She loved sitting by him while he played, watching his incredible hands, sensing the power of his concentration which was total and which sometimes almost frightened her. In his more taxing pieces, like the Schumann Fantasy, he finished with his mind exhausted. It was the only way she could think of to describe it. He didn't seem to be there at all for some minutes afterwards. If only her mother could appreciate a small part of the peculiar strains he endured, she wouldn't go on about electric airers. But nobody could know, who did not live with it. She had had no idea before. She didn't, even now, really understand quite how Pat worked, what drove him. It wasn't just for buying nappies, because he had been like it when she first met him. She wasn't sure if he knew himself.

Near the end of the Brahms sonata the doorbell rang again, three times for them. Nobody bothered. When the sonata was finished, Mrs. Hollis came in looking cross and said, 'There's a visitor for you. He says he's called John Bates.'

Pat said, 'God, did you say *Bates*?'

He got up from the piano and leapt across the room with rare animation. Ruth, having heard of Bates through hearsay, looked up curiously. She remembered the photograph that Mrs. Bates had shown her—a photograph that had been in the *Radio Times*—of a thin, bearded folk-singer; raising her eyes, she saw him, dressed in an old fur coat, with a bulging bead-embroidered satchel-bag in one hand and a guitar in the other, nervously expectant, smiling.

'Bates, you old fool! Fancy you turning up here. How did you find us? Where've you been all this while? Come in, don't stand there.'

Pat dragged him into the room. Bates looked round, blinking.

'This is Ruth,' Pat said, dragging him towards her. 'I'm married to her. This is Clarissa. This is my mother-in-law. Bates,' he added to them all. 'This is Bates.'

'And who is Bates?' Clarissa asked.

'We were at school together,' Pat said. 'He sings.'

'Sings what?'

'Oh, he'll show you, won't you, Bates? Have some tea. Are you hungry? Have you eaten?'

'There are no eggs left,' Mrs. Hollis said coldly.

'Cup of tea then?' Pat said. 'You'd like a cup of tea. Take your coat off. You can stay, can't you? You're not dashing off. How did you know where we are?'

'My mother's got your address.'

'Go and get him a cup of tea,' Pat said to Clarissa.

'Is this yours then?' Bates asked, looking at Ludwig. He gave Ruth a shy smile. He had a white, bony face underneath his beard, and dark tangled hair down to his shoulders. He moved in a clumsy apologetic way, as if unsure of his welcome; his eyes were dark and anxious, nervous.

'Yes, he is.' He answered his own question. 'He's just like you, Penn. How funny, you—' He grinned. 'He's lovely,' he added to Ruth politely.

'Take your coat off. Sit down,' Pat ordered.

Ruth went back to bed with Ludwig, and lay with the baby asleep beside her, while Pat and Bates talked, sitting on the hearth-rug in front of the fire. Clarissa brought some more tea and put the lamps on and sat in the best chair, and Mrs. Hollis came and sat on Ruth's bed with her knitting. Ruth lay propped on one elbow, looking at Ludwig. He was scowling just like Pat, his fists clenched up over his face. He had an aggressive underlip, and a lot of curly black hair.

'Ron called on Ted last week, did I tell you?' Mrs. Hollis said to Ruth. 'He's set up his own, you know, car-bodies—respraying, that sort of thing. I think he wants Ted to join him.'

'Good idea,' Ruth said.

'Ron's got a nice girl he's going steady with. I think he'll marry her, but no hurry. He's not a one for hurrying anything, not Ron.'

'No.' She had liked Ron. 'What's Peter doing?'

'Peter McNair? He's gone to work for a trainer in Berkshire somewhere. National Hunt—he wants to be a jockey. He's too heavy for flat-racing. He always asks after you when he's home.'

The horses had got him. She had always guessed they would. He was a beautiful rider, better than any of the others. She might have gone out with him, if she hadn't met Pat. She might have become the wife of a National Hunt jockey. As bad—worse—than being married to a concert pianist. Funny how the only two boys she had ever liked had such spectacular careers. She had known Peter better than anyone, almost better than she knew Pat. He was easier to know than Pat. Pat and John Bates were reminiscing about what they had done at school.

'. . . the time we took those bits left over from dissecting in the biology lab down to the incinerator, and Maxwell got that sheep's eye, with all the bits and tubes hanging off it, and it was the day the inspectors were there—'

'And he put it in his stew at dinner, and left it on the side of the plate, and the inspector came along—'

'And he didn't say anything, just looked, and Maxwell was chatting away as if it was all quite normal—'

'And that concert where I had to turn the pages for you, and I was dead drunk—'

'And you kept turning them three at a time until all the music fell to bits and I didn't know what I was playing, and that old geezer singing away, deaf as a post.'

'I had to get drunk to sing, do you remember? It still helps, I must say.'

'I'll get you some beer. Wilf's probably got some upstairs. Do you still sing the "Butcher Boy"?'

'Sometimes. Do you still play the harmonica?'

'I've got it somewhere. I haven't for years. Have you seen it around, Ruth?'

'Seen what?'

'My harmonica?'

'It's in your drawer with your socks and pants and things.'

'God help us,' Clarissa said.

'He's jolly good,' Bates said to her. 'He got me started.'

'Started on what? What do you do exactly? Where do you sing?'

'Folk clubs mostly. There's a few of us. I've got a bloke plays banjo with me. I play the guitar but only just enough to sing to. I'm not much good with instruments. Penn—Pat—ought to join us. We could do with a harmonica.'

'Do you make a lot of money?' Clarissa asked.

'Enough for all I want. We made a record and that's made us a bit, and a few stints on the BBC, and last summer we played holiday resorts, and we made a lot doing that. I've never been short of cash.'

'Hmm.' Pat, having found his harmonica, blew an exploratory run. 'Perhaps I ought to join you, in that case. Go and see if Wilf's got any beer,' he said to Clarissa. 'Tell him to bring his blowpipe down. He can play some nice tunes.'

Ruth looked at her mother, and saw that she was concentrating on her knitting, all screwed up with disapproval. Ruth knew she couldn't do anything to make it any better for her, and curled up in the bed, cradling Ludwig. Wilf was out but Rosemary came down with a gallon can of beer and Clarissa got some tea-mugs and set them all out in the hearth.

'Beer, Mrs. Hollis?' she asked politely.

'No, thank you very much.'

There wasn't anywhere else for her to go, unless she sat out in the kitchen. Bates was shedding his fur coat, revealing an incredibly thin body in a curious T-shirt with embroidered lions all over it and faded pink trousers. He got his guitar out of his case.

'How many pints do you need to sing the "Butcher Boy"?' Pat asked him.

'I work up to it,' Bates said. 'Start with something happy.'

'You never used to sing anything happy at all. All deaths, drownings, murder and suicide.'

'I've mellowed,' Bates said. 'Is that the same old harmonica? What key's it in? G, wasn't it?'

'Yes.'

He started to play something. Ruth wasn't very up on folk, although she recognized the tunes. She had never heard Pat play the harmonica, and was amazed to see him so animated after his hard day at the piano; it was as if Bates had tapped a fresh source of energy—or was it that this particular music was in fact easy enough to be a release, a relaxation? They certainly weren't taking it very seriously, larking about and breaking in on each other. Rosemary and Clarissa were talking. Ruth curled herself round Ludwig and lay admiring him, half listening, half dreaming, trying not to think about Saturday and Pat linked in that intense, musical effort with Clarissa, in the marriage of their two instruments. She supposed she was being a bit ridiculous about it, but she knew Clarissa wanted Pat. It wasn't her own jealousy that made her think it. She wondered if her mother had noticed anything. She was very astute about things like that. She would ask her afterwards 'Do you think Clarissa is in love with Pat?' She hadn't known Pat could play the harmonica; it was quite different, his playing the strange, sad accompaniment to Bates' voice, decorating the plain melody with a descant high above it; it gave Ruth a feeling of quite piercing nostalgia, unexpected and wrenching. Bates' voice was very unusual, a clear, high tenor with an in-built sadness. In the jolly songs it was competent and unremarkable, but in the softer, quieter songs it was moving in a way that surprised her. It had a sad, lonely quality of its own.

'I told you he was good, didn't I?' Pat said, as if he was responsible. 'Have another beer, Bates.'

'You ought to play harmonica with us, Penn,' Bates said. 'We could just do with you. I've never had a good harmonica since you used to do it with me. I mean, I've met them, but they were always tied up in another group. Some songs need a harmonica, or a penny whistle—it suits them.'

'Funny, I can remember all your songs, all the words and everything,' Pat said. 'We must have belted them out a few times, I suppose. Do you still do "Lowlands Away"? "Down by the Royal Albion"?'

They were off again. Clarissa was watching Pat. Ruth tried to read her eyes. She looked very happy, tender—but it could have been the music.

'How odd,' she said. 'Your being friends together at school. And both so talented.'

'I like your friend,' Bates said to Pat. He looked at Ruth and gave her a sympathetic smile. Ruth wondered if he had noticed the way Clarissa looked at Pat. Then she wondered if she was getting a fixation about it. Bates had a very sensitive face, nervous, sad—almost too gentle for a man. By comparison Pat didn't look like any sort of an artist at all, more like a soccer player.

'She says all the right things,' Pat said, not at all kindly. Clarissa only smiled. She was as hard as nails, Ruth thought.

'It's a coincidence, all the same,' Clarissa said. 'You could go to a hundred schools and not find two talents as good. And you both in the same form in the same school.'

'I'd be working on the farm with my dad if it hadn't been for your coincidence,' Bates said. 'Penn—Pat forced me. Bloody cruel he was.'

'Yeh, well, you needed it. You were so wet. Admit it. You only sang in public when you were blind drunk. And then we couldn't stop you.'

'That concert—and you poured that brandy down me. I nearly passed out, and you only trying to impress that girl— what was she called? She sang folk at that club.'

'Sylvia. I went home with her. And her mother made me play the flaming piano all night, and I got mad and went on and on, and they all went to bed, and I went on playing—her old man fast asleep in the armchair.'

'That's what started you off with that Professor bloke. So what are you beefing about?'

'Why did it?' Clarissa asked. 'You mean Hampton?'

'Yes. He was trying to sleep in the flat above. He heard me. Couldn't help it.'

They started on another song. Ruth wished she knew Pat as well as Bates did, since he was eleven. Pat hardly ever spoke about past things, only present and future. She had known that he had always been in trouble at school and with the police, been expelled from school, escaped Borstal by the skin of his teeth, and the Professor's timely intervention—but he had never told her any details. Bates had been in nearly everything with him, including the police-station. Bates could no doubt elucidate on the reasons for Pat's long history of argument with authority, and his hatred of the police which had so unnerved her when she first met him and which, though mellowed, was still apparent enough to unnerve her now when she thought about it.

Wilfred came home and heard the row, and brought his flute in. Rosemary went for some more beer and some chips. Clarissa made coffee in the hearth, and walked up and down with Ludwig when he awoke and cried. Ruth watched her with a confusion of feelings.

'Bring him to me,' Pat said. 'We'll play him a lullaby. Lullaby, Bates. Instant hush. Lud, are you listening?'

They played a sad, peculiar love-song, and Lud tried to focus

139

his eyes on the gleam of firelight on Pat's harmonica, flatteringly silent in Clarissa's arms. Ruth wanted him back. Her mother said to her, resigned, 'Does this go on all night?'

'Very likely,' Ruth said.

'There,' Pat said when they had finished. 'You can tell he's musical. He appreciates it. He wants some more, Bates. How about the "Butcher Boy"? You've had enough to drink.'

He started to play again and Clarissa sat with the baby, watching him. The song was about a girl's suicide, for getting herself with child, and Bates sung it with such compassion that Ruth felt herself stricken, sitting there, almost to tears. Her similar predicament, made so much less awful by the contemporary outlook, made her feel the girl's agony, so extraordinarily communicated by Bates, as a chillingly personal grief. Whether anyone else felt it or not she didn't know, but there was a long silence at the end of the song which she felt obliged to break by a great clatter with her coffee cup, to cover up her emotional embarrassment. Bates sent her a kind glance, smiling.

'Give me Lud,' Ruth whispered to Clarissa, and took him back in her arms with a great surge of her hysterical post-natal dottiness, that no doubt the doctors had a long name for, so that she had to hide her face in his woolly middle to cover up.

'Good, isn't he?' Pat said to her.

She nodded.

'I'd forgotten,' Bates said to Pat. 'What you did to that tune with the harmonica. It's far better than guitar accompaniment. If you were in with us I would sing that more often. Do you want a job?'

'That's the second you've been offered tonight,' Clarissa said.

'Yeh, I'm popular. I've got too big a job already, trying to play the bloody piano.'

'What's that thing you drove the whole school potty with, for that competition? Something by Mendelssohn?'

'Opus 14.'

'Something and something capriccioso. Play it. Go on, for old times' sake. I liked that.'

'If I can find the music.' Pat went to scrounge through the piles under the piano, and came up with a particularly dog-eared piece. He put it on the rack and started to play. Clarissa got up to go and turn over for him, but Bates politely insisted on doing the job, and when the piece was finished he gave a demonstration of how he had turned the pages for Pat the day he was drunk, for the song 'Cherry Ripe', which put everyone into a state of helpless laughter, except Ruth's mother.

'I want to go to bed,' she hissed at Ruth.

'Get in with me,' Ruth said. 'Pat can sleep in the camp-bed.'

'Don't be so ridiculous! I'm not going to bed in public. Give me Lud, and let me get him ready for the night, then I'll go and find a hotel somewhere.'

To Ruth's intense relief, by the time Lud was washed and changed and fed for the last time, the party had broken up. Bates was offered a bed on Wilf's floor; Clarissa made her parting arrangements with Pat and the upstairs trio departed. Pat then went upstairs with Wilf and Bates to give his mother-in-law a chance to get into bed, and stayed talking another hour; by the time he came down again Mrs. Hollis was fast asleep.

'Fancy old Bates turning up,' he said to Ruth, scrambling out of his clothes. 'That was nice. Are you still awake?'

'Yes.'

He put out the light on the piano and slid into bed beside her. 'He's doing well, isn't he? You'd never have guessed—if you'd known him earlier—you'd never have guessed he would ever do anything at all.' A long pause. 'Better than me.'

'Moneywise. But not for long. You're a better long-term bet.'

'Have you told your mother that?'

'She'll find out.'

Back to money again. The proposition Clarissa had put forward lay heavily in the ensuing silence. Ruth waited for Pat to say something, but he was silent, lying on his back with his hands behind his head, staring at the ceiling. Eventually she had to ask.

'Are you going to teach Clarissa?'

'It's eight quid a time.'

'She's after you.'

He didn't say anything.

'It's not my imagination,' Ruth said. 'At least, I don't think it is.'

'If we do it here, you could sit in on it. You know, knitting or something,' he said. 'If it worries you.'

'Hmm.' He was treating her like a child. It annoyed her. But justified, she supposed.

'I thought you said you couldn't teach?'

'For that money I will try. We need the money. Ask your mother.'

'Don't be horrible. I'm jealous.'

'It's purely work.' His voice sounded angry. 'Holy cow, you don't think I *want* to do it, do you? The prospect's bad enough without you getting temperamental! What else is there? If I win that competition, things might start looking up, and there's the Chopin audition. They're both in May—two big chances. And there's a recital with Alfred and co in June. After that—what? Damn all. No music-club work through the summer, and the only thing Mick thinks he might get me before next winter is the Brahms concerto, which isn't exactly a walk-over and will take all my practice time and more right up until the day. Some prospect! Clarissa's lessons will be a godsend, if I can do it.'

Ruth didn't reply. There was no answer. They lay side by side in the darkness in silence.

Eventually Pat said, 'If I work up the Brahms and it seems like a possibility, I might start working for Moscow. I'll talk to Mick about it.'

'Moscow?'

'The competition. The biggest of the lot. It's the year after next. You only have to raise your fare there. The Russians pay everything else.'

'God,' Ruth thought, and she was fed up with the thought of his going to Scotland . . . She buried her face against him, agonized. Proper pianists travelled all over the world, all the time. Sometimes she thought she didn't want him to succeed.

'Play the harmonica with Bates,' she whispered.

'It would pay me better.'

'No, I'm only joking. Go to Moscow. I shall be able to go out to work soon.'

He didn't say anything.

# Chapter 11

In actual fact, although he wouldn't admit it to Ruth, Pat suspected Clarissa's motives himself, and was nervous of being alone with her. He knew her pretty well; he knew she was very experienced at getting her own way and he wasn't too sure of his own strength of character, given certain conditions. It was nothing to do with not loving Ruth, which he now knew very well that he did; it was only to do with his own temperament, which he had never pretended to Ruth was anything that it wasn't, and which he had no great opinion of himself. There were times in the past when he had behaved with great irresponsibility and he had no reason to be sure that anything had changed. They might have, but, until faced with a sufficiently taxing situation, how could he tell? And he had a feeling that Clarissa might tax him, given the chance.

Going to Hemel Hempstead with her in her yellow Capri, he sat beside her in total silence. This was through no wish to repulse her, but merely because of the usual pre-concert absorption in what he was going to play, which came across to uninvolved people as a condition of irritable gloom. But as Clarissa too was involved, and in much the same state herself, the silence was reciprocal and without tension. They arrived at the school where the conference was being held an hour before they were due to play, while the conference was still in session, and one of the women preparing tea showed them the hall where they were to play, and the staff-room where they could change. Clarissa was able to practise, but Pat wasn't, as the hall was full of the conference. He lay stretched out in one of the staff-room chairs, feeling sick and cold and utterly miserable, oblivious of Clarissa's fiddling.

'Just like old times,' Clarissa said, when she had finished. 'You look like death.'

'Thank you.'

'They're having tea. I think it's time we changed.'

Pat had decided that six o'clock, the time of the concert, was too early to be deigned evening and to wear evening dress, but Clarissa had insisted on wearing a long dress, so he had been obliged to match her. This made him hate her bitterly. She had a dress of dark green-blue silk which showed off her creamy skin and chestnut hair to perfection; it was cut low enough to provoke Pat to remark, 'You'd better be careful when you bow.'

'I've practised,' she said. 'It's quite all right.'

They went downstairs and on to the platform at the required moment. There was a slight hiatus while someone asked for a volunteer to turn the pages for Pat, and he sat scowling at his music, desperate to start, while Clarissa tuned her violin with a great show of hair-tossing and furrowed concentration, which brought all their past performances back to him in an unnerving flash of memory, just when he least wanted to be distracted. An old girl of about eighty-five perched herself on the chair beside him and said, 'I'm ready, dear, when you want.' He wished suddenly, with a positive surge of longing, that it was Bates— sober. He lifted his hands off his knees and glanced at Clarissa, the intense, expectant silence of the hall engulfing him with the familiar panic to get moving, to galvanize the petrified fingers. Once away, things improved. It was never any different, time after time, the misery beforehand.

Clarissa stunned them with her visual performance, if not the musical one, only missing out three bars in the first movement and adding a few in the second. Her timing was far from impeccable, but Pat was grateful that they finished each movement at the same time. The Schumann, by comparison, held only known complexities. The piano was quite nice. Pat gathered his concentration fiercely. Failing in the Liszt had left its mark; he had not been aware of it till now. It was a spur of the most painful proportion, goading him to superb effort. It was not until he had finished that the enormity of the effort made itself felt; he could scarcely get up off the piano stool. The applause was more an affliction than gratification. He bowed, holding on to the piano and feeling the sweat running down his back between his shoulder-blades. He did not want to talk to anyone. He was stirred up, in a state unknown to anyone who had not done the same thing themselves, not quite sane. Clarissa knew. He wanted to lie down somewhere, in a quiet, dark place, but there were people everywhere, all wanting to talk, and when Clarissa said suddenly, 'Do you want to go?' he knew that he did. The place was unbearable. They gathered up their things and went out to the car, not stopping to change. Clarissa drove, turning the heater on, and the mechanical soft purring of the engine and the smooth road was a comfort, the womb feeling of the insulated travelling box, sealed from all outside pressures. Pat curled up in the front seat, resting his head against Clarissa's shoulder. She did not say anything, and he dozed, quite spent.

It was a warm spring Saturday and the traffic was heavy. About half-way Clarissa pulled into a lay-by and said to Pat, 'Will you drive? I've got a headache.'

He came to, feeling a lot better, and they changed places.

'I'm sorry it's not the Rolls you're used to,' she said.

He smiled. He liked driving, finding it restful after piano-playing.

'Do you feel better?' Clarissa asked.

'Yes.'

'You played beautifully. You are very good, you know.'

'I don't know. I wish I did.'

'Daddy says you are.'

'Good for Daddy.'

She pulled her legs up, curling herself round so that her head rested on his shoulder. As he in his exhausted state had used her in exactly the same way a short time before, he could not find any cause for complaint, but he felt himself instinctively retracting. She moved her head about, finding the most comfortable position, which proved to be with her eyelashes brushing his ear in a fairly suspicious fashion. He didn't say anything, concentrating on the driving. She rested there in silence for some time. He could not help being very conscious of the warmth of her body against him, and the shape of her thighs under the silk of her skirt pulled tight by the way she was sitting. Her hand fell on to his knee in a very easy, natural fashion, but she still didn't say anything. He concentrated on the road, which needed it, but it could not be said that his mind was wholly on his driving. This was the very situation he had wanted to avoid.

'You look very worried,' she said, slightly taunting. Her eye-lashes moved up and her eyes were looking at his, distractingly close.

'I thought you were tired,' he said abruptly.

She smiled.

'Relax,' she said. 'You're over it now. You scowl too much. You've got lines where you scowl. You'll be a hideous old man if you go on taking everything too seriously.'

'It won't worry you.'

'Ruth won't like it.'

He would not be tempted to discuss Ruth. He moved his knee away, but had to move it back almost immediately to change gear. Clarissa shifted slightly, and brought her other arm up across the seat back behind his neck. She did not touch him, but he was aware of it there, waiting its chance. He was furious. He pulled out to overtake a week-end car in front, but had to nip back in face of an oncoming lorry.

'Lay off,' he said. 'I can't drive with you breathing down my neck.'

'I told you, relax. You're exaggerating—I'm not breathing down your neck. I'm soothing you. You'll drive better if you're soothed. It's a scientific fact. You have a terribly bad temper, you know, Pat. You always had. I think you are mistaking my intentions, flattering yourself.'

He was pretty sure he wasn't. Clarissa's other hand was touching his hair, caressing it.

'I've always been very fond of you, Pat.'

If he did relax, he supposed he could enjoy it. He had to stop at some traffic lights, and the man alone in the car alongside sent him a glance that was quite clearly envious. It was true that he had a bad temper. He found Clarissa extraordinarily unnerving, which was a sign of something; he was very worried. He tried to put it right.

'Look, I'm quite fond of you too, but I'm not free to mess about any longer. I'm not interested. I don't want you to get any ideas.'

'It's you that has the ideas. I haven't any at all. I've told you, you flatter yourself. I just want you to stop worrying.'

'God, woman!' he thought. He shook himself free of her, but could not move far enough away to make it effective. He decided to drive into the next café or lay-by and get out; the road was too busy to stop by the kerb. But no sanctuary was forthcoming. He put his foot down and overtook three cars in front of him. Clarissa laughed, and kissed his neck, just under his ear.

'I love you when you're angry,' she said.

There was no defence at all. She had her hand in his hair, twisting it round her fingers. He only had to glance at her, to see the way her eyes were looking, and the way her white throat and chin were lifted up, her mouth mocking him, for all the old memories of her to come hitting at him—all the good memories, just to be perverse, not the quarrels and the bitchiness and remembering her eyes like stones with hate, but the early days when it was all new and fantastic and laughing and magical, which he had quite forgotten and buried and never even *wanted* to remember. It was so bloody unfair. He knocked her hand away angrily and she laughed. He put his foot down and overtook another car, saw a café forefront open up suddenly on his left, and zoomed in across the overtaken car to get into it. Another car was coming out. He heard the blare of the overtaken car's horn, wildly indignant, and missed the oncoming car by swerving on to a proudly mown strip of lawn and ploughing through a rose-bed. The car he had just missed was a police-car. Clarissa was laughing her head off.

Pat switched off the engine and saw the two policemen get out of the car and start walking towards him. Clarissa stopped laughing and looked at him.

'Pat, don't—'

He could feel it all mustering inside, as if he had been saving it up for all the past months—the fantastic indignation with his lot, the *injustice* of it, the great swelling rage with Clarissa, baiting him off his so carefully, painfully built holy path, and those bloody policemen sitting there waiting for him, as if they *knew*—

One of the policemen opened the door and stood looking down at him. Clarissa put her hand on his arm, not caressingly at all.

'Pat, don't!' she said very sharply.

But he couldn't help it.

'Because of Ruth,' Clarissa said. 'Ruth!' She almost bawled it in his ear.

'Get out,' said the policeman. 'Stand up.'

He got out. The policeman looked him up and down.

147

'Drinking *before* the party isn't wise. Come over to our car and oblige us by blowing into our breathalyzer.'

Pat stayed where he was, holding on to the door-handle. He needed to, to keep his hands down, to stop them doing what they wanted to with such passion that it was almost beyond his power to control them. He was shaking like a leaf. Clarissa got out and ran round and put her hand on his arm again.

'He's not well,' she said to the policeman. 'He hasn't been drinking.'

'We'll test him all the same.' The policeman gave her a hostile look. 'Step along,' he said to Pat. 'We haven't all night.'

Pat took his hands off the door-handle. Clarissa took one and held it tightly. Pat was glad of it. He remembered Ruth taking those shuddering breaths the night in the Rolls when the baby was coming, and he found he was doing the same. Only it was better. It was working. If only that cold-fish, pea-brained, stinking bastard of a policeman was civil to him, he might make it. He walked over to the police-car, and the two policemen fiddled about with their stupid apparatus. Pat was pretty sure that one pint of Wilf's beer last Wednesday, the last drink he had had, wouldn't register, and was proved right. The policemen were obviously surprised.

'Let's have a look at your licence.'

It was in his jeans pocket in the back of the car. They went back to the car and Clarissa got it out. Pat dared not open his mouth to speak, afraid of what might come out. One of the policemen copied all the particulars down into his notebook.

'It's my car,' Clarissa said. The policeman stared at her and she batted her eyelashes at him and smiled. 'It was all my fault,' she said. 'We were having a row. I started it. He told me to pack it in while he was driving, but I didn't and he lost his temper and told me I could damned well walk, and that's why he came in here.' She smiled again.

'Hmm,' said the policeman. He was a young man, and Clarissa's face was all warmth and admiration and innocence, held up to him with the expression in the eyes that Pat knew only too well.

'He's very tired—he's been playing in a recital, for the National Society of Music Groups. Schumann, Opus 17. Do you know anything about music? It's a very taxing piece. It was all my fault—I should have known better than to carry on at him.'

'You were quarrelling? About his driving, no doubt.'

'About his wife.'

'Hmm.' The policeman made a doodle on the edge of the pad, and looked carefully at Pat.

'You're a professional musician?'

'Yes.'

'My father will be along very soon,' Clarissa said. 'He drives a Silver Ghost—you ought to be able to spot him quite easily. He'll vouch for Pat. He's very reliable. He's on the board of the—' She reeled off a whole list of weighty establishment interests. 'Julian Cargill-Smith, O.B.E. You can check up. He was presiding at this conference where Pat was playing.'

The policeman wilted visibly.

'I've got a very bad temper,' Clarissa said. 'He'll vouch for that too. Enough to make anyone drive through a rose-bed when I'm on form.' She obligingly tendered up her address, which was as impressive as her father's directorships.

The policeman wrote it down and Clarissa smiled and spelt the name of the house for him, and the policeman smiled back and said, 'I suggest you drive the rest of the way, miss, and no quarrelling.'

'All right. I promise.'

They got back into the car, and Clarissa reversed out of the rose-bed and drove out of the forecourt with a cheeky pip on the horn. Pat sat slumped in the passenger seat, trembling. His past police grillings had come up out of his subconsciousness with the same uncanny vividness as his Pentonville dream a couple of weeks back. All the things he most wanted to forget, even his old relationship with Clarissa, shifted through his brain-box with an appalling reality, all the things he thought he had overcome and buried. And the near-mania he had just experienced, faced with a fresh encounter with the law, had left his whole physical body feeling shocked, as if an electric current had gone through it. The agonizing longing to explode, choked back with such phenomenal difficulty, felt as if it had detonated inside him instead.

'I think we could do with a drink—I don't know about their thinking we'd had one,' Clarissa remarked. She now looked shaken herself.

'For God's sake, you don't want to park this car outside a pub now.'

'A bit farther into London then—I'm shaking like a leaf. It was you—I thought—I thought you were—going to get yourself put back inside again—'

He couldn't bring himself to talk about it. He felt shivering cold and sick and as if he wanted to black out, sleep for ever. He put the heater on full blast, and dozed, but the dreams kept spiking him; the half-consciousness was like lying on the edge of a nightmare. He realized he was suffering from nerves, like a neurotic housewife. He longed for a black, drugged unconsciousness.

'Are you all right?'

Clarissa had parked outside his house, and was peering at him anxiously.

'Shall I come in with you?'

'Heavens, no.' He remembered Ruth's taut jealousy, his cow of a mother-in-law with her tight, disapproving mouth . . .

He moved himself cautiously, and climbed out. Clarissa gathered up his clothes for him and pushed the bundle after him.

'Okay?'

'Yes. It's all right. I think.' There were all sorts of things he ought to say, he knew, but he hadn't the strength.

'Good-bye then.'

'Good-bye.'

He let himself in and went into their room. Ruth was out of bed and sitting in front of the fire with Lud in her arms; her mother was sitting on the bed, and in the other chair across the hearth was Clemmie, the Professor's housekeeper. They were all obviously very cheerful, with cups of tea going and lots of gossip, cosy and feminine . . . Pat stared at them blankly, wishing them all in purgatory.

'Oh, God.'

He dropped his clothes on the floor and turned around and went out again. It was more than flesh and blood could cope with. He went upstairs and into Wilf's room. Wilf was writing letters, sitting in the hearth by his gas-fire. His bed was empty.

'Do you mind?' Pat gestured towards the bed. 'I'm knackered—room full of ruddy women—'

'Go ahead,' Wilf said cheerfully.

'Got any aspirins?'

Wilf got some out of a drawer and threw the bottle over. Pat took four, took off his shoes and got into bed. He was freezing cold. He pulled the eiderdown over his head and sank into a black pit of dreamless sleep. Ruth came up a few minutes later and looked at him doubtfully.

'Is he all right?' she asked Wilfred.

'Yeh. Post-concert blues. Quite normal. Felt like it myself sometimes.'

'He was terribly rude.'

'Not his fault really. Reaction.'

Ruth frowned. 'Tell him, when he wakes—' She shrugged. 'It doesn't matter, I suppose.' She paused. 'Did he say how it went?'

'No.'

Ruth went away.

Pat woke up at six o'clock. He had a splitting headache, but otherwise felt quite normal. Wilf was asleep on the floor, with some cushions underneath him and the hearth-rug for a blanket. Pat stirred him with his toe and said, 'Thanks, you can have it now. It's still warm.'

He went downstairs, carrying his shoes, and into the kitchen to make a cup of tea. He could remember everything quite sanely now, even to the point of being sorry for being so rude to Clemmie. He thought he could ring her up to apologize, then realized that he would probably get the Professor, and that would be impossible. But, standing over the kettle, waiting for it to boil, he realized that he had left a great deal unsaid to Clarissa. It seemed so urgent that he went straight out into the hall and dialled her number. Her father answered, and sounded reasonably cross.

'For God's sake, Pat—at six o'clock! Can't it wait?'

'No.'

'Wait a minute.'

Long, long pause. Then Clarissa, a bit slurry, 'Pat?'

'Clarissa, I ought to have said—'

'Do you feel okay now?'

'Yes. I've come round. That's why I rang.' In the kitchen the kettle started to shrill.

'What's the matter?'

'Nothing. It's just that I wanted to thank you for what you did. You were marvellous. You got me out of it.'

'All those lies!'

'You were inspired.'

'Well, I thought—I got you into it really, so I was obliged to do my best, wasn't I? I'm sorry about it. I shouldn't think you'd get a summons, though. You might, but doubtful.'

'Only an endorsement if I do. Better than another nine months for assault. Thank you for holding me down. That's all I wanted to say.'

'Any time, Pat. Anything for you.'

'No wrong ideas—'

'Yes. I'm full of them.' She rang off, and he put the receiver down, a bit disturbed by the last innuendo. Perhaps his impulsive telephone call hadn't been such a bright idea. But she had been fantastic, working on the fuzz; he couldn't not have told her so.

He went back into the kitchen and found Ruth taking the kettle off, silencing its row. She gave him a deeply suspicious look.

'Who on earth were you talking to?'

He considered telling a lie, but couldn't think of anything convincing. 'Clarissa.'

She gave him a very funny look.

'Was it all right? Nothing went wrong?'

'No.'

'Were you ill last night?'

'I felt terrible. I'm sorry if I was rude.'

'You were terribly rude. Clemmie nearly burst into tears.'

'Oh, God.' He didn't feel so good any more.

Ruth said, 'You could have taken your suit off.' He looked in the kitchen mirror and realized that he did look very odd for a Sunday morning, still in white tie and tails, covered with Wilf's leaky eiderdown feathers, a new beard struggling through. Then, out of the gloom, he remembered that he had played the Schumann Fantasy pretty well, all things considered, and he had stopped himself from exploding in the face of the law, which was a considerable feat. With Clarissa's help. The way she had physically held his arm—he had been right to thank her. She was a bitch, but a useful one.

'I think I'll have a bath,' he said.

'Tell me what happened,' Ruth said.

'I'll have a bath first, then I'll tell you what happened.' He could think up a good doctored version of the story in the bath.

'All right. I'll bring you a cup of tea. Give me your suit, you treat it dreadfully.'

'Okay.' He gave her the jacket and trousers and went to run the bath.

# Chapter 12

When Ruth had regained her strength and her mother left them, the atmosphere improved considerably.

'Summer's come!' Pat said, flinging open the French windows and taking big sniffs of an indubitably warm April morning. Ruth had Lud in bed with her, feeding him.

'I think it's time I went out to work,' she said. 'Can you fix something at the garage?'

'Oh, must you?' Pat said.

'You're a fine one to ask! Surely it will make it a lot easier all round? Just while you get started.' She was wondering if she had offended him.

'I like having you around. Anyway, what about Lud?'

'Well, I'd have to take him, wouldn't I?'

Pat scowled, coming back to the piano. 'I'll see. Perhaps with Clarissa's lessons it'll be okay. We can scrape through till next winter.'

'What does Mick say?'

'Oh, Mick's got this fixation about the Brahms concerto. For August. In Bournemouth. I think it's fairly definite now. He keeps asking me if I can play it. I told him I can play most of the notes, but whether I can actually perform it . . .' He shrugged.

'I thought you said you *had* played it.'

'After a fashion. My standards are getting higher in my old age. You should play it when you're forty really—spend twenty years of hard thinking on it, get it into your hands . . . after forty you'd be getting too feeble physically. It takes fifty minutes to play and it's mostly flat out for the soloist. But if Mick commits me I've no choice. I'll just have to do it well enough. I'll be pleased, in a way. It'll give me a clue as to whether it's worth preparing for Moscow.'

They were on a higher plane now than electric airers and nappies. Ruth had put up a washing-line between the lilac and the laburnum and the sun did the job.

'If I go to work, perhaps you could pack in the driving and have more time.'

'Wait till this competition comes off. If I win that, things will start looking up.'

There was a recital with Alfred and co, to play Schubert in Exeter; two letters from music clubs in Nottingham and Whitby asking what his fees were, which he had passed on to Mick; the competition in Scotland; and now Moscow . . . Ruth was beginning to realize that success was not wholly to her advantage.

'Anyway, we have Clarissa's eight-quids' worth this afternoon. That'll keep us in bread till Friday.'

Pat, after four lessons with Clarissa, was now sure that she had an ulterior motive for her piano-playing, but the money was a godsend. It had taken the edge off their desperate poverty. Ruth had taken his dress-suit to the cleaner's, and he had been able to buy his own music for the Brahms, instead of borrowing it from the library, also a white shirt. For that sort of luxury he was prepared to work very hard at teaching Clarissa, and to summon unaccustomed reserves of tact to turn her off him without offence. Ruth had strict instructions not to leave the room.

'She *has* got an eye for you still! I knew she had.' Ruth was glad Pat had had to admit it. It made her seem less neurotic. Pat was clearly embarrassed.

'Well, I'm not saying she—she—Oh, with Clarissa, anything in trousers—she can't help it.'

'Don't be so modest. It's your fantastic, intrinsic charm, your exquisite manners, your impeccable grooming—quite irresistible —'

Ruth had good cause for amusement, for Pat's distaste for getting involved with Clarissa again was quite evident. He had told Ruth a fairly unvarnished version of the day of their joint recital, and she had accepted—even been grateful—that Clarissa had come out of it with credit. No one had to remind Ruth of Pat's dangerous potential when faced with minions of the law, for she remembered her own experience only too vividly, which had parted them far more decisively than any trips to Whitby or Moscow that threatened. If Clarissa had prevented a repetition of that disaster, one could only be grateful.

'When I told Clemmie you were out for the day with Clarissa, her eyes came out on stalks. "Clarissa!" she sort of snorted. I told her it was only work, but I'm sure she didn't believe me. It was nice of her to call. She'd heard about the baby—indirectly, via Clarissa, I suppose. She's ever so nice. I told her how hard you were working and what a good husband you were and how charming you'd become with being a family man, and then you came in at the door and ruined it all. I might have saved my breath.'

'Serves you right for telling lies.'

The early-morning work was now devoted to Brahms. The Chopin for the audition was well in hand, and the programme for the competition was as well learned and considered as Pat reckoned he was capable of, needing only the awful tension of the competition atmosphere itself to spark it into what Pat hoped would be a winning performance. He had stepped up his practice hours to eight hours a day and the driving interlude he had come to consider as a rest in the middle. One day he overdid it and fell asleep while he was waiting for the bride. The best man had to come and root him out of his parking bay several hundred yards from the church, and Paddy the boss was justifiably annoyed.

Clarissa came for her lessons at four o'clock on Tuesdays and Fridays, the two days that Pat got home from work earlier. Ruth liked to take Lud out in the afternoons; by the time she had given him his two o'clock feed and got him ready, it was a bit of a push to get back again by four. Once or twice she was late and came in in the middle of the lesson. In each case Pat and Clarissa were working with impeccable rectitude, the first time discussing how to play a cross rhythm of three in the left hand against seven in the right, and the second time Pat was standing leaning against the mantelpiece while Clarissa played. The situation was on the point of settling into routine, and Clarissa evidently thought that she was getting her money's-worth. 'I don't find your lessons a bit boring,' she told Pat. 'I got bored before.' Ruth wasn't sure whether this was because the teacher was Pat, as opposed to old Zippy-Thumbs, who had known Elgar in 1910, or whether it was because, contrary to all expectations, Pat really could teach.

'Can you?' she asked him.

'Well, it's okay with Clarissa. I don't know about anyone else. I mean, I can say what I like to her. She doesn't mind. Tact isn't my strong point.'

'I've noticed.' Ruth remembered something. 'Next Tuesday I've got to go to the hospital for a check-up. Four o'clock. So you'll be all on your own. Is that all right?'

'I suppose so.'

'You're big enough to fend her off if she attacks.'

'I can't knock her under the piano and still expect to get the five quid.'

'No. Well—I'll put garlic in your sandwiches or something. That'll put her off. I shall have to leave Lud with you. Will that be all right? If he cries you can put him down the bottom of the garden.'

She left him in the garden before she went. The garden in spring had proved a heartening addition to their ground-floor room, the windows opening out on to a positive jungle of over-grown lilac and laurel and laburnum. The lawn in the middle was like a glade amidst the old-fashioned profusion of damp ferns growing against the smoky brick walls and the knotted sprouts of a mass of peony shoots. It was small and hemmed in, over-hung, and smelt of cats, but Ruth loved it. It was marvellous for Lud, and would be a godsend next summer when he was mobile. She was getting very domestic-minded. A cabbage. But it was hard to raise the mind above the immediate economics of the situation. Time enough to start advancing her thought-processes when Pat was able to supply enough money to stop her pre-occupation about the cheapest way to keep alive and healthy.

As soon as Pat came home from the garage, Ruth departed. Pat put the kettle on and went and sat on the doorstep in the sun. He was tired, but that was nothing new. It was always an effort to get started on the last hours of practice in the evening, the concentration growing more sporadic as the day progressed. All right once he was started, but so many reasons presented them-selves as to why he should delay the moment—sitting talking to Ruth, sitting in the sun now that it so obligingly shone into their room from the west in the late afternoon, drinking tea, doing anything but sit down at the piano. If he hadn't got a definite schedule to work to: the competition next week, Chopin the week after, and Brahms in August, he wondered sometimes if he would have the willpower to get on with it at all. Rather, drift off with Bates and play harmonica in a·folk group. Bates made more money than he did. Bates had asked him to. There were times when he was almost tempted. Sitting in front of the Brahms score, considering its problems, he was inclined to think that it was made for a greater mind than his would ever be, however well his fingers learned to scamper; he could get deeply depressed sometimes, when he was tired.

'Oh, just in time!' Clarissa had come in round the back, and the kettle was boiling. 'I'll make it,' she said. 'Isn't Ruth here?'

'She's got an appointment at the hospital.'

'Is she due back?'

'No. She's only just gone.'

That was his first mistake. He realized it immediately. 'We'll get started,' he said, getting to his feet.

'Oh, for heaven's sake, let's have the tea. Have you only just come home?'

'Yes.'

'Well, you need it. Sit down. I'll bring it over.'

He sat again. It was part of his weakness, to be tempted by idle chat and cups of tea. Earning his eight pounds—and he was very conscientious about it—wasn't all that easy. It needed considerable effort to articulate when it came to criticizing somebody else's playing; comparatively simple to know what was wrong, not so easy to put the helpful, constructive criticism into the proper five-pounds-worth of words—not for him anyway, who had always preferred to keep silent rather than expose too painfully his lack of a polished education. He did sincerely want Clarissa to improve (there was plenty of room for it) and it was as much effort on his part to effect this as it was on hers. More, he thought sometimes. He had learned quite a lot about teaching since he had started. He would no longer have described it as 'money for old rope', which is how he had·thought of it before. His thoughts had even flitted uneasily now and then to the Professor, who had been doing it for thirty years. But he still could not bring himself to think of the Professor without reopening painful scars . . .

'I've sugared it. Two. Here you are.' Clarissa brought the tea, and one for herself, and sat down on the step beside him.

'Oh, it's gorgeous—' She tossed back her hair and held her face up to the sun. It was very warm. The noise of the Finchley Road traffic, the distant throaty hum that accentuated their own lax content on the doorstep, was no match for the trilling of a black-bird in one of the lilacs. Lud slept blissfully. The big room behind them was bathed in sunshine; even the piano looked mild and harmless, like a basking cat stretched out, resting, across the door-way. Stupid, Pat thought, not to unwind when the moment suggested itself . . . five minutes. He leaned against the doorpost and felt the sun on his neck and face. Clarissa watched him reflectively. His eyes were shut. She sat holding her tea-mug, watching him. His skin was pale, indoors-looking; even relaxed, the lines of intense concentration showed on his face. He looked older than twenty. She put her tea-mug down, and put her hand out, resting it on his knee. His eyes opened abruptly.

In that second, Pat knew he should react with great decision. But he didn't. It was his second mistake. He knew perfectly well that he was being very stupid, but when he saw Clarissa smiling at him in the sunshine, he smiled back—not because he had any feelings for her at all, but just because he was comfortable and the sun was shining and she had made him a cup of tea . . . and it was so nice to stop, not to bother, not to think, and not, for the moment, to have any pressing anxieties: everything was going along quite nicely. With his eyes shut he had been thinking he would win the competition—and he knew he stood a good chance of winning—and then he would get quite a lot of work, and, all being well, their hard times would be over. His whole body was relaxed, soaking up the sunshine, optimistic, hopeful. These moments were rare, and it was unkind not to enjoy them when they came. So he smiled at Clarissa and Clarissa smiled back. And when she smiled, he remembered all the things as they had been once, long ago, before anything had gone wrong at all, when he had discovered for the first time his real talent under the Professor's discipline, after the years of groping, and Clarissa had blessed *him* with her favours when there was a queue of smoothies all avid for her smiles . . . He noticed, again, her quite undeniable attractions, and he knew at the same time that she knew he was noticing them, and that the whole situation was highly dangerous, but he still didn't move away.

'Pat,' she said softly. She moved against him and laid her head on his shoulder. Her arm slipped behind his back. She smelt delicious. He knew he didn't love her at all, but it was nice.

'You've no principles at all,' he said. 'I'm a married man.'

'Why does that change anything for me? Not my feelings. I've never been anything but potty about you, you know that.'

'Oh, come off it! Go and find some other poor fish. You had a funny way of showing it—am I supposed to have forgotten?'

'It was my mother,' Clarissa said. 'She wouldn't let me have anything to do with you after that spot of bother.'

'Well, it was all to my advantage in the end.' He felt almost paternal. She was like a purring, golden-eyed cat nestling against him. She had claws too. He was aware of them, almost tempting them. 'If I'd got hooked with you I'd never have had Ruth.'

'Do you love Ruth?'

'Yes.'

'But you only married her because—' Her voice dropped. 'Did you love her then, when you married her?'

'I think we'd better start the lesson.' She wasn't purring any more, and Pat didn't want to get embarked on any soul-searching. He had let it go too far already.

'No, answer me.' Her voice was sharp. 'I really want to know.'

He didn't know what the answer was himself. 'I don't know. I was scared, I suppose. But I know now.'

'What?'

He didn't reply. He went to get up, but Clarissa moved to stop him, burying her head against his neck and putting her arms round him. He remembered Ruth's saying he was big enough to fend her off, but Clarissa was a big, determined girl and her emotions were aroused.

'For God's sake, Clarissa—' He moved her hair out of his mouth, and remembered the eight pounds at the same time. 'Please,' (more gently) 'we can't—'

'Don't be so old-fashioned! You weren't once!'

'For crying out loud—' Eight pounds or no eight pounds, he'd had enough. He heaved himself urgently to his feet, dragging Clarissa with him. She was crying, but beautifully.

'I do love you so!'

'Yes, well—' He couldn't disentangle himself, and tried to back indoors towards the piano. She had both her arms round his neck, pressing herself to him, her face buried against his neck so that he was blinded by her hair. It was useless trying to be tactful.

'For heaven's sake!' He put his arms up to release her grip round the back of his neck and she started to sob in earnest. He got hold of her wrists and pulled her hands away by brute force, pulling them back in front of them and forcing her off him. She resisted like a tiger.

'Grow up,' he said. 'You're just a spoilt child, wanting what you can't have.'

He was fast losing patience, worried about the strain on his hands, for it was like holding dynamite. She was writhing and struggling to get free, and kicking as well. He had always known she had an uncontrollable temper, for he had seen it in action before, but he had never had it directed against him physically.

'You wanted me once, when it suited you!' she screamed at him. She wasn't beautiful any more, her face screwed up with rage.

'Well, I don't want you now and you might as well know it once and for all!' He was getting angry too. 'I've got all I want, and I'm not having you trying to break it up, pretending you want to learn the piano. I'm not hurting Ruth. God, you bitch—'

She aimed a kick at him which caught him painfully on the shin. He flung her away from him with considerable force, and she went staggering backwards over the doorstep, sprawling. He turned away, intending to beat a hasty retreat up to Wilf's room.

'I hate you! I hate you!' she screamed after him.

He half-turned, to see that she hadn't killed herself, and as he did so she snatched up one of the tea-mugs that was still on the doorstep and hurled it at him with all her might. He put his hand up instinctively and ducked, but her aim, stiffened by pure malevolence, was true. It was a heavy stoneware mug, part of a wedding-present set from Maxwell, and it caught him on the back of the hand.

'I wish I could kill you!' she said viciously. 'I wish—I wish—'

The tears were choking her. She snatched her handbag from the chair and ran to the door. The hurricane of her departure echoed through the house, door-panes and skirling mats, a frightened cat running for its life. Pat stood still, listening, still holding his hand up, too scared to move. He could not bring himself to look at the damage. He lowered his arm slowly and cradled his hand with the other one, trying to pretend that the pain was purely emotional.

'She can't—' he said out loud. 'It can't—'

But it was, he knew it was. He looked down very slowly and the hand lay there, held by the other one, looking perfectly all right. He dared not move. Perhaps it was his imagination— because he dreaded it so much. It was always at the back of his mind, that it might happen. While he stood quite still, like a stone, he could be comforted.

'It's my imagination. A mug couldn't—'

He then lifted the hand up out of the other one, and the awful, thick pain flooded up from the knuckle, through his wrist and right up his arm. It was so patently not the product of his imagination, that he had no possible doubt about its meaning at all. It was a fracture.

He could scarcely believe it. He just went on standing there, trying to pretend it hadn't happened. After Clarissa's skirmishing, the house was as quiet as the grave. The sun still shone in at the window, the kettle was still steaming on the ring in the hearth. While he kept his hand very still, supported, it felt all right. He didn't think that the mug, and a girl's strength, could possibly have done such harm, but he only had to try to move his fore-finger and it was quite apparent that it had. He had to accept it; it was useless trying to pretend.

He could easily have cried. An awful stifled feeling like crying felt as if it was throttling him; an amalgam of rage and grief and a piercing shaft of helpless, hopeless indignation at the *injustice* of it—a familiar feeling to Pat, mostly suffered in the arms of the law. But *this*—this was a new one, the eternal fear having come to realization and in such an unexpected fashion, when one spent one's whole life being particularly careful of car doors and bread-knives and not carrying anything heavy, and then this, of all things, a mere argument with Clarissa. But then arguments with Clarissa had never been mere—he should have bloody well known, when she started—instead of sitting there like a mental case, smiling at her. The fault was obviously all his, giving away an opening . . .

He would have to get down to the Casualty. The sooner the better. He couldn't wait for Ruth. He'd have to leave her a note. Holy cow, it was his right hand—he couldn't even write a note.

He started hunting around for what he wanted, something for a sling, a piece of paper, a pencil. Once he started moving, the hand hurt like hell. He found a scarf of Ruth's and knotted it round his neck, using his teeth, and laid the hand in it, then he wrote her a note with his left hand and left it on the piano. It said, 'Hurt hand. Gone to hospital.' All the music for his competition was on the rack, staring at him, and the Chopin study which was at last beginning to sound like something—it was like being fractured in the brain-box, thinking what had happened to him. It was really beginning to sink in now, along with the numbed suspended pain in his hand, what this injury meant. The choking feeling spread up his gullet again. He groped for some money in his back pocket—cripes, everything was geared to his right hand, he couldn't get at it without agonizing contortions—forty pence— but he couldn't face the underground; it was nearly rush-hour and the thought of his hand in the rush-hour made him feel ill. There were some five-pence pieces for the gas-meter; he took them, enough for a taxi, and went out. He never gave a thought to the baby in the garden.

When Ruth got home, the baby in the garden was yelling blue murder, and there was no sign of Pat at all. She went out and brought the pram in, indignant at Pat, for the sun had gone in and Lud was cold and hungry.

'He's a rotten father, Ludwig. Useless. I wonder where he's gone?'

She didn't find the note until after she had changed and fed Lud and laid him on the bed. She saw the tea-mug on the floor under the piano, went to pick it up and saw the note. She could barely decipher it at first, but when she had, her reaction was one of cold, bitter despair. She sat down on the piano stool, staring at the note. His right hand, obviously. There was no blood any-where, only the mug on the floor, which seemed odd. What hospital? The nearest. The quickest to get to was probably the one she had just come home from. He knew it too. She must go and find out what had happened.

At that moment, just as she was wondering whether to take Lud with her or not, Rosemary let herself in at the front door. Ruth deposited Lud into her surprised care and set off for the tube-station, running. She realized that she was shaking with fright; she could not sit down but stood by the door in a fever of impatience. When the train stopped she leapt out and ran all the way to the hospital, elbowing her way through the rush-hour crowds, shoving and pushing. The Casualty department had long rows of people sitting waiting, and lots more milling about, but there was no sign of Pat. She wandered up and down a few corridors and then went to ask at the desk. She had to wait for several people in front of her, filling in forms and being awkward, all the time getting more agitated herself. The girl had to look through all the admissions.

'What was wrong with him?'

'I don't know.'

The girl gave her a curious look. 'An accident?'

'Yes, to his hand.'

'Here it is.'

'He's here then?'

'Yes. You'd better go and ask Sister.'

Ruth wasn't sure which one was Sister. Nobody seemed to want to stop and chat. She asked a passing nurse who said, 'Try X-ray,' which struck Ruth as quite a bright idea. She followed the signs and came to a wide corridor full of people waiting. Pat was sitting there, hunched up and white.

'What is it? What's happened?'

He showed her his hand, which was now all swollen up and a peculiar colour.

'It's fractured. The doctor said it was—a fractured metacarpal —but I knew anyway. Only I've been here nearly a flaming hour and this queue just doesn't move. I told him I was a pianist but it didn't make any difference. They've got two radiologists off sick or something. Some of these people have been here two hours.'

'But with you—you ought to have a specialist see it, surely? It's not just any hand.'

'Yeh, I was thinking that. The Professor knows a bloke—I went to him before—he was marvellous. He knew it from the piano-playing end, as well as being a doctor. I don't think some doctors know what a piano is.'

'Can't we go to him? Do you know his name?'

'No. I know his address, though—Harley Street. We haven't any money and now we're not likely to earn any, are we? Not even the driving.'

'Whatever happened? What did you—'

'Clarissa heaved a tea-mug at me. I had to fight her off—I told her what I thought of her and she upped and started throwing things.'

'You mean it's *her* fault?' Ruth heard her own voice shake with pure venom. 'Clarissa's?' And all that money Clarissa was surrounded with! 'She ought to pay! Go to a specialist and send her the bill! What did she say? What did she do about it?'

'Nothing. She didn't know what happened. She just threw and ran.'

'Her father would pay—'

'No.'

'But you need help. It's no time to be proud. Not for a thing like this.'

'Not them.'

'But, Pat.' Ruth felt desperate. A baby was crying incessantly, and some women were voicing their complaints loudly and monotonously beside them. The queue hadn't moved at all.

'Two and a half ruddy hours,' one of the women said. 'I was here at half past three. The kids'll be home and nobody there.'

'I'll go and see someone,' Ruth said. 'I'll go and make a fuss.'

She got up and went searching for someone to complain to. It was only because she felt so desperate—she wasn't brave enough to complain as a rule. She broached a woman fierce enough to be someone in command, and got passed on to an Indian doctor who couldn't understand what she was saying. She gave up and cornered a very young student-looking doctor in a white jacket and explained the situation, but he only said, 'I honestly can't do anything about it. We're understaffed—everyone's off with 'flu. There's only one man working in X-ray and he's due off in half an hour.'

The system appeared to have broken down. Ruth thought of Clarissa with almost maniacal hatred, then took a conscious hold of herself. It was no good appealing to Pat. He would not ask the Cargill-Smiths for help, but there was another possibility. She went to the phone-box in the hall and groped about for a coin. The number was in her head and she dialled it quickly.

'Clemmie? It's Ruth. Is the Professor in?'

'Why, Ruth! Yes, he is, dear. Just this minute. Do you want to speak to him?' She was plainly surprised.

'Yes. It's urgent.'

'Just a moment then.'

The Professor came to the phone, also surprised. His voice was very cautious. 'Is that Ruth?'

'Yes. I'm very sorry to bother you, but Pat has had an accident to his hand. He's broken it and there's no one here who's got time to look at it—'

'No one where? Where are you?'

She told him. 'He's waiting in the X-ray queue but it's miles long.'

'I'll be over immediately. Wait for me outside the door. Don't let them touch him, whatever you do.'

He rang off without another word, and Ruth put the receiver down. Her feeling of relief was tempered by the thought of breaking the news to Pat.

'It's all right,' she told him. 'Someone's coming for you. We've got to go back again, to the reception.'

He got up and came without a word. They walked along the corridors and down the stairs. Ruth was trying to pluck up courage.

'It's—' She realized she was terrified. She couldn't tell him. She looked at him sideways. He looked drawn and morose, in his very worst temper.

'It hurts,' he said, as if he was six years old. It made her feel strong and maternal.

'It's all right. The Professor's coming. He's on his way.'

Pat stopped walking.

'The Professor?'

'Yes. I telephoned him.'

'You telephoned the *Professor*?'

'What else can we do? You tell me!' She was angry. It was like the night he had stopped playing in the middle of the Liszt sonata—he had to be goaded, nagged. 'You can't afford not to see to it—*I* can't afford! It's not a question of people or anything. It's only that—' She gestured angrily to his cradled hand.

He just stood there, looking stricken.

'All right, go back then, if you want to!' she hissed at him. 'If you're so stupid, and proud! Go and sit in that queue for the next hour and a half. You're not finished then, remember, only X-rayed. I'm going home. I've got Lud to see to.'

He was furious, she could see, but reason prevailed. He had no option. She began walking and he started to trail along behind. They went down through the Casualty reception and out through the swing doors into the car-park. Pat leaned against a waiting ambulance, silent, looking cold and mutinous. He had no coat, only a faded corduroy shirt and threadbare jeans. When the Professor came, he brought with him this aura of privilege: his sleek car and his gold cuff-links and impeccable suit, like a banker; his faint soap and cigar smell; it all struck Ruth with incredible force, the desirability of this privilege through money—that it was Harley Street, instead of the overworked Casualty, but only if you had money, not because you were a fantastic pianist with an injured hand . . . She felt as fraught and manoeuvred as Pat.

The Professor leaned over and opened the door.

'I'd better go back to Lud,' Ruth said. The car was only a two-seater. But Pat said urgently, 'No, you've got to come. You've got to.' He gave her no choice.

They got in, moving very carefully in the cramped space.

'Well, Pat, what have you done?' The Professor spoke, not looking at them, turning to see if the road was clear. It struck Ruth that he found the situation as difficult as Pat did; only the smoothness of his manners covered embarrassment. Pat would not say anything. It was not entirely temperament, Ruth supposed; he was having a very painful afternoon, both mentally and physically.

'It's broken,' Ruth said. 'Clarissa threw something at him.'

'I beg your pardon?' The Professor was startled.

'A tea-mug—a stoneware one.'

'Good God! Why are you children all so violent?' He looked shaken. 'You're sure it's a fracture? Have you had it X-rayed?'

'No, but it is,' Pat said.

'I rang Harper. He said he'd see you straight away. We'll go straight to the clinic, not to Harley Street. I don't think you need worry too much if he takes care of it. It's straightforward, as far as you can tell? Show me.'

Pat showed him.

'Tragic for you, all the same.'

Nobody disagreed. Now that everything was in hand, Ruth was beginning to feel shaky herself. Past making polite conversation, Pat looked awful. Whatever was he thinking? Ruth wondered. She could not guess at the depths of his despair. He had retracted as he usually did at moments of stress, so that he seemed not to be there at all. The Professor drove fast, without saying any more, and delivered them to a very smart, secluded Edwardian house near Regent's Park. He parked on the gravel drive and got out. Pat and Ruth followed him, not very eagerly. They went inside to an impressive reception, radiating calm and efficiency, as expensive-looking as was compatible with germ-combat. It reminded Ruth more of a beauty parlour than a hospital. She could not imagine anyone being admitted if they were vomiting or bloody, or not ill in good taste.

'Dr. Harper?' the Professor said to the smooth beauty at the desk. 'John Hampton. He's expecting me.'

Dr. Harper duly arrived, very charming and handsome, and after a short chat about nothing to the Professor, he looked at Pat's hand and said, 'We'll go and do something about this then. How about if I ring you later,' he added to the Professor, 'and let you know what's happening? All right?'

'Perfect.'

'If you'll come this way, Mr. Pennington . . .'

Pat hesitated and looked at Ruth, and the Professor said, 'Don't worry, I'll look after Ruth.' When Pat had disappeared, Ruth had a feeling that he had wanted her there, to hold the good hand, and she had this extraordinary feeling of surprise, which she had experienced once or twice before, that in some things her Patrick, whose strength she trusted and rested against like God Almighty, was very vulnerable.

'Well, young lady'—the Professor was looking at her with his old expression of tempered suspicion—'I'll run you home, shall I?'

'Yes. Thank you.'

She wondered if he was going to dump her, and then take over the reins again for Pat. She knew he would like to.

'He won't be staying here, will he?' she asked. 'He'll be home tonight?'

'Oh, I should think so.'

'Pat didn't know I rang you up.' She thought she had better make the situation plain. 'I did it because I thought it was very important. How much do you think it will cost?'

'I wouldn't worry about that,' the Professor said. He opened the car door for her, and held it while she got in.

'I'd rather know.'

'Dr. Harper is a good friend of mine.'

'I wanted your help, to get the treatment, but not for you to pay. You will tell Dr. Harper to send the bill to our address?'

The Professor was smiling. 'Of course.'

How they were going to pay it was not something she was prepared to think about. Later. Their prospects were now so bleak they didn't bear thinking about.

'How long will it be, an injury like that?'

'Hard to tell. About five weeks to mend, but rather longer, I suspect, to get back its agility. Bad enough, I'm afraid.'

Ruth didn't want to think about it. She couldn't bring herself to ask any more. Perhaps Mick would be able to help? She would have to go out to work. She would have to get Lud weaned on to a bottle. Her thoughts were zooming all over the place.

'Don't worry about Pat tonight. I'll bring him home when he's ready, or I'll ring and let you know what they're up to. What's your telephone number?'

The Professor delivered Ruth to the door, and wrote the number in his diary. Ruth thanked him.

He said, 'I'll do all I can to help. Don't be afraid to ask.'

Ruth hesitated, standing on the pavement looking down at the Professor. 'You are very kind,' she said spontaneously. She had honestly never thought so before, but now she did. He shook his head and smiled, and drove off without saying anything else. Ruth let herself in. She felt very tired.

Pat came home a couple of hours later in a private car belonging to the clinic. His hand was in plaster from the knuckles to half-way up his arm.

'Have you rung Paddy?' he asked. 'He'll have to find another driver for tomorrow.'

'No. I haven't rung him.'

'I'll do it.'

That was the only thing he said for the rest of the evening. Ruth decided that it would be better to save all the questions she was dying to ask until a less charged time. She got herself something to eat but Pat wouldn't have anything. He just lay on the bed staring at the ceiling. Lud, as if sensing the atmosphere, wouldn't stop crying. Ruth fed him early, in desperation. She sat down on the hearth in front of the gas-fire, leaning against the bed, and held him against her, smelling his lovely clean-washing smell and stroking his funny black hair. The thought of leaving him all day and going out to work was terrible. He was the cause of all the difficulties they faced; he had been the reason for their getting married at all; he had a lot to answer for. It was strangely quiet, with the pianist out of order, only the muttering of the gas-fire and the spring wind fluting round the windows. Ruth felt charged, nervous and shaky, as if it was she who had had the accident.

'Poor Ruth.' Pat put out his good hand and touched her hair. 'You shouldn't have married me.'

She didn't answer.

She fed Lud and soothed him and put him to bed in his pram, then fished out her nightdress and got undressed, and turned out the fire. Pat lay watching her.

'Am I supposed to be sorry?' she asked.

'You married me? Yes, of course.'

The look on his face was quite different now. She was smiling. 'No,' she said. 'We shouldn't ever have got married.'

She lay down beside him and put her arms round him. 'The worst thing we ever did.'

'The very worst,' he agreed. 'I'd never do it again.'

'No, not to anybody else.'

They started to laugh. They should have been crying. But this was what it was all about, Ruth remembered thinking—that nothing, not anything at all, really mattered, as long as . . . God, life was too stupid . . . he could have gone to bed with Clarissa and not broken his hand at all and what would she have to laugh about then?

# Chapter 13

They were awoken in the morning by the doorbell ringing. Ruth had already got up once and changed and fed Lud—he was in bed with them; she had been dozing, but Pat was still sound asleep.

'What's that?' he said, jerking awake. The sudden movement hurt him and he remembered what had happened. 'Oh, God. Oh, hell . . .'

'It might be Mick,' Ruth said. But nobody had told him. She pulled her dressing-gown on and shook back her hair. 'I'll go.'

It was the Professor.

'Oh, heavens,' Ruth said involuntarily.

'Am I too early? It's nine o'clock.'

Pat was usually up before six, but today was different.

'There wasn't anything to get up for. I'm so sorry,' Ruth explained. 'Do come in.'

'How's Pat?'

'I don't know. All right, I think.'

The sunlight shone through the stained-glass window-panes, making the hall look like a cathedral. It was a bounding spring day, when even the blown newspapers were the urban equivalent of gambolling lambs, and the Hampstead cherry-trees were being lured into flower. Their own room, facing west, was dark and cold in the morning. Ruth, remembering everything, felt with a sudden shiver that this sunlight was not for them; it was right that she should lead the retreat to their cold lair. Pat was still lying in bed, hunched up with Lud under the blankets.

'It's Professor Hampton, Pat.'

'Oh, cripes.' He sat up, groaned, and lay down again.

'How's your arm?' the Professor asked.

'It hurts.'

After the first shock of the meeting, Pat must have reconsidered his manners, for he slowly sat up again, combing his hair back with his fingers, and looked at the Professor.

'I'm sorry.'

'No, please. I'm rather early. I had a reason, though, something I wanted to mention.'

'Do sit down,' Ruth said, bringing up the chair. 'I'll make a pot of tea. Pat, give me Lud—he'll suffocate.'

Pat groped under the blankets. 'I can't—he's all right. He can stay here.' He heaved the baby up a bit and Lud lay beside him, frowning with his black eyes at the bright plaster arm lying on the blanket before him.

'That baby is extraordinarily like you, Pat,' the Professor said, intrigued. 'Clemmie told me, but I wouldn't have believed.'

Pat looked at Lud, as if expecting to see his own face staring back. Lud squinted at him, hiccuping gently.

'I'm not cross-eyed.'

'Don't be so horrible,' Ruth said. 'It's the focus, not a squint. They're all like it. Aren't you going to get up?'

'No. I'm ill.'

'What did Dr. Harper say about it?' the Professor asked. 'No complications?'

'No.. Five weeks, he said. Then when the plaster comes off he'll treat it to get it moving as quickly as possible. He wasn't very optimistic about my being back to normal before next winter.'

'Next winter!' Ruth was horrified.

'Well, back to standard. Brahms' number two standard.'

'Is that what you're working on?'

'I've got a date for it, in Bournemouth in August. I must ring up Mick and break the news to him. It will be another year now.'

'What are you going to do—now this has happened?' the Professor asked. 'This is what I came to see you about. Have you any idea? Have you talked it over?'

'Not yet.'

'No—well, I did think—it's just an idea—' The Professor hesitated, looking embarrassed. 'I don't want to interfere, you understand, but I did think—if you want a little breathing-space, a short rest, there's a nice flat in Brighton you can borrow—have a bit of a holiday. I understand you've been working very hard. It wouldn't cost you anything. A few of us use it whenever we feel like it, and there's no one there now.'

Pat looked at him suspiciously. The Professor smiled. 'No strings attached, Pat, I assure you. If you are financially embarrassed—to put it nicely—I suggest you have a talk with Mr. Zawadzki. It would be quite in order, you know. He is likely to make a lot of money out of you in time to come, and it's only right that he helps you now. He is a very astute young man. He won't risk offending you.'

'I don't want to lose this room, and the piano,' Pat said. 'It's not very cheap.'

'No. A place like this is hard to come by.' Hampton glanced at his watch. 'You needn't decide anything now. I'm on my way out to Winchester, and I thought I'd just drop by and suggest this flat business. It would do you both a world of good, this time of year. And afterwards, if you want any help—well, I won't say ask for it, because I know you won't, but there are a few of us who want to see you get on, Pat—a purely selfish interest, if you like, and if you want to drop round, any time, you will be more than welcome. Just to talk.'

Pat, propped on his elbow, was examining Lud. He didn't say anything. Ruth was glad of the kettle noises, and made a clatter of the cups and tea-jar to cover up his silence, but the Professor didn't seem put out. The thought of a holiday in Brighton appealed to her enormously. Such was the pace of Pat's normal working-day that she realized they had never had any time off since they were married, apart from Christmas Day and Boxing Day. They had never been home except then or to Pat's parents; in fact Pat's parents only knew about the baby because Ruth had prodded Pat into writing them a postcard, and Pat's mother had rung up one evening and delivered some rather sarcastic congratulations. Two days later she had called with her husband and spent the evening arguing with Pat and rocking Lud in her arms until he was sick. She had promised to call again, but hadn't, fortunately.

Ruth made the tea and offered the Professor a cup, wishing that they had a table and that everything wasn't quite so squalid, and the Professor talked to Pat about left-handed compositions and promised to bring over what music he'd got.

'I could learn the Ravel concerto, perhaps,' Pat said. Then he changed his mind. 'No, I can play the Brahms left-hand for five weeks.' It will be a good chance,.'

'Try it in Brighton. There's a piano there too.' The Professor smiled, and shortly afterwards took his leave for Winchester.

It was as if they always did what the Professor wanted, Ruth thought—in the end. But this time she had no regrets at all. People were unexpectedly kind. Paddy the car-boss agreed to pay Pat half his usual wages until he was fit again; Mick agreed to pay the rent, but Wilf said, 'Oh, let it go for a week or two. No one will say anything,' so Mick gave it them in cash and they had something to go to Brighton with. The flat was luxurious, and the refrigerator and pantry were freshly stocked with food by the woman who 'kept an eye on it' when it was unoccupied, presumably on the Professor's orders. Ruth's parents wrote and invited them to come and live at home for a few weeks, and Bates followed them to Brighton and left six five-pound notes under a milk-bottle on top of the refrigerator, saying, 'Pay me back when you do a gig in the Festival Hall.' They prevailed upon him to stay, and he persuaded Pat that he could play the harmonica, plaster or no plaster.

'Can't get the effects,' Pat said.

'Play the ruddy melody, man,' Bates said. 'I'll do the effects.'

He took Pat out to a pub with him the following evening, and came back with ten pounds.

'Five pounds for me, five pounds for you,' Bates said.

How come you can make ten quid just ruddy enjoying yourself?' Pat was confounded.

'Because we enjoy ourselves so ruddy well,' Bates said.

It was all a bit too good to be true, considering what had happened. Ruth was a cautious optimist. She knew there was a long time to go yet, and they spent as little as possible. Pat played left-handed Brahms all morning, and after lunch they would go crunching down the beach for a couple of hours, sometimes taking Lud and sometimes leaving him with Bates.

He was more relaxed, more ready to laugh. It really was a holiday, in spite of the way it had been forced on them. Ruth didn't want to go back. Bates came and went, a gentle, congenial presence. Once he said to Ruth, when Pat wasn't there, 'I will help you—moneywise, I mean—until Pat gets going again. I don't need much, the way I live. I give most of it away anyway. And it's true, you know, if it hadn't been for Pat early on, I wouldn't have ever done anything. Only worked on the farm. I'd have been quite happy, I daresay, but—' He shrugged. 'There's something about Pat.'

Ruth had always thought so too, but had supposed she was biased. But it was curious, now, to find how many people were so well disposed towards him, enough to offer very real help although he had never put himself out to be kind to them, or even polite.

Bates said, 'It's because you feel, with him, that he won't ever give in. He was like that at school. They just couldn't win, whatever they did. And now with this, there's this colossal will-power —single-mindedness. It drives him. And when you think what it's for—although he knows it's got to make him money, he's playing for money, if you like, it's only got to make him money so that it justifies his going on playing, which is the only thing that means anything at all to him. And most people, I think most people feel like me—you feel you want to have a hand in it, somehow—you admire it, you know you could never do it yourself, so the best you can do is tag along and want to be his friend.'

'I thought it was just me who felt like that.'

'No, I don't think so. It's something he generates. The only people who can't stand him are the ones who are jealous. As long as you aren't jealous, you think he's marvellous.'

'I don't think he thinks of it like that himself.'

'No. I'm sure he doesn't. He doesn't think about it at all. He doesn't think he's anything exceptional.'

'He thinks he plays well enough for it to be worth going on with. That's all. He thinks about playing all the time. Even when he's driving, he takes music to read while he's waiting about. He doesn't talk about it, but I'm sure it's all he thinks about. He doesn't talk to me, anyway—he might to people who know about it, like Mick.'

Mick came down at the beginning of the second week, and they talked about it all night. Ruth sat curled up in one of the elegant armchairs and listened. Some of it she understood, and a whole lot she didn't, but the atmosphere was so charged with dynamic intentions that it was impossible not to be involved. 'I have received as many inquiries about possible dates for you to play, since your recital at the Society conference, as you would have got anyway if you had won that competition,' Mick told Pat.

'I would have got them *as well*,' Pat pointed out.

'Yes, but this is so encouraging—these are the people who actually heard you play, and want you to play in their clubs. I want to get out some literature on you—it's fairly urgent. We shall want a decent photo. Perhaps we can get one taken tomorrow —unless you've got one?'

'No.' The only ones he had ever had taken were for police records, and he wasn't going to admit this.

'We'll do that then. And make out some recital programmes. That's the important thing.'

'This is for next winter, I take it? We can't think about much earlier.'

'It depends, of course, on everything going smoothly with your hand. I've seen Harper.'

'Oh?'

'He's got your convalescent programme all laid on, exercises and what you can play and what you can't play until something or other gets its strength back—all highly technical and involved. I should think, talking to him, that whatever we have to pay him will be well worth it.'

Ruth noted the use of the plural in the last sentence and felt a bit happier. Pat looked surprised. 'You mean we have to submit the programmes to him first and he marks them up: "suitable sixth week post-plaster-removal, seventh week, eighth week," etc.? How about Brahms' number two?'

Mick laughed. 'I didn't mention that. We'll work up to it. But you don't think it's too optimistic to offer it for next year?'

'Hand permitting, no. If we make it definite, then I know I've got to do it. I would rather work to deadlines, if you like. Otherwise you would give yourself ten or fifteen years. If you had any sense you would. I can do the Rachmaninov two and Liszt one. The Beethovens I want to do more work on, especially the G Major. But nothing else now. Not with the Brahms.'

'No. And for solo recital—your main works would be—?'

'The Schumann Fantasy. Brahms' Handel Variations. Of the Beethoven sonatas I would prefer "Les Adieux", the "Waldstein", and the 109, but most of them if necessary. The Scriabin four. Chopin's sonatas—B Minor preferably.'

'The Liszt sonata.'

'No.'

'Why not? I thought that was your best piece.'

Pat hesitated. 'I stopped—you remember.'

'So?'

'I'd like to forget it for a bit. It shook me.'

'But your playing of that sonata is one of the best things you have to offer. The best, if you ask me. Just because on one occasion you stopped—' Mick shrugged. 'It can happen to anybody.'

Ruth said, 'I think you should play it.'

'It scares me now, the thought of playing it in public.' Pat looked worried at the thought.

'If you played it successfully, just once,' Ruth said, 'it would be all right again. You've got to do it. It's like throwing away all that time you've worked on it, to drop it now. Anyway, it's marvellous. Your best.'

'It is,' Mick agreed.

'It might be. But if you were me, sitting there—'

'I thought the Professor said,' Ruth said, 'that the more it mattered, the more you rose to the occasion. So if the occasion matters very much—'

'He said that, did he?'

'Yes.'

'I agree with Ruth,' Mick said. 'It's a terrible waste to drop it. As far as I'm concerned I would like you to play it at every recital you do. It's a splendid showpiece.'

'Played in one piece,' Pat said.

'Next time,' Ruth said.

Pat shrugged. 'Ruination to my metacarpal. It's not that I haven't given it a great deal of thought—'

'No. Well, think again,' Mick said. 'If you're considering Moscow, you can't afford to be put off by a minor lapse. We'll put it on the list.'

Pat did not protest but his expression aged two or three years. Ruth wasn't sure how serious he was about Moscow: the fare was a major stumbling-block, but if Mick wanted it—and if the Professor had come back into their circle. . . . Mick had a list of the music clubs who had inquired about Pat's playing for them, and they were from all over the country, not just the London suburbs. The more his career succeeded, the less she would see of him. It was the lot of the twentieth-century musician, to be a high-powered travelling man. Sitting there, watching the two of them, it occurred to her that in this point in Pat's career, fractured metacarpal or no, *she* was as likely to be as happy as she ever would be. If the engagements flowed in, she could not see Pat turning them down to stay at home with her. And even if he wanted to, there was no longer the choice, for his career was in Mick's hands. And Ruth could see that it was in very capable hands, but equally Mick was successful because he was a pressure man. He had the same nervous energy as Pat, but his nervous energy was channelled into making money out of Pat. He had been to Dr. Harper, chafing at the delay, because the engagements were coming in. Watching him, Ruth recognized that there was an aggressive streak in his nature. He was one of life's pushers and shovers, for all the charm; he was shrewd and sharp and demanding—exactly as a good agent should be. Ruth wasn't sure if she liked him now. She was a romantic at heart, and Pat's music had wrapped her love-affair in a pink cloud, like a bad film. She wanted her life with Pat to be sentimentally happy, with him playing the piano and the sun shining and the children running in from a big garden full of flowers and birds singing, but now she saw that—however dedicated his own approach—to exploit his art for money was as business-like and commercial an undertaking as stockbroking. She could see it in Mick's attitude. No doubt Pat knew it too. The music would remain inviolable, but their way of life would of necessity be tautly organized and full of stress, for to tie the temperament of the artist to a commercial schedule was surely an incompatible task? Or was Pat already trained, through his scrupulous years of practice, to perform according to schedule? She supposed he was—to play gentle, introspective Schumann straight out of the rush-hour on a wet night in Ilford was already part of the job, or all-consuming Liszt when your wife was having a baby—but the training was not infallible, because this was why he went to the lavatory to be sick, or stopped in mid-movement, and wouldn't talk to anybody. It didn't just come out of the soul, born of joy and passion, as her romantic dreams would have it. It was tempered to time-tables and cold Town Halls as it always had been, even for the dying Chopin playing in Glasgow for sixty pounds so that he could pay his doctor's bills, so who was she to want it any different for Pat? She watched him talking to Mick, very practical and matter-of-fact, about the hardest problems of the Brahms concerto, demonstrating with his good hand in the air, the plastered one lying on his knee, and she felt something very like affection towards Clarissa for being the cause of this respite, this nice holiday, this breathing-space. To be happy for the day was what mattered, and she was happy now.

Mick wanted to watch something on the television. Lud was asleep and Pat said to Ruth, 'Let's go out for a drink. It's nearly closing time,' so they went out and walked along the sea-front. It was too nice to go into a pub; the air was warm and the sea calm and not many people were about. They walked in silence for some time. Ruth thought Pat was thinking about his music, but after a while he put his arm round her and said, 'Like old times.'

'Yes. I was thinking that. Thanks to Clarissa.'

'Old married couple. Nearly a year.'

'A lot has happened.'

'This time last year I was still in Pentonville.'

'Seems ages ago.'

'We haven't done enough of this.'

'Nothing, you mean?'

'Yes. We haven't done nothing ever since we've been married.'

'Well, I have. It's you.'

'I can't. Later I shall.'

Ruth doubted it. She said, 'Funny, that it was Clarissa—giving us a sort of honeymoon.' They hadn't had one before. 'Does she know what's happened?'

'Yes, of course. Mick called on them, but she knew already through the grapevine. Mick said the old boy was very upset. I don't suppose Clarissa was, mind you.'

'Perhaps he'll pay the doctor's bill.'

'Mick said we needn't bother about it.'

'Really? Is he paying it?'

'I'm not sure. I didn't ask.'

'Perhaps the doctor will do it free, being a friend of the

Professor's. When he takes the plaster off, can you start playing straight away?'

'I don't know. I suppose so. I hope so. There's an awful lot to do if Moscow is going to come off. If I can afford to enter for it.'

Ruth didn't want Pat to go to Moscow, or work for it either, but she wanted him to be happy, and one was dependent on the other. She couldn't win. It was what her mother had said way back. But she didn't want to change anything. They walked back. They went home the following week and Pat started his driving job again, and Dr. Harper removed the plaster from his hand. The hand was stiff as a board. When Pat tried to play the piano with it he became acutely depressed and went out and got drunk. Ruth was angry, appalled. Pat wouldn't speak for several days. He did the exercises that Dr. Harper prescribed, but for too long, and suffered severe pains which depressed him still further, and tried Ruth's philosophy to its limits. She knew now that she was only happy if Pat was happy, and during the weeks of his recuperation she was sorely tried. For normal usage the hand was acceptably cured, but for the extremes to which Pat wanted to drive it, it was sadly out of condition. Dr. Harper's therapy was highly skilled, but he hadn't the power to alleviate Pat's frustration at the slow rate of progress. The doctor wouldn't agree that progress was slow, but Pat, finely aware of the hand's former capabilities, found it almost impossible to accept its present limitations.

'Cripes, it'll be as long as Pentonville all over again! He never told me this early on! He calls this "a most satisfactory improvement"—and we're still on ruddy grade three stuff. How long does he want?'

'Don't be ridiculous! He can't work miracles. He's not God! You've got plenty of time. It's only July.'

'I shall have the best bloody left hand in the business, at this rate, while the right hand messes up everything it's put at. Nobody ever wrote music like I can play—it wasn't intended that way round.'

Mick came and listened anxiously, while Ruth lay on the last patch of evening sun at the end of the garden with Lud beside her, trying to pretend it didn't matter, and knowing very well that their very lives depended on it coming right. She had a job as dogsbody to a solicitor's family in Hampstead, where she could take Lud with her, and with her money and Pat's driving wages they made just enough to pay the rent and barely live on. The job exhausted her, the solicitor's wife being an exacting woman and the mother of four spoilt small children, and Ruth came home with little appetite for Pat's moods. She tried very hard to be patient and sympathetic, but being so tired herself made her inevitably short-tempered. The weather was hot, and the end of the garden was the best place when Pat was practising, and Lud her dearest joy and comfort in what she euphemistically thought of as 'a bad patch'. It wasn't that she didn't understand how Pat felt, for she understood only too desperately well, remembering how the 'Winter Wind's' right hand had stormed through the keys the days before the accident, but she hadn't the strength to be patient and constructive in the face of Pat's bad humour: she merely felt mangled and at the end of her tether. Her money was essential, otherwise she would have saved her energy to pander to him. He hated her being away all the time. He was hopeless at feeding himself, even at getting something out when he had finished driving, and when she came home tired and with the baby-washing to do and Lud to see to, he was always ravenously hungry and demanding a meal. After supper he would go on practising, left hand only after the right had given out. Ruth couldn't decide whether he was a male chauvinist pig or a genius. 'Both,' Pat said, and went on practising. His right hand hurt him nearly all the time. Ruth wished she had the energy to make an effigy of Clarissa, so that she would have the satisfaction of sticking pins in it.

'It's improving fast,' Mick said, one evening. He dropped in fairly often, anxious about the programmes that were booked for the coming winter. 'Watching his bread and butter,' Pat called it. 'When you feel you're ready to play something to an audience, let me know. Old Cargill-Smith was asking.'

'He doesn't want me to accompany Clarissa, I hope?'

'No. She's in Vienna at the moment. He's got something up his sleeve—"Ask young Pennington to dinner," he said, "and we'll have a few people in. He can play." From anyone else it wouldn't mean much, but from him—it's different. I might find out more for you later. Just thought I'd drop you the hint, though. When do you think you might be able to manage it?'

'Autumn some time.'

'He feels he owes you something. We must make the most of it.'

'He doesn't owe me anything at all.'

'As you like. Clarissa owes you six months' working time—put it that way. He must feel responsible.'

Pat growled something.

'And your old professor, Mr. Hampton—he keeps inquiring about you. Doesn't want to interfere, but you might go and see him. Wouldn't do any harm.'

'It would do *me* harm,' Pat said angrily. 'I don't want to get involved. I've learned to do without him, because I had to. I don't want anything from him now. I have a bad conscience—I want to forget it.'

'Relax! Just be friends! Conscience needn't come into it at all. You don't have to be so prickly.'

'Well—it's the time factor. I've no time.'

'He said to tell you if you want to use his tape-recorder, or if you want him on the second piano, to practise the concerto— entirely friendly and well disposed.'

'That gives me an even worse conscience,' Pat said.

'It's up to you. Useful bloke, though.'

'Yes.'

'And you still want to go to Moscow?'

'Want to—yes. I've been going through some stuff—Stravinsky, Rachmaninov—reading it. But I don't want to make up my mind to go unless—well, there's so many ifs and buts at the moment. It's no good getting excited about it. Money, for one. And being good enough so it's not just a waste of time.'

Ruth noted that he put money as the first problem, and being good enough the second. She didn't think he lacked confidence, in spite of his hand. It was true that it was improving fast, but in his gigantic appetite for work Pat couldn't accept that it was fast enough.

For Ruth, the summer passed under the cloud of the solicitor's wife and the endless chores in the large, smart house. At least she had Lud with her. Even if she had been a highly efficient secretary by training, instead of a useless nonentity, she would hardly have been able to find a job where Lud would have been welcome alongside the typewriter, so she counted her blessings, trudging to and fro morning and evening with her pram from the seedy environs of the Finchley Road to the more elevated residences where such as she were welcome in the kitchen. Lud enjoyed every minute of it, and Ruth supposed she was happy. At least there was Pat to go home to every night, hungry or no. He wasn't yet in Moscow, or doing a recital in Ashton-under-Lyne or Swindon or Clacton-on-Sea. When he was, presumably, they would have enough money for her not to work. 'I don't know what I want!' She had to scold herself for the perversity of her feelings. But she was too tired to be objective.

'Look.'

Pat got up from the piano and showed her the card on the mantelpiece.

'Mr. and Mrs. Julian Cargill-Smith request the pleasure of the company of Mr. and Mrs. Patrick Pennington to dinner . . .' Underneath, scrawled in pen, 'Would you be prepared to play something after dinner? We should be so delighted if you would.'

'I've nothing to wear,' Ruth said.

'No. Nor have I. At least, only the trousers.'

'Go like that. Black trousers and red braces and your Beethoven medal.'

They got giggly. Ruth opened a tin of spaghetti, and Pat lay on the hearth-rug with Lud sitting on his chest, trying to pick up his shirt-buttons.

'What will you play?'

'Something to go with the coffee and liqueurs. Not to give them indigestion. I'll think about it. To be accompanied by the tinkling of teaspoons and the clicking of false teeth on wine-glasses. Performing monkey—free.'

'Mick said—'

'Oh, Mick wants to believe all sorts of things. What does Julian C. Smith care who plays at his dinner-party? I'm near, in need of a square meal and likely to be grateful. We'll go for the dinner. I'll borrow Wilf's dinner-jacket and perhaps Rosemary could find you something.'

'I'll ask her. It'll swamp me. She'll have to look after Lud too— unless we take him. We can take him in the pram, I should think.'

Lud pulled off a button and put it in his mouth. Pat scooped for it. 'I need that. Give it here. Hey, he's got a tooth. He bit me! Did you know he's got teeth?'

'Yes, of course. I told you in bed the other night and you said, quote, "I wonder if I could get the Petruschka Suite out of the library? Or perhaps the Professor's got a copy."'

'Did I? The Professor *has* got a copy. I remember now. I might go and see him. No, he'll be at this dinner, I daresay. I can ask him then. Do you think Lud still looks like me?'

'It's going off a bit, luckily.'

'He's wet.'

'He'll curl the hair on your chest. Give him to me. I'll change him. What have you been playing today?'

'Liszt. Chopin. All fireworks, and my hand doesn't hurt.'

'Splendid.'

They duly borrowed some clothes, and Rosemary agreed to have Lud for the evening. Ruth cut Pat's hair to coincide with the collar of the dinner-jacket and Mick picked them up in his car. Mick had just come back from Germany, and was talking about the possibilities of playing in Europe. Ruth was tired after her day with the solicitor's wife, and was looking forward to a good dinner, and hoping that the safety-pins that were holding her dress together didn't show at the back. Pat had a recital in Coventry in a fortnight's time, the first since the night Lud was born, and it sounded from the way that Mick was talking that things might be getting rosier.

'Thank God your hand has made it in time,' Mick was saying. 'That's the main problem solved. What are you playing tonight?'

'I'll sound out the old boy. I thought the Chopin preludes, or some quiet Brahms—whatever seems best.'

Mick opened his mouth to say something, but thought better of it and drove on in silence. The Hampstead house was all lights and smart cars outside. Mick parked and turned off the engine, and they sat for a moment, looking. Ruth realized, hungry as she was, that it was work, when all was said and done. Pat had gone quiet. It did seem a very long time since he had played in front of an audience.

'Is there a catch in this?' he said suddenly to Mick.

'If there is, it's entirely to your advantage, if you want to make use of it.'

They got out and went up to the front door, which was opened by Mrs. Cargill-Smith herself in a cloud of yellow chiffon.

'My dears, how lovely to see you again!' She kissed Ruth and shook hands with Mick and Pat. Ruth wondered if she had any qualms about taking Pat's hand, but she never then, or afterwards, made any reference to what had happened. 'Do let's go and find my husband. There are several people he wants you to meet tonight. Do you want the cloakroom, Ruth? It's over there, the last door.'

They had no coats to give the hovering maid, not having been able to produce a respectable garment, male or female, in the whole household, so Ruth went to comb her hair and gather up courage, feeling terrified of the first glimpse of what was in store, and Pat and Mick went into the sitting-room with their hostess. Ruth could not find anybody apparently under the age of forty, and was quite relieved to be nobbled by a comparatively harmless-looking old dear just inside the door who said to her, 'Are you a friend of Clarissa's? I understand Clarissa is in Vienna?'

'Yes, she is, and I'm not a friend of hers,' Ruth said, not even for the sake of politeness being able to admit to liking Clarissa.

'Such a relief, I have to admit,' the old lady said, confidentially. 'We won't have to listen to her play.'

Ruth felt apprehensive. A waiter offered her a drink and she took one nervously, and the woman continued, 'Such is parent-hood, that our charming hosts, quite the most astute judges of instrumental playing that I know, are completely blind to how well below their own standards dear Clarissa falls. She is im-possibly spoilt, I'm afraid.'

'Yes,' Ruth agreed.

'I understand there is to be some music tonight, that's why I wanted to be sure about Clarissa. Now I can look forward to the after-dinner interlude with real enjoyment. Clarissa apart, one is never bored by music in this house. Judging by who is here, I suspect that whoever plays tonight will be very well worth listening to; Julian won't want to lose his reputation in such company.'

'What do you mean?' Ruth asked nervously. She looked into the room, to see if there was anybody she recognized, but the company looked to her extremely sober and dull, mostly rather quiet elderly men and very well-dressed women. Pat, standing by his host, stood out by reason of his hair and his youth, but looked more sober than anyone in the room, in fact positively miserable. Ruth recognized his pre-recital withdrawal symptoms and realized that the situation was a bit tricky for him, having to be polite because the circumstances demanded it; it wasn't a job for money tonight, but a . . . Ruth felt her stomach give a nasty lurch.

'Who is here?' she asked the woman.

'Some extremely discerning people, my dear. The man with his back to us, talking to Julian, is Ernest Brunow from New York, the conductor of—' She proceeded to list several names, some of which even Ruth had heard of, all in the musical world. She remembered Mick's saying, it seemed a long time ago, something about Cargill-Smith's saying he would have 'a few people in' when Pat was ready to play, but she hadn't somehow connected it with this invitation and Mrs. Cargill-Smith's scrawled 'we should be so delighted . . .' It was a bit different from playing to a lot of wet mackintoshes in Wembley. Had Pat had any idea? He probably had by now. He was looking desperately serious, being introduced to a man with white hair and a white moustache. Ruth excused herself from the elderly woman and sought out Mick, who was talking to Professor Hampton.

'Did you know? You didn't tell Pat—' she started.

'Tell him what?' Mick was looking amused.

'What important people would be here—to hear him play.'

'Isn't it lovely!' Mick said. 'I guessed. I thought there might be one or two, but Julian has surpassed himself.'

He was obviously delighted, and not at all worried.

'You could have warned him!'

'Dear Ruth, I did all I could. But he is so spiky—you know it— if there had been any suggestion of Julian's doing him a favour, he would have gone communist on us. You know how he is.'

'Julian is very conscience-stricken about what Clarissa did,' the Professor said. 'For my own part I'm surprised no one has physically attacked Pat before now, the way he treats people, but—' he shrugged and smiled. 'He brings the most fearful consequences upon himself, and somehow, for him, it all comes right. It wouldn't for anybody else, but for Pat life is like a game of snakes and ladders. Down to the depths, and then the struggle back. I wouldn't say that he thrives on it, but it appears to do him no harm. I suspect that his upbringing has something to do with it, and it taught him this *tenacity* . . . one can only admire, in spite of everything. And his work has this extraordinary strength and feeling, out of such difficulties—no one else I have taught has possessed this elemental quality to such a degree. Allied, of course, to the impeccable musicianship which I taught him.' The Professor smiled. 'What have we to worry about? Dear Ruth, stop looking so worried.'

Ruth was amazed at the Professor's speech. Neither he nor Mick was in the slightest way anxious about the evening's work for Pat—they who cared more for his progress than anyone else apart from herself. Had she got it wrong, all this time, that she worried so for Pat? She only took it from Pat himself, and how she knew he felt. And yet his mentors here had such confidence that they were laughing at her doubts. The Professor put his arm round her.

'Come, it will be a lovely evening. You have nothing to worry about. Didn't I once tell you about Pat rising to important occasions? It's the greatest talent of the lot. You are a very lucky girl, Ruth. You are looking very charming. Pat is a very lucky man too.'

Ruth thought the Professor had had too much to drink. But he did not appear to be drunk in any other way. Perhaps it was herself. Mick said to her softly, 'You see that man Pat is talking to now?'

She looked and nodded.

'That man is prepared to finance any young pianist he feels worth encouraging to go to Moscow. He told me so himself.'

Ruth looked more closely. Pat was staring at the man's shoes, scowling.

'Fortunately his judgement will be based on Pat's playing, not on his drawing-room manners,' the Professor said.

He and Mick both laughed.

Ruth looked round, still feeling far from serene about the evening's eventualities. The way both Mick and the Professor appeared to see Pat diverged sharply from her own experience of living with him. This bland optimism overlooked entirely Pat's own day-by-day worries: they only saw the result. Although they knew it happened, they did not actually live with the exacting concentration that Pat brought to bear on his work every day. They did not sit in on his dawn starts and listen to his hardest current problems being given the treatment, as she did, and know intimately the parts that had caused him the hardest thinking; they did not witness the fraught allocations of their two wage-packets to the most pressing of their debts, her deliberations over

187

the most economical ingredients with which to assuage Pat's healthy appetite, their ridiculous borrowing of acceptable clothes for any out-of-the-way events, like tonight's, the constant 'borrowing' of gas-meter coins and shunning of the occasional temptations, like a good film, or a drink at the local with Wilf and Rosemary, even her having to cut Pat's hair tonight—it was miles away from the Professor's avuncular comments about having nothing to worry about, and being lucky. They both got so tired and so screwed-up and Pat wouldn't talk and Lud cried all through some punctilious pianissimos so that Pat threw the music across the room and went up to see Wilf . . . What did the Professor know?

They went in to dinner and the Professor took her arm and said, 'Perhaps you could both spare the time to come and see me one day next week? I would like to feel that any differences we had in the past are quite forgotten now.'

'Yes, of course.'

But she couldn't think about next week, only now. Pat was next to her at the dinner-table, and Mick on her other side. Pat had Mrs. Cargill-Smith on his left, and presumably she understood about his not feeling talkative, so Ruth was relieved. The Professor was opposite, next to the Moscow financier's wife. Were they really lucky? She couldn't stop trying to work it out. Only that she wouldn't change anything. And so terrifyingly precarious to think that good fortune or bad depended only on what Pat was able to do within the next hour or so. She could only see it like that, not as the Professor saw it; she didn't have his confidence. And whether Pat had it or not she couldn't tell. Pat wasn't giving anything away. He wasn't eating a thing, nor drinking.

'Do you feel all right?' she asked him.

He didn't answer. He sat crumbling his bread roll into little pellets and piling them round the edges of his plate. His fingers were moving all the time. Ruth realized that she felt as sick as he did, although she was so hungry and the food was delicious. Mick was saying to her, 'Of course, everybody comes here for the food. It's renowned throughout London. And what with all the wine, whoever plays afterwards can only be a roaring success. So don't waste your opportunities.' It was true, Ruth thought, she had never seen anything like it out of a film, with candles all down the table and the food served by waiters from silver dishes and a different wine with every course. Just like an Edwardian dinner.

She began to wonder if it was all quite real. It took ages, and Pat's mounds of pellets grew like fortifications, and Ruth began to think she had drunk too much, she felt so tensed up. She tried to think what she would feel like if it was only a dinner-party and no piano-playing to think about, and she realized that she would be laughing and gorging just like Mick, and enjoying the Professor's compliments. But linked so closely to Pat, she could only feel with him, and this time it was agonizing. Would it always be? Was that part of the luck? Yes, she thought. If it all came right, and the luck saw them through, it would one day be like this waiting in the wings of the Royal Festival Hall. It would be like this the first time he played the Brahms concerto. But perhaps by then the confidence would have grown, and feeling sick would no longer be part of the job.

'Coffee and liqueurs will be served in the music-room,' Mrs. Cargill-Smith announced at last. The table was a sea of crumpled napkins, the silver candelabra sailing serenely above. Everyone got up and began to drift out across the hall to the music-room, but Pat went up the stairs on his own. Ruth followed him. He went into the bathroom on the first floor and shut himself in the lavatory, where she could hear him being sick. She went and opened the window and leaned out, looking out on the garden. There was the scent of late roses; she could see the beds of them below, immaculately tended, the pale, opened blooms gleaming in the light that flooded from the house. She had been here before, the first time she had met Clarissa, and Pat had been playing Beethoven downstairs. She had looked out of the window at these same roses, and not known then what was going to happen at all. It was the same day that Pat had been taken to prison. It seemed a very long time ago. The night outside the house was calm, with the smell of autumn that reminded her of home. It was very comforting. She suddenly felt that the confidence that had so surprised her before dinner was not so misplaced after all.

Pat came out and ran the taps into the wash-basin and leaned on them, dangling his hands in the water. Ruth took a Cargill-Smith face-cloth from its elegant gold ring and handed it to him.

'It's all right,' she said. 'I know it is. The last time I was here, in this bathroom, do you remember?' No, she supposed he didn't, for he had been downstairs.

'Pat.' She put her arm across his shoulders. 'It will be all right. I know it will.'

He said, 'Don't worry about me. I can't help it.'

'There isn't anything to worry about.'

He straightened up and dried himself. Ruth found him a comb in her handbag and he combed his hair and she did hers. They looked at each other and Ruth smiled. Pat's expression reminded her of the day in the clinic when he had gone away with Dr. Harper, as if he had wanted her to go with him and hold his hand. But then, as now, there was absolutely nothing she could do to help in the thing that mattered. Only on the sidelines. That was her job for life. She was beginning to get the hang of it.

'Come on. The old girl will think you've run out on her.'

He gave her a faint smile, and they went downstairs. Mrs. Cargill-Smith was just coming out of the music-room door. Her face beamed at them.

'There you are. Splendid! We're all ready for you. Everyone knows who you are—I don't think you need any introduction. Go straight over to the piano and tell them what you're going to play. Then it's all yours.'

They went into the room. Ruth could not get any farther than inside the door, where there was a convenient chair, but Pat threaded his way through the semi-circle of chairs and coffee-tables and went to the piano. Ruth knew he would waste no time at all.

He turned to the audience and said, 'Liszt's sonata in B Minor.'

Ruth bit her tongue with shock. Then she remembered what the Professor had said about 'the greatest talent of all', remembered that there wasn't anything to be afraid of, and sank back in her chair. The first quiet staccato notes sounded across the room. He could have gone on being a chauffeur, after all. It was only what he had chosen.